A
Harlequin
Romance

OTHER
Harlequin Romances
by ESSIE SUMMERS

THROUGH ALL THE YEARS

by

ESSIE SUMMERS

HARLEQUIN BOOKS   TORONTO
WINNIPEG

Original hard cover edition published in 1974
by Mills & Boon Limited.

© Essie Summers 1974

SBN 373-01854-1

Harlequin edition published February 1975

Printed in Canada

The Author records her thanks to the *Australian Woman's Mirror* for permission to use Jane East's poem, *Country Cemetery*.

To keep in memory
my
Snelson forebears
My grandparents, Edwin and Elizabeth, née Temple Watson,
My great-aunt Adelaide who went to Canada so long ago,
My great-uncle Thomas who fell on active service in India.

CHAPTER I

Thomasina Meade sat in her favourite thinking place on Green-chester Hill and looked down on the smiling valley of the Tyne showing here and there a glimpse of the Roman Wall that had been part of her childhood scene for as long as she could remember and for the thousandth time wondered how she would find the courage to leave it. But leave it she must, and soon.

Most times when she'd sat here the rock had been warm against her back, but not even the brilliance of this summer sunshine could warm her today. Usually it was the twin hollow she occupied on the other side of the outcrop, but today she couldn't because it meant looking down on their old cottage where soon no cottage would be.

It was something you *couldn't* fight, this, which was a pity because, given a just cause, she was a bonnie fighter. If it had been one of the stately homes of England there'd have been no talk of demolition, but it was only a shabby cottage of no particular historical charm or architectural beauty and it stood in the way of a big new road complex.

The other residents of Greenchester thought it no less than a miracle that the whole village wasn't under threat. There had been an agonized time for them when it was first being surveyed, till the engineers came up with a solution. Only the Meades' cottage stood in the way of that one.

There would be compensation, of course, but only to the tune of the value of the cottage, not the cost of buying another place to live in. The amount Thomasina was to receive wouldn't as much as pay a good deposit on a house in town and a big mortgage was beyond her means. If only there had been some sort of cottage to rent in Greenchester itself, but there was nothing.

So it must be a flat in Newcastle. The children, her half-brother and sister, were desolate. They had always lived in the country because Stephen, their father, had so craved for his three children the inestimable happiness of a rural upbringing. No matter where they had to live in later life, he wanted them to associate with their childhood, the singing of a lark high in the sky, the sound of a brook purling over mossy stones on its down-ward course, poplars tall and slim against a sunset sky, dew on a

7

field at daybreak and the incomparable beauty of rolling hills dotted with sheep.

If only Madeline, Thomasina's stepmother, hadn't died so soon after Dad. Somehow she and Maddy would have managed. As always the thought of Maddy stabbed with nostalgic poignancy. She had been such fun. There had always been another giggle round the corner when Maddy was about.

What courage she must have had to take on, at twenty-two, a stepdaughter of twelve. But then they'd always been such pals. Dad had chuckled and said he never even got within distance of having his fair share of Maddy because she and Thomasina were such cronies. For Dad to die at forty-nine when he was just starting to make a name for himself as a novelist was bad enough, but for Maddy to follow him a few months later at thirty-five was beyond bearing. What a stupid thing to think—one just had to bear these things.

What a year it had been, the good and the bad happening in one twelvemonth, event after event. It had been so wonderful when Dad had been able to give up his office job in Newcastle to which he'd commuted each day, to write full time. They'd worked out that if they lived extremely reasonably for a year, his increased output of words would mean a greater security for them in the future.

Thomasina herself had been offered a better position than her office job at a local mill. She was now secretary to a big estate nearby that, in order to preserve its buildings, ran a model farm for dairy and crop produce very successfully. This had been marvellous. It was nearer home, had higher wages and shorter hours—this last the greatest bonus of all because Thomasina had inherited her father's knack for words and this meant she could do quite a lot more freelance writing.

'Get at it while you're young,' Daddy had urged. 'You're doing well with short stories and poems and articles. But put the extra time into a bigger work. Try a novel. Don't be like me, always postponing the chance of long-term success for the quicker rewards of journalism, simply because we needed extra cash immediately. If I'd had the courage earlier to live on a shoestring for a few years I'd have been an established thriller writer sooner instead of leaving it as I did, till too late.'

'Too late?' Thomasina had picked him up sharply on that. 'Dad, you're only forty-eight. Don't be absurd.'

He'd laughed. 'Well, Tamsin, at twenty-four you feel life

8

stretches out limitlessly. At my age you get a strange feeling that it's later than you think, that the years from now may go too fast. That's why I'm leaving my steady job and buckling down to eight hours a day of creative writing. And I love it.'

Nine months later they had realized Stephen Meade had already suspicioned a long life was not for him, because by then he was sleeping in a sunny corner of the old churchyard in Greenchester that he had so loved. His performance in the last few months had been no less than magnificent, writing to the last to provide as much as possible for his wife and family.

He'd said to Thomasina, ' I'm so glad you're with Madeline, Tam, and that you're such pals. She's going to need you.' He'd grinned, his eyes like blue lamps in his gaunt face, 'I daren't say it to her now, but you can tell her—after. I'd like her to marry again. She's too young to spend forty years or so alone.'

But there hadn't been even one year for Madeline, just four months and, with no more warning than a sigh, one night when she and Thomasina were watching television, she was gone—an unsuspected heart deformity.

Thomasina was fiercely glad for her stepmother's sake that she'd had no warning. She would have grieved to leave her children, to know Thomasina would have to assume such responsibility. Not that the burden had seemed so formidable till this last blow had fallen, the imminent loss of their home. She could have managed fine with the cottage freehold, her own wage, and Dad's modest royalties, even if he had just become known. If only there had been more books behind him! But now, very soon, she must tell Matthew and Edwina that a move to town was the only solution. They were still hoping against hope a cottage here might fall empty. However, they would adapt, and at least they would have this to remember. And so would she.

Dad had proposed that before she took on the new job he and she should go south for two or three weeks, just as they had at Easter, for gathering material for a new book. Her shorthand was very useful to him. He had a lot of research to do round Portsmouth and London. Maddy had been so generous in sparing them, never possessive, sending them on their way declaring that for her it was a blessing in disguise. She could now get on with her spinning in peace, perfect peace, with loved ones far away!

Thomasina could re-live every moment of that three weeks. She would never forget their ramblings round that lovely, exciting, historical coast. She could still see Dad, high on the keep of

9

Portchester Castle, gazing out over the shining spread of the harbour towards France, saying: 'Just imagine, Tam, here Henry the Fifth assembled his men for Agincourt.' How wonderful it was to have memories like this, laid up in one's mind's eye.

Other memories . . . prowling round Fleet Street, treading the very stairs where Samuel Johnson's feet had trod, in his house just off the Street; Dad as eager as a boy, shivering over the cruel place of execution in the pleasant green courtyard of the Tower, standing on bridges over Father Thames, and wondering how many unrevealed stories it had heard through all the centuries.

Then had come that magic, though ordinary seeming, day when they had gone into New Zealand House in the Haymarket. Dad had had an inspiration during that holiday for another book to come when they had visited one of the museums and he'd become enthralled with the South Pacific section, and with its weapons in particular. He thought he'd glean the material he would need there and then. Later, who knew, if the books did well enough, he might be able to travel out there? He took copious notes on greenstone articles from the books in the New Zealand House Library, then they'd dipped into the newspapers on the tables for an insight into the contemporary scene.

Suddenly Stephen Meade became very engrossed, then thumped the table with his fist and said, 'It beats all! I just can't believe it. We've always believed him dead.'

Thomasina jerked her head up. This was an intriguing statement. Why, it was the very essence of a plot for a thriller. But who was alive? Who had been presumed dead? 'Who can you mean, Dad? Someone from World War Two? Someone you used to know?'

He laughed, still staring at the page. 'No, not in World War Two. Not in World War One. Not even in the Boer War! He was in the regular Army. We thought he'd died in a skirmish on the Indian Frontier, way back in the eighteen-seventies.'

Thomasina blinked. 'Dad, it's not making sense. What do you mean? *We* thought him dead? You weren't even born. Even your mother wasn't born then!'

'Sorry, Tam. It's just so unbelievable. I mean the odds against my even seeing this must be millions to one. This paper—' he tapped it,—'the *Christchurch Argus*, has been running, evidently, a series of recollections of pioneer ancestors. Written by their descendants. This one is one, of all people, on Thomas Swainson!'

Something stirred in Thomasina's mind. 'Swainson. That

was—let me see—your mother's maiden name. Your grandfather was Edwin Swainson. Edwina is named after him.'

'Aye. And very like him from what I've heard. Not that my mother could remember him, she was only three when he died, the youngest of a very large family. Her sister Jane was more than twenty years older than her. She said he was fair and blue-eyed and very gentle.'

Thomasina burst out laughing. 'Well, that last doesn't apply to our Edwina. She was born ready to take on the world. Not only her own battles, but everyone else's.'

Stephen laughed. 'True. But this article. Edwin married Bessie Swainson, your great-grandmother. Can you remember much of the stories my mother used to tell you?'

She concentrated. 'Yes, a fairish bit, I think. Let me see . . . I think I know more about Bessie than about Edwin. That side of the family seemed to die out. Bessie was Elizabeth Temple Watson. And Temple is my own middle name. Oh dear, now what do I know about the Swainsons? They were orphaned when very young. Two boys, one girl, Adelaide, who went to Canada. Gran said her mother finally lost touch with her altogether. And Thomas—' her eyes widened—'went to India and was killed there.' She made a clutch at the paper. 'So *he* couldn't have been a New Zealand pioneer. Must be someone else, Dad. Oh, I see . . . he wasn't killed, after all.'

He put his hand over the page. 'It all fits, Tamsin. I want you to see first how much you actually remember of the old story. It's so long since it's been mentioned.'

She closed her eyes in an effort to remember, shutting out the ultra-modern surroundings about her and trying to slip back into a past she had never known except by hearsay. 'There were three Swainson children left orphans. Edwin, Thomas, Adelaide. Edwin, the eldest, was only nine. There seemed nothing for them but an institution, and in those days orphanages weren't like they are now. Then an uncle said he could take them in if Edwin went down the mines with him, leading the pit ponies. You see, he had seven of his own, Gran used to say.

'He had a burning determination to work above ground, in the sunshine, to provide some sort of independence for his brother and sister. In time he became a French polisher, loving his work of restoring old furniture. Bessie, his wife-to-be, was just a sweet seventeen, youngest of the family, and a spoiled darling, who had never had to work in her life. Her father owned a boot

11

factory. Her brothers and sisters were all fair, she was gipsy-dark and tiny. The others were all married. When her mama developed an incurable cancer, her one desire was to see her youngest married. Edwin was a frequent visitor at the home and the mother contrived. Edwin adored his child-bride with a romantic fervour, yet she remained unawakened. They lived with the mother, whose illness was arrested, for some time. Their first daughter, Jane, came within the year.

'Adelaide had gone out to Canada and married a French-Canadian and wrote glowing letters home of the opportunities there. Edwin went over to make a start in a new world, planning to send for his Bessie. He was there three years, doing well, then sent for his wife and child, but Bessie wouldn't leave England, so he returned.

'Just before his brother came home, Thomas had come to England on leave from India. A glorious June it was, Grandma said her mother told her. Bessie had never been so happy. Thomas took them picnicking in the valley of the Tyne, showed them Hadrian's Wall, took them to Alnwick Castle, gave his brother's young bride a carefree, never-to-be-forgotten time. Thomas was dying for his brother to come home to share it all, something they hadn't known as children.

'Bessie didn't even guess why it was the skies seemed more blue than they had ever been, why the days were so short, the roses so richly perfumed, till a moment of revelation when she and Thomas knew they loved each other. Both were too honourable to lose control of the situation. Bessie had never known a grand passion for her husband, but she had loved his gentle, understanding ways, and Thomas owed his brother so much . . . for him and for Adelaide Edwin had spent those wretched years in the darkness and chill of the mines.

'They kept their secret well and Edwin remembered his brother's last leave with nothing but happiness after his death on service was reported some months later. He and Bessie longed for a son so they could call him Thomas. But daughter after daughter arrived. Then, to their great joy, they had a little son. Small Thomas died at eight months, of a convulsion. Then, in 1890, when Bessie was thirty-seven, your mother was born and they called her Thomasina. Three years later Edwin died of the asthma that was a heritage from his years below ground. He was only forty-four.

'Your own mother wanted a little son called Thomas too, to

please her mother, but her little Thomas lived only a few days. You were born many years later, when she was thirty-five, and to please her, when I was born you called me Thomasina because by the time I was a week old you knew Mother couldn't have any more children.' Her eyes dropped to the article in the paper. It was simply headed : ' Thomas Swainson, a sterling pioneer.'

It said he might not have arrived in Canterbury in the First Four Ships, but just over a score of years later he had reached there from India where he had been reported missing, believed killed. He had been carried off by hill tribesmen, escaped, and after gruelling adventures reached civilisation again. Because of his wounds it would have been impossible to rejoin the Army, and he went first to South Africa to decide about his future. He knew he could never return to England. He could never take the risk of betraying his brother. Edwin and Bessie would have mourned him as dead, for months, and by now would have adjusted themselves. It was better that way. One day he took ship for New Zealand, furthest away from all he loved

He had married later in life and the article was written by his youngest son, born near the end of the century, one Ebenezer Swainson, who was still farming his father's property on Lyttelton Harbour, Banks Peninsula. It had a romantic name, Ngahuru Marama, the Bay of the Harvest Moon. He had lived a full, useful, and happy life, the only shadow being the nostalgia that sometimes visited him for word of his brother, and of his sister in Canada.

Most of the article, naturally, was taken up with the early struggles to establish himself as a land-owner and to play a fine part in the early affairs of the province.

That night in their hotel, Stephen asked Thomasina to write to this cousin of his mother's, care of the *Christchurch Argus*. ' I feel if I do, just putting Stephen Meade on the back of the envelope, it won't mean a thing, but if you put Thomasina Temple Meade, I reckon his pulses will quicken and he'll leap to recognition, knowing you must be a descendant of Elizabeth Temple Swainson's.'

Ebenezer's reply to them had been started within minutes of receiving that letter. It had given him the thrill of a lifetime. He even envisaged the chance of the whole family visiting him, saying they could tell by the photograph of the old homestead that there was no lack of rooms and at present just himself, his housekeeper, and his nephew rattled round in it! Stephen wrote back in light vein, saying if he sold television rights any time they'd be on the next plane. Ebenezer had read two of his books the year before.

Thomasina had begun to dream, for her father, of him being able before too long to go on his own, to get the gen for a new novel, perhaps basing it on this long-ago family story. She and Maddy, secretly, began to save towards his fare. The blow to her father's future came before they had even broached the subject to him.

He hadn't told Ebenezer of his illness till the last . . . a pity to shadow so happy a correspondence with it, he'd said. Ebenezer had naturally imagined an author to be fairly comfortable, and not till this last reverse in fortune had Thomasina written to tell him their circumstances. Then it had been only because soon now she must give Ebenezer a new address. Till then he would have imagined the books were established enough to provide them with security.

Now all the dreams of a more affluent future for her father and Maddy were gone, and her thoughts were exhaustedly occupied throughout each day with questions of ways and means, trying to reach sensible decisions, to act wisely. And the hours of sleep that should have 'knitted up the ravell'd sleave of care' were woefully short as night after tossing night she lay awake, trying to decide their future.

Today, now, she knew it could be postponed no longer. There had been a letter from the authorities yesterday giving a deadline and asking had she succeeded in obtaining alternative accommodation. If not, they were prepared to do what they could to secure her the lease of a flat in town. So what was she doing sitting here dreaming about New Zealand?

Suddenly, on her rock perch, she grinned to herself. Unless, of course, she won that competition. A thousand or more to one chance, probably. The children had egged her on to enter, and she'd done so merely to take their minds off other, less pleasant things. They had all three worked out the code in the advertisement of the airline sponsoring the competition. It turned out to be a slogan for air-travel; they had answered the written quiz on New Zealand. She had spent more time than she could sensibly spare swotting up New Zealand history and geography, and finally she had submitted her essay on the set subject: 'Why I want to visit New Zealand.' She probably had a head start on

14

that. She had simply told the true romance of Bessie and Thomas, and of the article they had found in London. It had needed no embellishing. A trip to New Zealand was the prize. But what a hope!

It was then that voices floated up the hill and broke into her dreams. Children's voices, Matthew's and Edwina's. She'd call out to them as soon as they reached the top. But she didn't . . . because as they neared she found they weren't rambling just for delight, they were discussing something serious.

Matthew's voice was much too grave for a boy of eleven. 'We've just got to do something about Tamsin, Edwina. She's worrying like mad about us. Thinks we can't take it, living in town.'

Edwina's voice was bleak. 'Matthew, I don't think *I* can! Can you?' She sounded incredulous about it.

His quick answer was unchildlike in its philosophical acceptance. 'We've *got* to take it, Ed. There's no show of staying on here. Not a cottage to let anywhere. Tam's even charged round the farms to see if any of the old stables could be sold to her for converting into living quarters. But there's nothing. She's going mad thinking about it. So listen. We've got to somehow convince her we think it's rather exciting, after all, going to the city. You're good at pretending things. I heard Mrs. Bruce telling Tam children are more adaptable than she was giving them credit for, that after a spell of homesickness, we'd adapt. She said, " If you don't stop worrying you'll make yourself ill and then where'd they be?" '.

Edwina's voice had a catch in it and held real terror. 'Matthew! You don't think *she'll* get ill? *Die*? I couldn't bear—'

Matthew seemed wise beyond his years. 'Of course not, you great nit! Really, girls do like to meet trouble head on! Tamsin's as tough as a nut. Only what's the good of her getting the collywobbles over something she can't help? So when she comes in tonight—I think she must be at Bruce's—we'll play it up, make her think we've got used to the idea instead of moping. But don't overdo it. I'll say it'll be awfully easy getting off to the cinema on Saturday afternoons when we live in town and you could spark up and ask if you could take roller-skating lessons. You've always wanted to and there's no place here. See?'

Edwina said rebelliously, 'I'd rather get a placard and make a demonstration outside the Council offices!'

Matthew burst out laughing. 'Just like you! Fine demonstra-

15

tion that'd be—one nine-year-old kid. It's just not on, Sis. One little cottage is small beer. We've got to give in. And you're going to look as if you like it! C'mon, I'll race you back!'

He was evidently away before Edwina could protest any more and she went flying down the hill after him. Not till Tamsin, peering round the outcrop, saw them cross the stepping-stones of the brook, and get lost to sight among the orchard trees, did she emerge. She would accept that gallant pretence and maybe in time the kids might even come to believe there'd be compensations in city living.

Poor lambs. They'd be unnaturally quiet and grave tonight.

Quiet? Not a bit of it. As she reached the house they came tearing out of it, helter-skelter, yelling at the top of their voice range, each trying to drown the other out in a desire to be the one to impart news. It only added up to incoherency.

Edwina used a crafty elbow to wind her brother temporarily and win the day. She gasped it out. 'A letter—from that airline. I think we've won it! The trip to New Zealand. That's all it could be.'

Matthew drowned her out. 'Open it, quick!' He thrust the envelope at her. 'It's *bound* to be good news, isn't it?'

Bound to be good. How resilient children were. Even after the year they had had, blow after blow, they still had this lovely confidence. Thomasina knew an inner shrinking. She said hastily, 'Don't count your chickens. It might be just a query, or even one of the consolation prizes.'

All the time her fingers were tearing at the tough envelope, her hopes as fervent as the children's. It would give them such a lift. Her glance at the first sentence told her all she needed to know. They had won it—a trip for two adults or one adult and two children! A very generous amount of spending money went with it, and a wardrobe of clothing for each of them. Suddenly her legs wouldn't support her and she sat down quickly on the old circular seat round an apple tree.

The children boggled. 'What's wrong?'

She pulled herself together. 'It's silly. Only my knees are knocking. *We've won it!*'

'Great green grasshoppers!' said Matthew, and turned a double somersault out of sheer joy. Then he sat up, his face sobering, and said, 'Thomasina, would it be possible to exchange the prize for cash? I mean add the price of the fares to the spending money and put it towards a house to live in?'

She shook her head. 'No—I found that out, too. You see they use a trip like this as a publicity stunt here, and carrying three people doesn't cost a fraction of normal fares—they'll just give us empty seats, you see. But it was sweet of you to suggest it. It said in the rules that the trip must be taken or it would go to the runner-up. It's two months, with everything provided. That means we'll save our keep all that time. And it'll give us the holiday of our lives!. Now just a moment. There's more here I haven't taken in yet.' She read, looked up with sparkling eyes. 'This is a real bonus! They liked what they called my journalistic style, they note I'm Stephen Meade's daughter—they'd get that from my essay, of course, about the newspaper in New Zealand House—and they say I seem to have inherited his gift. Oh, how marvellous—this executive seems to know Dad's books and they wonder if I would care to write up all the ports of call for their publicity issues, as from a *bone fide* traveller. They say they'll pay well for these! Oh, thank goodness I haven't gone job-hunting in Newcastle yet. That can wait till we get back. We can stay with Mrs. Bruce when we return.

'Let me see the time-table . . . goodness, we'll be on our way before we can realize it. This itinerary gives us a week in Christchurch at the end of our tour of New Zealand as we leave from there again. I'll ask if we can extend that by about a fortnight, and we can go over to Harvest Moon Bay and stay with Cousin Ebenezer Swainson. Won't he be excited when we write to tell him?'

It was just on bedtime when Matthew had his bright idea. 'Wouldn't it be more exciting not to write to tell him? We'll be on our way so soon. Let's just ring him from Christchurch.'

His sister thought it over. 'Yes, it would probably give him an even greater thrill, Matthew, if he suddenly heard our voices on the phone.' Oh, how glad she was that they could stop worrying about ways and means and be able to plan something that would be sheer fun. All sorts of chaotic thoughts were chasing through her mind. If she wrote those articles up well enough, it might lead to something permanent in the publicity line. Oh, tonight she could believe in anything. She wouldn't worry at all about what would happen when she came back. Nothing must spoil this wonderful opportunity. In fact, with a two months' respite, there might even be a cottage to let or for sale in Greenchester by then. And there were always jobs going at the mill.

They revelled in everything, the exciting shopping particularly. They'd had to be so cheeseparing for so long, it was sheer joy to spend like this. Edwina was in raptures, even forsaking her beloved patched jeans for gorgeously feminine garments. The whole village was thrilled for them. Thomasina guessed their feeling of guilt that their houses had been spared at the expense of hers was being lessened by this, and when they heard the airline was presenting Thomasina with an expensive camera to take pictures to illustrate her articles, with ones more personal than the run-of-the-mill tourist ones, the people took up a subscription and presented the children with a camera each. They planned a grand send-off party for them.

Nevertheless packing and storing their furniture and other treasures, in the loft Mr. Bruce put at their disposal, caused Thomasina a few pangs. The worst moment of all was when she locked the little green door with its enormously old-fashioned key for the last time, knowing she would never open it again; knowing that no more fires of aromatic apple-logs would burn on that hearth; feeling a traitor to walk along the brick path and click the white picket gate shut because soon great transport lorries would thunder unfeelingly over the macadam that would seal beneath its smoothness for ever all traces of a home that had stood there for more than two hundred years.

Thomasina braced herself, flung back her tawny hair and walked down the lane to the Bruces' house with never a backward glance. She would put on a happy face, glad with anticipation for the exciting future as she got near. The children mustn't guess at her feelings.

They were wildly excited. Tomorrow they would take the Flying Scotsman from Newcastle to London. The next day the airline was giving them a luncheon and the following one they would leave England in late summer to arrive in New Zealand just as spring was waking the southern hemisphere. They would take off in the early afternoon for Los Angeles, racing the sunset and beating time by hours and hours. Matthew was primed to the ears with information about how time changed as one circled the globe, and data about international date-line crossings and all the places they would visit en route was just about bursting out of him.

They would see Disneyland and Hollywood and a vast area of

18

California. There would be days spent in the magic of Hawaii and Fiji, then the flight to Auckland would bring them to their New Zealand tour. Thomasina hoped no word of it would leak out to Cousin Ebenezer. She would so like to surprise him. It wasn't likely to be featured, she thought; the publicity was really aimed at prospective British tourists.

She had a wonderful gift for Ebenezer, packed flat at the bottom of her case: an old, well-preserved photograph of the 1870s, taken of Thomas and Bessie and her small Jane in Bessie's mother's rose-embowered garden.

How fortunate it was that she had decided to discard the heavy old frames of the other family portraits for the sake of taking up less storage room. Under the one of Edwin, Bessie, and their family of daughters, she had found it. She guessed that Bessie had hidden it under there so that sometimes she could swivel the catches round and look at it. It must have been taken when Edwin was still in Canada—and was just too revealing. The photographer had caught them when Thomas was laughing down at his sister-in-law and niece, and all Elizabeth's unguarded love was in her eyes as she laughed back up at him. Thomasina was sure old Ebenezer, a born romantic from the article he had written, would rather have it than any other gift from England.

CHAPTER II

Now on this last week of September their official travelling was past. The last month had been a kaleidoscope wonderland of impressions, all jotted down by Thomasina as they travelled, and just yesterday they had been despatched to the airline offices in London. They had forsaken their more glamorous accommodation for a couple of rooms in a modest Christchurch boarding-house for Thomasina to accomplish this, and she'd arranged to stay on if, when they visited Harvest Moon Bay, she decided Ebenezer's housekeeper might be a little too old to be bothered with two children.

Mrs. Fairweather, their landlady, had nodded her head sagely. 'Very wise. Some people are very set in their ways. You'll know as soon as you've been there an hour or two if she's the right kind or not. Mind, you've nothing to fear with those two. The day you were busy typing and they came to the Museum with me, I thoroughly enjoyed it myself. I'll have them any time you want to be off on your own.'

They had by this time decided not to even ring Ebenezer. Just to knock on his door and say : 'Guess who?' Therefore, it was rather a pity the night before, after answering the phone, Mrs. Fairweather came through to say she was going to visit her daughter at Lake Coleridge and Jill had said she could bring those two children if she liked. Matthew could see through the power-house. Nothing would have held him back. So now Thomasina was on a sightseeing bus that would let her off at Ngahuru Marama. The garden city of the plains was garlanded with all the flowers of the springtide, daffodils and bluebells lay in sheets of azure and gold beneath huge oaks and beeches home-sick pioneers had planted in this sweep of fertile farmland enriched by the watershed of the great Alps that rimmed the westward horizon, and it seemed as if each tree had set out to catch up in size, if never in age, with its English forebears, to lessen the nostalgia of the adventurers.

Forsythia rose in fountains of gold, almond and cherry and peach trees were rosetted with pink blossoms, grape hyacinths girdled trees growing in the stretches of lawn that bordered the pavements, and many houses had narrow strips of polyanthus and anemones growing outside their street fences. The geraniums that

20

grew outside all the year round looked as if they were trying to turn spring into summer already.

Thomasina knew that the bus would take them away from the flat city with its Roman-like precision of squared-off streets and avenues, up and over the Cashmere Hills that kept watch and ward over the city and finally circled the green waters of Lyttelton Harbour, and reached out to enfold in its great arms Akoroa Harbour too, in the embrace of Banks Peninsula that had been named for Cook's great naturalist so long ago. But aeons before this, these harbours had been the craters of two enormous volcanoes, and the more gentle years had filled them with translucent water and created havens for ocean-weary vessels.

Before long they reached the summit of Dyer's Pass well above the houses that clustered the lower slopes, and were dipping down to Lyttelton Harbour by a road just like a question mark, scrawled hugely on hillsides that were much greener this side, away from the blazing sun of the north. Arms of headlands reached out into the colourful waters and one island lay as if God had leaned down and marked it with a cross because it was crisscrossed from corner to corner with gigantic lines of dark blue-green pines—Quail Island.

One of these headlands must curve round to shelter and form Ngahuru Marama. What a gem of a setting! A strange emotion suddenly stirred in Thomasina. Almost like homesickness acting in reverse. How strange. How could one be nostalgic for a place never seen before? For a spot one hadn't known existed this time last year?

It must be something to do with this country, with its clear air and mountain heights, sapphire lakes and rivers holding the refracted light of the blues and greens of the ice-falls and glaciers and snows whence their waters came. You could still call it a young country with space like this. True, there were cities that knew crowding, and high-rise buildings springing up in those areas, but for people who loved the country there was so much of it. That was natural enough, for it was larger than Great Britain and the population hadn't yet reached the three million mark.

Why not stay here? Thomasina almost flinched as the thought hit her. Could she? Perhaps in some suburb of Christchurch near good schools for the children? Houses were expensive, she knew, but perhaps she could get a small flat to begin with, till she had a chance to weigh up pros and cons. To find out what secretarial jobs were offering. Wages were good, food was, in the main, less

21

costly, though inflation had pushed it up. Clothes were dearer. She mustn't get carried away with the idea, but they could make a new start here. Dad's mother's sisters had been so much older than her that their children were more like aunts than cousins to Thomasina, and they had drifted apart somewhat because of this. What had she to return for? Ebenezer Swainson could be a sort of grandfather-figure to the children, somewhere for them to visit, situated on a farm so that the children could retain a link with the country life they had known and loved.

The bus stopped for morning tea at Governor's Bay, a place sweet with smaller farms than most New Zealand ones, dotted with cherry orchards and holiday houses, looking up the Harbour to the Heads. Thomasina thought the tourists would never be done eating and buying postcards and souvenirs. She wanted to get on, to meet Ebenezer, to find in him this link with her own forebears.

Then on they went, through Allanton and Teddington, with a road called Gebbie's Pass snaking off to the right through the hills, to take those who wanted to, further south. They kept to the harbour road, and at the deepest U-curve of the head of the inlet, went up and over a road that cut straight over a headland. At a crossroads the bus stopped. The driver turned round, said to Thomasina, ' The tourist buses don't go right into Harvest Moon, but it's less than a quarter of a mile to the village. If you go straight on down, you'll be at the Harvest Sickle—the pub—in no time. They'll tell you how to get to Swainson's place. There's a short cut that's much quicker than going round by the road.'

The tar-sealing, as they called it here, stopped soon and there was no footpath. Thomasina was glad she'd put flat thonged sandals on, laced up round her ankles, and that she'd worn a light-weight trouser suit in green crimplene. She'd clipped her slightly longer than shoulder-length hair back with an Alice-band in green, and had a golden scarf tucked triangular-wise into the cream silk revers of the top of the suit. She carried a green suede bag swinging from her shoulder, but clutched to her was the flat parcel with the precious photograph in it.

This road had certainly nothing of the symmetrical design of the Christchurch ones. It must have been a sheep-track originally, surely. It would have widened in time as more and more settlers arrived at the Head, to a walking track, then horses and buggies would use it, forming great ruts in winter. Then someone, tiring of the mud, would spread shingle from the shore on it, and they had planted poplars and willows and silver birches among the gnarled and spreading gracefulness of the ngaios and the feathery slenderness of the kowhais that were as golden as their English cousins, the laburnums, this glad, sunshiny September day.

A narrow humpy-backed bridge, formed of the volcanic rocks of these hills, spanned a little creek that wandered over the road, then dropped out of sight among native evergreen trees that hemmed in the gully that conducted the waters, presumably, to the salt waters of the harbour below.

Birds sang from the trees, trying to outrival the song of the creek, Red Admiral'butterflies gleamed brightly, and dragonflies iridescent in green and blue. Sea-birds curved in glorious flight against the cerulean sea, their wings glinting silver in the sun; somewhere a calf was bawling and lambs and ewes constantly baaed to each other. Thomasina turned a corner and stopped enchanted. This was the nearest to an English village she had seen in all New Zealand.

The road was so white, almost chalky, and in the old days the pioneers had built small cottages closer to the road than most New Zealand houses were. Indeed, the old stone hotel, the Harvest Sickle, rose straight up from the side and had not only preserved its hitching rail and rings, but there was actually a horse tied up there now, its gleaming chestnut flanks reflecting the sun. There was a horse-trough full of water and a blacksmith's shop beside it with the name Aaron Copperfield across the doorway.

Thomasina grinned to herself. Ebenezer had told her the Bay of the Harvest Moon was almost an anachronism, a village founded by Obadiah Cherrington, a Yorkshireman who liked Biblical names. They must have carried on the custom through the generations. Hence Ebenezer, she supposed.

Just as she came up to the hotel, out strode a fair giant of a man with hair that looked as if it tried to be brown but was bleached into straw-colour. Oddly enough, for so fair a man, he looked forbidding, hatchet-faced, in fact. Perhaps it was those overhanging eyebrows or the fact that he seemed to be in a temper. But perhaps that was too imaginative. That was what happened to people with a writing flair. He could be just worried and in a hurry.

He positively flung himself into the saddle and dust spurted up from under the hoofs of his mount as he took off. Just like a western it was. Thomasina almost expected shots to break out.

23

She went on into the hotel. The interior was cool and dark, flagged in the old style, in black and white. She could hear voices.

'Aye, she's a bad-tempered wench, that,' said one, a man's voice. 'I hope he knows what he's doing, and that they make it a long engagement. Give him time to find out what a bitter tongue she has.'

A woman's voice in answer. 'I'd ha' credited him with more discrimination. It's no' as if he's just a boy. But I daresay they fall the hardest, the older ones. I don't think I've ever wanted to put a spoke in anyone's wheel before, but if I saw a chance of it, I would, so help me. But it looks as if someone else has put the rift in, and good on him, too. I thought it was her voice when I answered the phone. She knew he was here. He was beyond caring we were within earshot. He knows we're safe, anyway. He must've fair infuriated her. The way he said, with that icy politeness, "You've gone too far. I won't hang up in your ear, but I'm terminating this conversation right now!" I'd have liked fine to see her face.'

Thomasina thought she'd better cough. Out came the woman; such a rosy-faced pleasant-looking soul, Thomasina couldn't credit she had just expressed herself so forcibly. 'Can I help you, love?'

'I wanted to know the way to Corrieside, please? The short cut.'

'Oh, what a pity you hadn't come a few seconds back. Luke Richmond was here. He could have taken you, not that it's far.'

'Luke Richmond? Works at Corrieside, does he?'

The woman smiled. 'In a way. Not that I mean he doesn't. He works hard, too hard. But he's not hired help. He's the owner's nephew and partner, and I daresay his heir. Mebbe you saw him —he just rode off.'

Rode? The man with the penthouse eyebrows and the ferocious expression. Oh dear! Nephew to her own kinsman. Then he'd be some sort of relation to her. Not the happiest of thoughts. Just as well she hadn't brought the children. Thomasina had a feeling she wasn't going to like this Luke Richmond.

The woman said, 'Do I detect an English accent? Do you know—?'

Thomasina didn't mind this; if it was curiosity, it was a friendly interest. 'I don't really know Mr. Ebenezer Swainson, other than by letters, though I'm a sort of second cousin of his. He doesn't know I'm even in New Zealand yet. I thought I'd like

24

to surprise him. I got in touch with him when—'

'When you read his article in the *Argus* in New Zealand House. Bless you, and welcome. What a lift it'll give Eb, a lift he sorely needs just now. He'll be fair beside himself with joy.'

'He's home, then? I'm staying in Christchurch with my little brother and sister, but they're out for the day. I thought children might be a bit much for Ebenezer and I'd be best to make my first visit on my own.'

'Eb's wonderful with children. Pity he never had any of his own. But his brothers' grandchildren are forever there. He'll make them very welcome.'

'But his housekeeper—I mean it's not like a wife. She mightn't like having her routine upset. I know there's only the nephew there—though Ebenezer never mentioned him by name. He's been writing mostly about the family history.'

'Och, Louisa Stirling would make nothing of a bairn or two extra in the house. She's a grandmother several times over and all wee 'uns are welcome with her, but sorry to say, she isn't there. She's in hospital in Christchurch—gallstones. Just three days since the operation, but she's doing fine. If I know Louisa she'll be rarin' to go in no time. I hope you aren't just paying a flying visit, she'll be that vexed to have missed you. She said it gave Eb a new lease of life.' A thought struck her, as if something had just connected. 'Can it be you're here to stay? Eb did say you'd lost your folk. We were that interested in that story he wrote we feel we know you. Might you think of settling in New Zealand? What I was after thinking was that mebbe you could help out at the big house. They could do wi' it. They have some help. Their hired man's wife does a few days. Not easy to come by in New Zealand as a rule, help in the house, but here in the village there's not much for women to work at part-time. Corrieside's far too big a house for one woman to manage, even a demon for work like Louisa, so they get Peggy Bancroft in three days a week. Just now she's cooking their dinners too, but those men have to manage their own breakfasts and lunches. So if you could come over with the children, I'm sure it would be a happy solution. I think Eb would be right pleased with me for putting it before you. He mightn't like to rush you right away.'

Thomasina felt a little overwhelmed. She said cautiously, 'I might possibly be able to manage that for a couple of weeks or so —providing they want that. But I'll see how they are—first. I'm only here on a visit. I won a competition with an airline—yes,

25

truly. But I daresay I could help out for a bit till this housekeeper gets on her feet again, but only if they propose it themselves.'

The woman burst out laughing. 'I ken fine they'll want it. That Luke is no more fond of rustling up his own meals than most men, especially at this time of year, and Eb will want you under his own roof for sure. You've no idea what it meant to him, that contact with you. He'd missed his wife terribly. We thought, Jake and me, that he was starting to slip, but from your first letter he perked up.' She shook her head sagely. 'I'm no' a betting woman, but I'd lay a thousand to one he'll never let you go back to England. I'd like to ring and say you're on your way, but I mustn't spoil your surprise.' She peered at Thomasina, 'I wonder if when he answers the door he'll leap to the right conclusion. Are you like your great-grandmother, or whatever she was? I expect Eb will have an old photograph of Bessie and Edwin.'

Thomasina said, laughing, 'It won't be much good to him if he has. I can give Bessie about five inches and she didn't have a tawny mop and freckles like me, nor eyes neither one thing or the other—green or blue—she was a tiny, gipsy-like creature, my grandmother told me, with smooth raven-black hair, and had almost black eyes and an olive skin. I shouldn't think Mr. Swainson would leap to so wild a surmise.' She looked down on herself deprecatingly. 'And she wouldn't be wearing a trouser-suit. It would be a bustle and leg o'mutton sleeves and a whaleboned waist!'

Finally she managed to get away, but not before she learned that Drusilla Babbington had been born in the Bay, so naturally had been given a Biblical name, same as her mother's, but her father had been a Scotsman. She had known Eb all her life and her husband, Jake, had been baptised Jacob. Thomasina promised she'd let her know how she got on, and how Ebenezer reacted when he knew her identity.

It wasn't Ebenezer's reaction she was worrying about, it was this scowling nephew's. How stupid of her to feel such unwarranted apprehension. He wouldn't be cross with her, a stranger. Anyway, now she knew the circumstances it was probably only indigestion, not temper, if they lacked a housekeeper.

She was hardly past the bakehouse next to the pub when she heard the sound of hooves and turned her head. Another horse being ridden hard. Heavens, Harvest Moon Bay wasn't the sleepy hollow she'd imagined. It was more like a Wild West Show!

She had an instant admiration for the horsemanship and the picture this girl made. She had long straight black hair flowing out behind her and one would almost think it was an emergency. Even if it looked like sheer curiosity, Thomasina stopped to watch. The girl reined up short, gazed blankly at the empty hitching rail, she thought, swung round, gazed uphill and began to move, but at that moment Jacob Babbington came out.

The black-haired beauty wasted no time on polite preliminaries such as good-mornings. She demanded, ' Where's he gone? Back up there, or on to see me?'

Jacob showed no resentment. He said mildly and rather uncaringly, ' Home, I'd think. I saw him pass this window.'

She said no words of thanks, finished wheeling her grey round, dug in her heels and was off. Thomasina was sure it was Luke she was after. She began to wonder if coming as a surprise was such a good thing after all. But perhaps she was reading too much into it. Perhaps the girl was just cross she'd missed Luke at the Sickle. When she met them up at the house they'd seem perfectly ordinary. Curb your imagination, Thomasina, you're at it again. Stephen used to call it, excusingly, to Maddy, their extra-sensory perception. Maddy called it overworked imagination. Anyway, it was Ebenezer she wanted to see. No doubt his nephew would be out all day. The lambs were still very young. He'd be riding round the sheep all day.

She took the lane across the street, climbed a little hill, crossed a bridge over a tiny stream, and saw a path beyond a stile leading into a spinney. Beyond that, she'd been told, lay the stables, and nobody would mind her approaching the house from there. Everyone went that way on foot, Drusilla had said, because it was a mile round by road.

As she emerged from the trees she came upon the stables, built of a stone that was almost golden, and twined round with virginia creeper and wistaria, just starting to leaf. She was to go past the stables, up a bank by some steps cut steeply into it, and she'd find herself at the house.

But as she drew level with the stable she heard voices. She hesitated. Perhaps she should look in to see if Ebenezer was there. Little use going up to the house if she had to come back down here to find him, and by then he could be anywhere on the farm. She walked in and realized the voices came from inside the next section of the building. She had her mouth open to call out : ' Anybody there?' when the very tone of the voices stopped her

27

dead in her tracks.

It wasn't an old voice, such as Ebenezer's would have been. It would be the voice of the man with the eyebrows and he was still in a temper.

'How in hell could I have stopped him?' it demanded. 'He's not gaga, you know. He's merely a very alert seventy-five. And in any case, at first it seemed merely a pleasurable exercise for a lonely old man. It took his mind off losing Aunt Georgie. And anyway, what are you getting in such a flap about? Not every-one'd want to live here, even for a sugar-coated pill. She'll probably say no. And in any case, what did you think I could do? Say : "Oh, no, you don't, Uncle, *I* want the lot ! " '

He finished up with an inexpressible sound of contempt and anger.

The other voice was cool. It would belong, Thomasina knew, in that frozen moment of indecision, to the black-haired beauty on the grey horse. It said, ' Don't be absurd, Luke. Who'd want to be as blunt as that? You've no finesse. You ought to have seen the way the wind was blowing. Surely to goodness you could have got in a few seeds of doubt long ago. You'd only have had to say, " My goodness, she *is* crying a poor mouth, isn't she? Hope she's not on the make. Don't let your sympathies run away with you, Uncle," and he'd have been on his guard. The whole situation has grown up out of your complete stupidity, your inability to assess other people's motives. You're too high-minded by far and much too easy-osy about money. That was fine when you were single, but as a married man you'd have more than yourself to think about. One has to be practical to succeed in this world. And you've me to think of now !'

Thomasina had been pivoting around on one foot ready to flee, hoping that the very fury of their raised voices would cover the sound of her footsteps on this concrete floor. Plastic soles were such giveaways. But at that moment the voices ceased. Were they simply holding their breath, glaring at each other, or had they become aware someone was in the outer part, listening in? Oh, how horrible ! It was like a nightmare. Thomasina stood petrified, gazing with fearful fascination at the archway to the inner chamber where any moment two wrathful figures might appear. Oh, if only she hadn't decided on giving the folk at Corrieside a surprise !

To her relief the man's voice broke the silence. But it had gone to a low pitch, with a cold intensity worse than the heated anger of a moment ago.

'Aren't you jumping the gun? Aren't you surmising a definite conclusion to our innocuous outings? Am I suffering from amnesia or what? But for the life of me I can't remember proposing to you! *Or* giving you a ring!'

There was another ominous silence. Thomasina was inwardly imploring that girl to shout in anger, to make enough noise to cover her retreat. But suddenly the other voice was placatory.

'Luke, oh, Luke! You're just saying those things because you're angry with me. But I've had to say what I've said because there's not time for you to give me a ring. This thing has got to be checked here and now. We've got to work out a campaign together immediately. Besides, modern couples don't go in so much for sugary proposals these days. We've gone everywhere together for months. Everyone's expecting us to announce our engagement any moment. It's so obvious. There's been a great deepening of friendship that could only mean one thing and you—'

She was cut off. Luke said: 'Ilena! That's far too prosaic. Which shows how unsuited we'd be. When I want to marry a girl she'll get a definite proposal and a ring immediately after. I hadn't got to that stage with you, believe me, and let me tell you something . . . if there'd been any chance of it before you revealed yourself as mercenary as this, there's none now. I'll tell you here and now I never *will* propose to you, so you can—'

His voice had risen. Here was the cover Thomasina so badly needed. She turned and fairly flew out of the stable, running on tiptoes. As she fled through the doorway she kicked a tobacco tin that had been dropped there. It shot before her like a hopscotch block to ring clangingly against the drystone wall that kept the bank at the right from slipping downhill, and all she could hope for was that they were still at it hammer and tongs and mightn't have heard her.

She gained the cutting in the bank just as someone came flying out of the stable into the yard. Thomasina shrank against the far wall of the cutting. She dared not go on ascending, the movement could draw attention. How ghastly if they knew they'd been overheard by a stranger. All she wanted to do was get away. She wouldn't go on up to the house. She'd sneak off from the top of the bank if she could, go down into the spinney again and wait somewhere, anywhere, till she could get a bus back to the city. Then from Christchurch tomorrow she'd ring Ebenezer and ask if they could come over to see him.

Then, just as she felt hopeful about this, it hit her. Drusilla Babbington knew she'd come. Drusilla, who was aptly named, a babbler, if a kindly babbler! By now everyone who'd come into the pub since would know Ebenezer's newly-found relation from the north of England was in Harvest Moon Bay. Oh, what was she to do?

Frozen into immobility, she saw the tall girl, dark hair flowing out behind her, put a hand on the rail and vault over into the paddock where the grey was. She unhitched him from the rail, flung herself into the saddle and rode off. She took a fence some distance away with consummate skill, though Thomasina, very much a novice rider herself, held her breath in case she came off and broke her neck. Then the rider was lost to view across rolling hills.

Thomasina half expected Beetling-Brows to tear after her, flinging himself into the saddle in the same style, but he didn't. What on earth did it mean? When she got away from here she'd sort it out in her mind, if she could. Somebody had made mischief, that was for sure. Imagine stumbling on a family brawl about money or inheritance or something when you'd come thirteen thousand miles to meet an unknown kinsman. Mrs. Babbington had mentioned other nieces and nephews. Looked as if they wanted to cash in as Ebenezer's beneficiaries too.

Thomasina put her hands up to her temples and groaned inwardly. What would that irascible man in there do? It was so nearly lunchtime. Would he go up to the house soon? Presumably Ebenezer would be up there, all unaware of the domestic storm in the stables. Would it be best for her to go up to the house, seemingly ignorant of any quarrelling, and meet Ebenezer? Then perhaps when Luke came up to the house, seeing a stranger, he'd keep his inner turmoil to himself. No man would want to give away any hint of a lovers' quarrel in front of a complete stranger. Thomasina found herself drawing in a great breath of relief. That would be the way of it.

The next moment she knew a great alarm. There was a sudden rush across the courtyard; she made a convulsive movement herself to flee upwards, but someone bounded clean up the steps and in two great leaps was facing her.

Beetling-Brows himself! Thomasina gave a yelp and was furious with herself for so doing. It underlined the guilt she felt at her involuntary eavesdropping.

Luke Richmond said, the eyebrows right down, and eyes sparking, 'Ah! I thought I heard someone kick a tin! How long were you there? What did you hear? And what the devil do you want, creeping about like that listening to private conversations?'

Guilt fled. Thomasina jerked her head up, lifted her chin and said disdainfully, '*Private* conversation? You've just got to be joking! *Private* conversations aren't carried on in a roar like the Bull of Bashan's! My guess is that they could hear you down at the village. I was merely wanting to see if anyone was home, told to take the short cut by the woman at the pub. I had to pass the stables, heard voices and hoped to find Mr. Swainson. I thought it'd be silly to go on up to the house if he was here though I soon realized a voice like that could never belong to a *gentleman*! I heard just enough to realize it wasn't the sort of situation for a stranger to intrude on, so as soon as you started yelling again, I made for that door and kicked that damned tin! I rushed up here —to save you and that girl embarrassment. *She* didn't see me, by the way. I was just waiting here wondering what to do next. I even crouched so no one could see me.'

He made another of his indescribable sounds. Thomasina flinched visibly, taking a step away from him. It seemed to infuriate him still further. An angry red rose in his cheeks.

'Wondering what to do next? That for an excuse! Who do you think you're kidding? You were enjoying every moment of it. Better than a soapbox opera, wasn't it? You were hoping for another instalment! Maybe you thought I'd take after her? Oh, no, she can go and good riddance! I've *had* women! And anyway, who are you and what do you want?'

Thomasina said slowly and coldly, 'It's just possible you may have heard of me. I'm a distant relation of yours from Northumberland. The name is Thomasina Temple Meade.'

She'd never seen such a look on anyone's face. His jaw positively dropped and he appeared bereft of speech.

So she took up the tale. 'Surely your uncle's told you about me? My father—my late father—saw an article in the *Christchurch Argus* your uncle had written about his father, Thomas Swainson, the brother of my great-grandfather, Edwin Swainson. Mrs. Babbington at the pub knew about it, so you must. I came over here from Christchurch to give Ebenezer a surprise because—'

His speech returned with a burst of fury. '*May* have heard of you? *May*? That's rich! It's the understatement of the year. You

31

sworn laughter leapt into his eyes. 'But then I'm *not* a New Zealander,' he said. 'If you're interested, I'm English—like you!'

This time it was Thomasina's jaw that dropped. Then she rallied. 'Well, all I can say is that right this moment I'm less proud of being English than I was two seconds ago!'

He said, all anger having fled, apparently, 'Couldn't you pick it? My voice? Most New Zealanders think I haven't lost my accent.'

'Well, probably they can pick a lingering trace. I couldn't. But it's nothing to do with what we're discussing.'

'No, it's not, but then you brought the subject up, not me. And the reason for my bellow—I trust that's the correct term . . . you did say bull, didn't you?—is that I just don't believe you! Saying you're just here in Christchurch visiting and thought you'd pop over to see us. Good heavens, you may think me thick, but I can see through that. Uncle Eb gave me your last letter but one to read—when you told him about having to give up the cottage. How your father's books had just been beginning to sell well, and you'd have to take a flat in Newcastle-upon-Tyne. It's not likely you'd suddenly make a world trip with two children unless you thought you might profit financially from a newly-found relative.'

Fury rose in Thomasina again and spilled out of her. 'You— you horrible, suspicious, beastly man! If this is what money does to you I'd rather have to scrape and scratch all my life. I know what you think . . . you think I've come here to see if I can worm something out of Ebenezer. How utterly ridiculous! I never as much as thought of such a thing.'

He laughed. It didn't sound any more pleasant than the bellow. 'My dear girl, you must think I'm easily gulled. Why, you couldn't have come more quickly. You wasted no time. You must have fairly burned a track getting to London Airport. I can't think how you managed to even get your injections done in time.'

Thomasina clutched her temples again. Then she said slowly and distinctly, 'Would you mind telling me, preferably in words of not more than two syllables, exactly what you're talking about?'

His lip curled. 'It's easy. Not that you don't know. But here's a direct accusation. The moment you got my uncle's letter saying if you liked to come out to New Zealand to make your home with us, he'd see you didn't lose by it, you upped and offed! Women! Their talk about Women's Lib is all nonsense. They want to feather their nests at the expense of the male community as much

T Ý—B 33

—I'll tell you in a second why I didn't get that letter and how I could afford to come! Now take that disbelieving look off your face and start digesting the truth! Well, I take it Ilena must have got wind of this and thought you ought to have stopped him making such an offer. So you had that slanging match. Well, none of it concerns me and neither you nor Ilena need worry about me. I stand on my own feet, always have and always will. My—our—return flight is booked for mid-October and we'll never see you again.'

'Then why come?'

'I'll tell you why. I entered for a competition for a free trip and won it.'

He laughed. 'That for a fairytale! The chances against anyone winning such a thing at the very moment so much was at stake are too great. I suppose you read about a competition and thought you'd pretend you'd won one—it makes you look less mercenary. Now you'll pretend to be persuaded by Uncle Eb. Against your inclinations, of course.'

'You make me tired! I can prove it. I've got umpteen carbon copies of articles I've written for the airline that ran the competition, in our lodgings in Christchurch. You'll peruse every one of them if I have to glue your nose to the papers to make you do so! And it wasn't just a lucky chance. It was tied up with Ebenezer's story. You had to write an essay saying why you wanted to go to New Zealand. Most, I suspect, would be just an itch to travel, mine had good, warm human interest in it, having just discovered a long-lost relative. The uniting of a family. Added to that, they discovered I was capable of journalism and asked me to do publicity articles for them.

'I expect I left England too long ago to have got your uncle's letter. It's probably following me round. Some mail has already reached me at Christchurch Post Office. I wanted to surprise Ebenezer. It was my little brother's idea. He thought it would have been fun. So just before I left, I wrote an ordinary letter, just saying we were looking for a flat in Newcastle. Now I don't think your uncle should know we've had such a shindy. He'd be distressed to think it had happened. I expect he'll have to know, in time, about your break with Ilena. If you're wise, you'll make it up with her, anyway, seeing there's nothing in it. But I expect, here and now, a full apology!'

She waited.

The brows were down, considering it. That made her madder

35

than ever. Why couldn't he just accept it?

Finally he said, ' There's such a thing as coincidence. I can accept the fact that you won this competition.'

He got a flash from those indignant greeny-blue eyes. ' How big of you! Of course you'll accept it. You've got to. You can't argue with facts . . . carbon copies of facts.'

' Just a moment. But how do I know you didn't receive that letter? It seems a long time ago he wrote it.'

Thomasina's cheeks hollowed in below her cheekbones with the force of the breath she drew in to steady her temper.

' You could of course take my word for it, but seeing you can't seem able to recognize the truth, we'll amble up to the house, outwardly amicable as two people who've just met might be, and you can ask your uncle when he sent that letter. We left Greenchester in the middle of August. I can show you the butts of our tickets—Matthew has kept them as souvenirs. I've no idea when your uncle wrote his letter, but I presume it must have been after that, since you've expressed amazement at how soon we got here. I can only hope he knows the exact date.'

A voice from beyond the inner archway spoke and they jumped.

' He doesn't, quite,' it said, ' but it looks as if it must have just missed you. Right, Luke, a full apology to the lady, please.'

Thomasina was appalled. So too, she saw, was Luke. They both stared, then rushed into the other compartment. A chuckle above them directed their gaze upwards. A ladder led to the loft, and there, hanging downwards, was a very handsome old head, crowned with silver hair. It was pulled back and the next moment Ebenezer Swainson was descending, his back towards them. He reached the floor, turned round, dusted himself down.

He was tall and spare and handsome, in fact even beautiful, with a patrician cast of features that was remarkably like that one-hundred-year-old picture of the gentle Edwin. There was just nothing for Luke and Thomasina to say. They could only stare. It was too much for Ebenezer, he crumpled into laughter, really helpless mirth that made him hang on to the ladder.

' I heard the lot,' he gasped. ' I was over here mending that bridle. Then Sukey came down from the loft, so I guessed that was where she was laying away. I went up for the eggs. When Ilena chased in after you before I'd a chance to call out to you, I thought I'd better lie low. My word, it was revealing! You've had a lucky escape there, my boy.'

36

Luke looked at his uncle coldly. 'Don't play the innocent with me. You'd been chatting Ilena on the phone. She let it out when she phoned me at the pub. You did it purposely! *And* told her I was at the Sickle!'

Ebenezer didn't look a bit abashed. 'Well, I thought it would be interesting to have her reaction to my news. Her behaviour the last few weeks had been very possessive, so I thought it time she knew I'd invited the Meades out, that I hoped they'd stay. That I thought it would be very fitting if Bessie's descendants benefited in some way from Thomas's good fortune. You ought to be grateful to me.'

Thomasina wanted to implore him to stop, not to make a bad situation worse. He added casually, 'Don't *you* think you've had a lucky escape?'

Luke said, quite evenly, 'I'm sure I have. I'll stay single. There are worse things than bachelorhood.'

Ebenezer said quickly, 'Oh, all women aren't tarred with the same brush, Luke. But I knew that one was. And, Luke, I'm waiting for that apology.'

Thomasina said even more quickly, 'No, don't bother. I don't think it would mean a thing. It's just been unfortunate.' She looked across at Ebenezer appealingly. 'Would there be any chance of forgetting all this? It can all blow over because I'll be at the other side of the world in two or three weeks' time and I'd like this shelved now. We can look upon it as a misconception, and I'd like to enjoy meeting you as if it had never happened. I'd like to bring the children over and explore the Bay. It's so lovely and the children would love to come over for a day at a time.'

Ebenezer snorted. These men were good at snorting, she thought, though this was a kindly one. 'For the day, nothing! You must come to stay. Fancy paying for lodgings when you've got blood relatives here in a house big enough for three or four families! And we're supposed to be noted for hospitality at Corrieside. I'm only sorry Louisa Stirling, my housekeeper, isn't here. It means you might have to get our breakfasts and lunches, but I dare say you could manage that, eh?'

Thomasina said, rather unhappily, 'Yes, of course I could, but I think that under these circumstances it would be better to pay two or three-day visits.'

Luke Richmond pulled a wry mouth. 'Not domesticated, eh? Well, few writers are, I hear. They like to push the breakfast

37

dishes to the back of the table, pull the typewriter forward and type on, regardless.'

Stung, Thomasina turned on him. 'I can only surmise that you've not known any writers. My dad was a member of a writers' group in Newcastle. Quite a few women writers among them. They use to visit us and we would pay return calls. They cooked lovely meals for their families. Not just snacks, either, good honest North of England fare—Yorkshire puddings, hotpots, steak-and-kidney puddings, treacle tarts, apple dumplings, pan-haggeldy, the lot! *And* looked after their husbands and children well, *and* by their writing were able to help educate their children. I was brought up by my own mother to turn my hand to anything, and after she died by my own young stepmother, who despite being just a girl herself was the most marvellous homemaker.'

Ebenezer was trying to control laughter again. His tone was most affectionate. 'Oh, Luke! It's years since I've seen you act like this—so belligerent. It does me good. You were turning into a staid old bachelor.'

Luke looked grim. 'And I'm staying one.'

Ebenezer was unabashed. 'And even if Thomasina hadn't bowled you out middle stump, I would have. I still can't resist it. With regard to writers, how about Elizabeth Stirling? I mean Elizabeth Ffoulkes.'

Luke actually grinned. 'You've got me there, Uncle. Elizabeth is a gem—so gloriously ordinary despite being a novelist. Okay, okay, maybe all of them aren't Bohemian, sitting cross-legged on floors, poking at Chinese meals and Indian curries and despising roasts with two veg. and spuds, but I didn't want you letting yourself in for more than you'd bargained for.'

Thomasina, exasperated, said, 'This is the most uninhibited morning I've spent in the whole of my life! Are you all always as outspoken as this? And if so, does it mean that that outburst I so inadvertently overheard doesn't mean a complete break in a relationship? That it'll blow over by the time lunch is finished and all will be sweet harmony again?'

Luke's voice was grim. 'It does not mean that. Ilena surmised far too much. I'm not taking her out again. It's come to some-thing when you can't partner a girl round without her hearing wedding bells.'

His two listeners both decided to ignore that. It was too controversial by far.

Ebenezer shrugged. 'Well, my watch and my stomach tell me it's noon, and fighting always did make me ravenous. How about lunch? It's a fair go, isn't it, telling a guest she's got to cook it, but I'm sure you'll enjoy your own cooking more than mine and Luke's very little better. I'm hardly able to rustle up more than bacon and eggs.'

'Whereas,' said Luke sarcastically, 'no doubt our Miss Meade will dish us up omelettes at a moment's notice, that wouldn't disgrace à Paris chef!'

'I might at that,' cried Thomasina rashly, and could have bitten her tongue out the instant after, because she didn't know what sort of a stove they had, or what utensils, and the blessed things would probably turn out as tough as bootleather and about as thin. She didn't think shaky knees were conducive to feather-light omelettes.

'Right,' said Ebenezer, taking her elbow, 'armistice. Come on, Luke. We'll all help. From now on the late fracas is forgotten.' He looked down on her. 'Better call me Uncle Eb. You can't possibly call me Cousin-Ebenezer-forty-times-removed.'

Thomasina said, 'I would like to, as long as it doesn't occasion a jibe from your nephew. He might think I was trying to worm my way into the bosom of the family.'

'Well, as long as I don't, it won't matter. And you don't need to worry about Luke. You're a pleasant fellow as a rule, aren't you, Luke? Right, march!'

It was just as well he had her elbow, because Thomasina felt so battered and dazed she was almost light-headed. They went up the steps in the cutting in the bank. They were dappled with fallen peach petals and a mosaic of leaf shadows moved across them as the lightest of sea-zephyrs stirred the trees above their heads. As they gained the top of the bank and Corrieside lay before them she stopped dead, halted by the beauty of its setting and architecture.

CHAPTER III

It was fittingly named Corrieside because it had been built in a great semi-circular sweep indented into the hillside, and natural outcrops of rocks and native trees had sheltered the garden from the east winds that sometimes beat up the harbour.

Now, a hundred and ten years since the first cob cottage had been built there, a gracious garden had grown up about it, with the most magnificent specimens of European trees to lend their own splendour and variety to the evergreens. A wave of spring fragrance from the narcissi and jonquils and hyacinths was borne to them, and the ceaseless murmur of bees burrowing into orchard blossom on half a hundred trees was the sound of pure happiness.

Violets sprang from every rock in the first bed at their feet and Iceland poppies danced in a gay abandonment of gold and white and tangerine and coral, while in a flowering-currant bush little wax-eyes hung upside down, penetrating the bell-like flowers for the honey they loved.

But it was the house that caught and held Thomasina's eyes. She'd loved the bright modern homes of the city suburbs with their spick-and-span neatness and big landscape windows, but here was an older Colonial house, added on to through generations, loved and benign, mellow and liveable. Probably too large for convenience, but a darling house.

It had large gables and here and there dormer windows poking through its roofs, and had been built upon different levels to suit the terrain so that it appeared as three-storeyed. There were quaint little sheltering roofs peaked out over entrance porches and a very attractive string-course projected horizontally along the face of the building, with fine moulding. The north windows, facing the sun, were protected from too much glare by over-hanging hoods supported on heavy brackets, beautifully in keeping with the massiveness of the structure, and the spoolwork banisters of the terraces were wreathed with clematis and with wistaria that was just beginning to show a blue bloom on its bare, gnarled branches.

Thomasina remarked on it. 'I've not seen any out in Christchurch yet.'

Ebenezer nodded, well pleased. 'We're so sheltered here. We grow many things that are hard to establish elsewhere. We even

40

have bougainvillea. And grapevines and banana-passion vines. This spot is similar to Akaroa—over in the next harbour—where some almost tropical stuff grows. They even have a few stunted olives. We'll take you over there. It was originally a French colony and retains many French characteristics. Though they all call themselves New Zealanders now.'

They came into the house by a side door. At a glance Thomasina knew that this was a house that had been loved and cherished through many years. There was a patina on the old furniture that had been achieved only by elbow-grease, and modern conveniences served only to enhance the atmosphere. There was no striving here to achieve a showpiece of one particular period. It wasn't all early colonial. The furnishings as well as the house itself had grown with the years into a harmonious blend of family living. Oh, what a pity Ebenezer and Georgiana Swainson had had no children of their own to inherit this. Then this lovely house, seemingly steeped in peace, would have known no bitterness of dispute about ownership of the future. Then she could have come as a welcome visitor, no more.

But she hadn't much time for such musings. The necessity to produce those wretched omelettes hung over her. She'd been practically dared to do so. She said briskly, ' I'd love to see over the house now, but I'd like to do it leisurely, so how about lunch right away? Could you show me where things are, please?'

Luke said, ' I'll do that. Believe me, I know far more about cooking than my uncle.'

They came into a long beautifully modernised kitchen whose end windows looked right out on to the bay below and beyond. It was all daffodil-yellow and black-and-white with a shining-vinyl-tiled chequered floor. A table stood in the window and Thomasina said quickly, ' May we have lunch on that? No need to stand on ceremony with me.'

Luke said suavely, ' Of course not. You're family, aren't you?'

' Very distantly so,' she said just as smoothly. ' I'm not anxious to claim a closer relationship than exists. Now I'd like a pinny, please. This trouser-suit is very new and I don't want it splashed with egg.'

' A pinny! Good grief, you sound just like Cousin Louisa. I thought modern girls didn't wear pinnies any more, only smock tops.'

' Well, if you can produce either, I'll wear it. But I thought Louisa sounded more a pinny-type.'

41

He grinned, rather evilly, she thought, went to the back of the door and unhooked a mammoth apron. He held it out at arm's length, surveying it. 'Cousin Louisa is—um—well, cosy, to say the least. Very rounded. I won't blame you if personal pride makes you turn it down.'

'Oh, give it here,' she said impatiently. 'I couldn't care less. To me it's just a protection. I'm not thinking about how I look all the time.' She slipped her head through the loop, reached round herself, brought the strings round her waist twice and tied them in front. 'Now eggs, please, and some milk and butter, salt and pepper, and if you've any dried herbs I'll add a pinch, but not to worry if you haven't. And I'd like parsley and tomato for a garnish if there are any. And which hot plate on the stove is the fastest?'

He brought her everything with exaggerated deference. She stooped to swing open the doors of the cupboard under the sink. 'Would Cousin Louisa have an omelette pan? If not I'll use a small frying pan.'

He laughed, went off into a pantry off the kitchen and returned bearing an omelette pan. 'Before she went into hospital she said she'd murder me if I used it for anything else but omelettes. I told her it was safe enough with me, I'd not be using it at all!'

Uncle Eb strolled in. 'Ah, you're lending her a hand, Luke. Good. My forte is more in the line of setting tables. Where's one of the tablecloths?'

'She wants it in here,' said Luke. 'As she says, we're all one family now.'

His uncle looked at him suspiciously but said nothing, and Thomasina decided to ignore him too. For a man Ebenezer made a good job of the table, flinging a blue-and-white checked cloth over it, and willow-pattern cups and saucers from an old kitchen dresser against the wall. He disappeared outside, came in with a few sprays of almond blossom and filled a glass to receive them and placed them in the centre of the table. 'This is so I can assure Louisa we did you proud.'

Some of the wariness departed from Thomasina's bearing. Luke cut brown bread, put out butter, peach jam, honey-in-the-comb. Thomasina concentrated on the omelettes, warming the plates to receive them, slicing a tomato and chopping parsley. The first one, to her horror, she overdid, but she'd have that one, and anyway, the last ones were always the best. They turned out perfectly, and at least they didn't talk madly to her all the time she was doing them.

They sat down and old Ebenezer said grace. Suddenly Thomasina was seized with a mad desire to laugh. If anyone had told her three-quarters of an hour ago when they were going at it ding-dong in the stables that she'd be sitting down beside Luke Richmond, acquiescing in giving thanks, she wouldn't have believed them.

She bent her head, hastily forking up some omelette, and the laugh rose in her throat again and she had to cough. To her great surprise Luke Richmond laid down his fork and burst out laughing. 'Don't hold it back, it *is* ludicrous, isn't it?'

Thomasina flushed to the roots of her hair, said hastily, ' I am *not* laughing at the idea of saying grace—we always said it at home—that is, unless we had anyone we thought it might embarras, but very nearly always. I was only giggling because—'

'Because you have a sense of the fitness of things—which is only another name for a sense of humour—and it's damned funny, after being bawled out by a complete stranger, to offer thanks for the blessings of the day! Don't be so touchy, girl. Of course it's funny. Look at Uncle Eb.'

Uncle Eb said, sobering up, ' Lay off it, Luke. If I laugh I can't enjoy this excellent omelette. And Thomasina's not to be teased. She's a darling girl and most strangers would have stormed out of the stable after smacking your face and be on their way back to Christchurch right now instead of cooking your lunch!'

'And a very good lunch it is too,' said Luke, returning his attention to his plate.

Thomasina said, 'Well, praise the saints, hostilities seem to be at an end.' She put a hand to her midriff. ' I was all tight here, like a board, And either I was going to sit here and say nothing and look as if I were sulking, or else it would have made me babble like a brook out of sheer nervousness.'

She caught a strange look in Luke's eye. Might it mean that hostilities were not at an end? That she mustn't presume too much. It was as well that at that moment Ebenezer began asking her about the trip over. She welcomed this. It gave her a chance to underline the publicity work she had undertaken for the airline.

They washed up, Thomasina at the sink, Luke wielding a tea-towel, and Ebenezer stacking the dishes away with such familiarity she realized he'd let Luke take over earlier with producing her needs, merely to leave them alone, working together. He

43

regarded them as children who had quarrelled and would soon forget. Not if Thomasina knew it. She would be very wary with this man. Thank goodness it wouldn't be for long. In three weeks they would be gone from sight and sound of here. A pang struck at her. She had thought they might settle in New Zealand. Maybe, however, it wasn't wise. If people doubted your motives, you were better back amongst friends and neighbours who knew and trusted you.

She wished Luke hadn't accompanied them on their tour of the house. It was difficult to praise as it deserved. She had the horrible feeling her cousin's nephew and heir would read into every appreciation she uttered an appraisal of the values. She wished she had never mentioned in her letter how straitened their circumstances had become. It had seemed natural to admit it when Ebenezer had asked were her father's royalties enough to keep them in comfort. And she'd had no idea her kinsman in New Zealand owned such an estate. On the way up Ebenezer had pointed out over quite a number of rolling hills to the boundaries of his property. She had pictured him on a small holding, probably mortgaged. Certainly she'd never dreamed there might be anything in it for her and Matthew and Edwina.

As they went through the house Thomasina realized they'd had the money to modernize it in the most attractive way, with new windows faithful but larger replicas of the old small-paned ones. Nothing of the original design had been spoiled. There was linenfold panelling in the halls and a beautiful curving staircase led up from the main one, to the bedrooms. She loved the master bedroom that faced the sea. Ebenezer had been born in it. It was covered in a carpet that had a soft floral design of lilac and rose and blue that toned in perfectly with the chintz-petticoated chairs that were drawn up to a basketwork table in the bay window under the gable, and the windows were flung wide to gentle sea-breeze coming up the harbour. What a place to sit and dream, to see ships from all over the world coming through or leaving by the distant Heads.

This was the harbour where, in December of 1850, the First Four Ships of the new colony, under sail, had made safe rendezvous. Ebenezer said, 'It was little short of miraculous, that distance, the length of time it took them, through all the hazards of those days, the storms, the becalmings, that they came in so closely together. They left, three of them, the *Charlotte Jane*, the

44

Randolph, the *Cressy,* on the seventh of September from England. The *Sir George Seymour* left on the eighth. The *Charlotte Jane* came into Lyttelton Harbour, or Port Cooper as it was then, at ten in the morning of the sixteenth of December. At three-thirty in came the *Randolph.* The *Sir George Seymour* arrived the next day and the *Cressy* ten days later. Here they are, as they lay at anchor, all four of them.' He turned to show her a sketch on the wall. Oh, the grace and beauty and gallantry of those four small ships!

They turned back to the view of the glistening water again, the cradling hills. This was a harbour which Captain Scott had known, sailing on his voyages to the South Pole, the harbour that had hoped to welcome him back, victorious, but instead had known the sadness of a mourning ship returning. A harbour where, on Ripa Island, the gallant Count Von Luckner had been sent, where he had planned an escape, unrealized, and had lived on to be respected by all and welcomed back many years later as an honoured visitor. And the island marked by the cross of pines had once been a refuge for the lepers from far Pacific islands. Ebenezer could remember that well. And during his lifetime, happily, numbers were so reduced that they could now be treated in less isolated quarters nearer their own people, in their island territories.

Thomasina could have listened to Ebenezer's stories for hours. Oddly enough, the beetling-browed nephew wasn't in the least impatient with his uncle's string of tales, though he must have heard them time and again. Was it true that, mostly, he was even-tempered? What was it Ebenezer had said, a stupid bachelor? Well, he could sure have fooled Thomasina on that!

There was something sad about so large a house lived in only by a childless widower, a hardened bachelor and a housekeeper. There was a room off that master bedroom that had obviously been for the latest addition to the family.

Ebenezer said, 'I can remember occupying this. Evidently it was for the current baby, but I was the youngest of seven, and an afterthought at that, so I was in it for ages. Spoiled, I suppose.'

There were other rooms, some of them nostalgically individual and indicative of past occupancies. A cot still held a row of soft cuddly toys, home-made. Amateurish attempts at chocolate-paper pictures of the thirties era hung on the walls, there was a dart board, a scallawag set, dolls' prams, cupboards for toys, maps framed on the walls, with territorial features completely out of relation to this present-day world that was carved up and re-hashed by victorious armies and courts of international justice.

Ebenezer said, 'It's sheer sentiment to keep them like this, but every few years a new generation of my sisters' and brothers' grandchildren seem to come to enjoy seaside holidays here. Some of their parents own farms, but none near the sea. I'm always thinking some day one of them will propose flinging all this stuff out and starting off with modern decorations, but each lot of children seems to want it to stay this way. They mostly live in smaller modern houses with little room for the paraphernalia of hobbies. But it beats me that they find this so fascinating.'

Thomasina found she had to blink. Then she said softly, 'I think it's because it gives them something stable and unchanging in an otherwise unstable world. It's so marvellous to find something like this, resting on the old values, the simple pleasures.'

She looked up to find Luke's brows lowered. The glance under them seemed piercing and she said defensively, 'You think I'm being grossly sentimental, Luke Richmond, and perhaps you even think I'm playing up to your uncle. But I don't care. I feel as I do because this very month that little cottage that meant every-thing to my father and stepmother could be shuddering under the bulldozers that will clear it away to make room for a new motorway. You can't have any idea what it means to lock a door for the last time and look at a key you've no further use for; to turn your back on windows that were always warmly lit for your homecoming on winter nights, windows with red curtains to shed a glow . . . and to think how foolish you were to latch the gate so carefully, because it didn't matter any more if wandering stock got in and ate the lilies and the roses. Because soon the trees would be felled and the bulbs of last spring would be buried next spring under tons of concrete and macadam!'

Ebenezer, with the patience of the not-so-young, waited for his nephew's reply.

Luke said a little roughly, perhaps resentful of the fact that her eloquence had stirred him, 'Wasn't there any chance of appealing, protesting? Did you *have* to take it lying down? It's all so changed since I lived in Britain. Was there no way at all to prevent it?'

She said slowly, 'At first it seemed as if the whole village was going to be demolished. So there *was* a protest. The solution they came up with was to bear to the west. We lived west of Green-chester. So it tied my hands.'

He was silent then. Finally Ebenezer spoke. 'Lassie, you don't know what's ahead of you. Something compensating, I'm sure. I've proved this so often in my three-score and fifteen years. Every time I've had a reversal, something comes along. Though it's only when we look back we can see the pattern in it. For instance, you and your father coming into my life. Luke here would tell you how apathetic I was for a time after Georgiana died. She was quite a bit younger than I. I never dreamed she would go first. She was so full of the zest of life right to the day she died. It didn't seem possible anyone as vital as my Georgiana should so suddenly be gone from this world. I felt my mainspring had gone.

'Because we had no family of our own, the loss seemed more severe, though I've been so grateful for Luke, Georgiana's youngest sister's boy. His parents live in Christchurch. None of my own nieces or nephews want this place, they all have farms of their own, or businesses. Then suddenly, due to that series in the *Argus*, I began looking back into the past and I found you. There was no photograph of Elizabeth among my father's things, though we have that one of his brother on our walls, but he had written a description of her in his memoirs, which he compiled after my mother died. You may have very different colouring, Thomasina, but other things fit. He said she had a proud walk to her, a lilt in the step, and, to his sorrow, because it was for him, a hint of pain in her eyes. You had that just now, thinking of Greenchester, my dear.'

Thomasina felt a constriction in her throat and a fear too. This was what Ebenezer was setting his old heart on . . . having her here. He felt it would make a storybook ending, if Elizabeth's descendant, in want, could find a home amongst Thomas's broad and wealthy acres. She didn't want to wipe that eager look off Ebenezer's face, but Luke Richmond was watching her every expression, hawk-like in his intensity, and he thought, she was sure, that she was playing up the situation. Oh, they mustn't discuss anything like settling here so soon. Not in the first flush of seeing her. Not with this shadow hanging over the situation. Because she knew, with a certainty that was instinctive, that the black-haired Ilena would not let Luke go, and that one would have no compunction in making their lives a misery if she thought there was any chance Luke's inheritance might be divided.

So she looked for a diversion and found one, seizing on

Ebenezer's last words. 'No picture of her, you said, but there is one in existence—in fact more than one, a group taken later, of Edwin and Bessie and their daughters. But the one I mean must have been taken that summer they fell in love. I discovered it only at the last, hidden underneath another one I was divesting of its bulky frame for packing. I think perhaps Bessie was afraid to hang it on her wall in case her eyes, going to it in some unguarded moment, might give her away. I've got it here with me today. I put it down on the hall table as we came in, with my bag.' She turned to Luke. 'I expect it doesn't mean much to you, and you might be regretting all this lost time with the farm chores. Don't feel you have to stay.'

'Oh, Josh is attending to the sheep. He'll sing out if he's in trouble. It's not like earlier in the month. And you're wrong —I'm most interested, not to say intrigued.'

Now what did that mean? It could mean interest in his uncle's father's lost love, or interest in her technique for endearing herself to a wealthy cousin.

Nevertheless, despite the nervousness this engendered, she felt she had indeed brought Ebenezer a great pleasure when she unwrapped the old photograph and brought it to his view. That long-ago photographer had grouped them well in that lovely setting. There was a wall, with fruit trees expertly espaliered against it. You could almost feel the warmth of the sun on the bricks. The corner of an old house showed, and a steep roof, and there, in the archway of the rose-garden, Elizabeth Swainson, with hair piled high, wearing a dress that was obviously sweeping around to trail out from a bustle. It had long tight, frilled-edged sleeves, and a frivolous ruffle of lace round the neck. Her little daughter Jane, in a frock almost reached her ankles, was clutching at her mother's skirts. Bessie was looking up at her brother-in-law, her heart in her eyes, and Thomas, young, fair, handsome, was laughing down at them.

Ebenezer looked and looked and had the air of a man very much touched, as if he had had a dream fulfilled. How Thomasina wished that cynical Luke Richmond would go away, but he didn't. She had an idea he felt he dared not leave her alone with his uncle in case Ebenezer made her some rash offer.

When Ebenezer handed the photograph back, she said. 'It's yours, Cousin Ebenezer. I want it to find a place on your walls. I'd like to think that in some way Bessie came here to the place where Thomas lived out the rest of his life.'

Ebenezer said, 'Oh, but I couldn't take it from you. It's of your own great-grandmother. She's just my aunt by marriage.'

'Please, oh, please? You see, I've not got much of any worth to give anyone, and I know you'd treasure it.'

He stood looking down on it and she knew he craved it. Suddenly he looked up and grinned boyishly and mischievously. 'I'll make a bargain with you. I'll accept it on one condition ... that you and the other great-grandchildren of Bessie Swainson spend the rest of your time here with us.'

She looked doubtful. 'They aren't angels. Edwina looks like one—she's very like her namesake, the gentle Edwin, but only in name, believe me. She's about as gentle as a man-eating tigress at times. Thinks she's been born into the world to fight other people's battles. Matthew's easier, though he's sort of accident-prone. And he and Ewina fight a lot, though basically they're good pals. And they're adventurous. They're biddable, I'll hand them that, but unpredictable. I think a little of them could go a long way. You could find them tiring.'

Ebenezer said, 'I've told you all the kids of the family come here in January. It's like Bedlam let loose. The house comes alive then. In a place this size they aren't for ever under the grown-ups' feet, anyway. Now how about it? I'll take the picture if you come!'

Thomasina capitulated. She looked a little apprehensively at Luke. His eyes were on his uncle and it was to him he spoke. 'Very very clever,' he said softly, but Thomasina had an idea the words were meant for her.

Ebenezer wouldn't hear of her picking up the tourist coach on its way back. 'You'd find it tiring. They go right round the bays to Lyttelton and over Evan's Pass to Sumner. Fair enough, it's a wonderful trip, but you've all the time in the world to see those views.'

'Not long really,' she cut in anxiously. 'Remember I said we're booked for an October return.'

He shrugged. 'Well, even in that time we'll show you round by car, but in any case—' he broke off and looked wistful. Then he added, 'Would it be rushing you to take you over to town now, and bring you back here tonight? Otherwise a whole day will be wasted. Could you pack in that time?'

'I could—we're travelling light, naturally—but I feel—' she looked defensively at his nephew.

Luke shrugged. 'Makes no difference to me. Uncle pays the

piper and calls the tune.'

His uncle didn't seem to resent this one iota. Thomasina found herself wondering how far that was true. She said slowly, 'Mrs. Fairweather, our landlady, said Lake Coleridge was a long way. They won't be back till seven. Told me to just make myself a snack and they would eat whenever they got back. Maybe I'd better just go back, and bring them over tomorrow.'

Ebenezer wouldn't hear of it. 'No, we'll go round the sheep early, you'd enjoy that, lassie, we'll take the Land Rover, and we'll have dinner at the Sickle and then go over and get the children.'

Luke said, 'In that case I'd better be off. I've a few things to do before the rounds. See you in about an hour, Uncle.'

Thomasina heard herself say a sudden, 'Wait!' He turned back, brows up this time, and she said, 'You had—er—a very interrupted morning, not to say upsetting. I think I should make it tomorrow to arrive to stay.'

He looked at her coolly. 'Don't fuss, girl. I was interrupted, yes. But not upset. Women's tantrums aren't important enough, or as infrequent, to matter too much. I can take them in my stride even if I don't exactly welcome them. It'll suit me better to get you over here this evening than to break into another day's work tomorrow. I find this situation interesting. It will be intriguing to see how it will work out.'

'There's nothing to work out. It's merely a brief visit. Don't worry, Mr. Richmond, in three weeks' time I'll be back at the side of the world where I belong, looking for a flat in Newcastle-upon-Tyne, and remaining an occasional correspondent to your uncle. No objections to that, I suppose?'

'None at all. *If* that's the way it works out.' All of which had the effect on Thomasina he was evidently hoping for. She'd die rather than stay here permanently. Oh, well, not to worry. By the time old Ebenezer had had two lively children for more than a fortnight, he'd probably be glad to see the back of them too. She turned, and the beauty of her surroundings, from this loggia, struck her afresh with that unaccountable impact of nostalgia.

As Luke disappeared through a path in the shrubbery, Ebenezer Swainson burst out laughing and rubbed his hands together with glee.

'Capital, capital! I think I put the cat among the pigeons all right when I told that Ilena straight out what I'd offered you.'

Thomasina gazed at him in astonishment. He looked so saintly,

50

but he was anything but. 'Luke *said* you'd done it on purpose.!'

His chuckle was rich, and unrepentantly mischievous. 'Aye, that I did. I've never been one to hold myself back from getting involved in trouble. The times I've seen parents hesitate when their sons and daughters have been going to make fools of themselves, just because they're afraid of being called interfering, are legion. Well, I've never been lucky enough to be a parent, but Luke's like my own son. I was terrified he was going to drift into marriage with yon woman. He wasn't serious, I'm sure, but she was, and today proved it. Money's her greatest interest in life. Luke's not the man for her, he's too easy-going.'

Thomasina boggled. 'Too easy-going? Why—'

'Oh, yes, like most easy-going ones, when he does blow his top we all go for cover. You should just hear him if any of the men are rough with the animals. But this time I was afraid he wouldn't blow it soon enough and wake up one morning to find himself engaged to that one.'

Thomasina wished she didn't find his attitude so endearing, like a roguish schoolboy one couldn't help liking. She said, 'I wish you hadn't brought me into it. It puts me in an invidious position. Everyone round here will think I've come out with an eye to the main chance, and really,' she fixed him with a stern eye, 'you took an awful chance. No wonder Luke was furious. Even if you only did it to make this Ilena think Luke mightn't necessarily be the heir to the whole estate, what if I'd taken you seriously?'

'Oh, you were meant to. It wasn't just with the idea of throwing a spanner in the works. I saw the hand of Providence in it . . . you, Bessie's descendant, needing a roof over your head for the younger descendants. It's a good life. Think on it.'

Thomasina heaved a huge sigh. 'I couldn't. No, I couldn't. I like my freedom. I don't like anyone to call the tune. I'm much too independent, but thank you. I can't just take. We'll manage back home. I reckon Dad's royalties might pay our rent for a year or two, and what I get in compensation for the cottage will educate the children. Thanks to the competition we have an abundance of new clothes and secretaries get good wages. I can also implement by doing a few freelance articles. That's pretty good and will keep us.'

'But only just. Let's wait and see.'

Time flew. Ebenezer told her to pick out rooms. Thomasina took a fancy to a small wing that jutted out. It was the original

51

cob cottage, Ebenezer said, built long before Thomas had reached these shores. Thomasina saw it was furthest from Luke Richmond's bedroom—less chance of the children disturbing him. It even had a little back stairway of its own. There was a small sitting-room, even a kitchen.

Ebenezer hunted out linen for her, helped her make the beds up, switched on the electric blankets in case the beds had become damp. Thomasina's tension gradually lessened and she was glad for the children. Heavenly to be settled for two or three weeks in a home. Travel was fascinating, but how one longed to be able to stay put for longer than one or two nights at a time.

The old man was in his element. He went off and returned with armfuls of children's books both old and modern, dolls, an electric train, model cars and planes. Matthew and Edwina would think this a haven of refuge. She turned to Ebenezer. 'I wonder if you'd do me a favour? Please don't hint to the children that this could be any more than a visit before going back to Northumberland?'

His lips twitched. 'You mean you think they too might bring pressure to bear upon you to throw in your lot with us?'

She nodded. 'The decision must be mine alone.'

To her surprise he didn't argue about that, just said, 'Fair enough. I'll say nowt.' Oh well, perhaps he already realized that there was one person who wouldn't dance to his piping.

Uncle Ebenezer must drive the Land Rover, Luke said, coming in; he'd go on horseback. Thomasina was very conscious of mixed feelings . . . this was the life she loved, the life the children loved, but it wasn't going to be unalloyed delight, even for less than three weeks. There were too many undercurrents.

The lambing was almost finished. By the time Ebenezer and Thomasina joined Luke, however, seeing they'd had gates to open and shut, he and Josh, his man, were in trouble with a sheep that had fallen in between some uprooted willow trunks over the stream, and was lambing, with difficulty, in a confined space.

Ebenezer said, 'Come you over here with me, Thomasina. We're having a bit of trouble over here. The mother's quite good, but one of these twin lambs just won't suckle. Perhaps you could hold her while I hold the stupid thing on till she just has to drink. We almost got her drinking this morning.'

It was just as well Ebenezer had given Thomasina a pair of dungarees belonging to him to put on over her own things, because by the time Ebenezer had expressed milk from one of the teats to get it flowing strongly, and had sprayed her liberally, to say nothing of the lamb backing up against her all the time, because she preferred that to holding the ewe, her trouser suit wouldn't have been in clean enough condition for dinner at the Sickle.

Suddenly the wretched lamb got the idea, and began to suck vigorously, a comically surprised expression on its little face.

Ebenezer said, 'You've done plenty of this before?'

She nodded. 'Yes, on the estate I worked for it was mostly dairy produce and crops, but ever since I can remember, I've helped Mr. Bruce, our neighbour, at lambing-time. Dad said it was the right way to view farming. Not the idyllic one of snow-white lambs and fields for gambolling in, with sunshine and blue skies above, but the one of difficult births, and sleet and driving rain, and weak lambs yellow and slimy with mucus.' She looked at him with shining eyes. 'It's odd, it's a dirty job, but I think there's nothing to compare with helping a lamb into the world.'

Ebenezer nodded. 'Yes, it's not all just riding round on magnificent mounts, and having people admire you for show-jumping expertise.'

He meant Ilena, of course. Thomasina laughed. 'I'm a dud on a horse. I'm plain scared.' The lamb had had enough and was being butted by its twin. Luke and Josh were still busy in the creek.

Ebenezer might be slimly elegant, but he was tough, like whipcord. He could certainly handle these heavy sheep. He was busy with a ewe that wasn't going to give much trouble, then he looked across at one, not far off, and said in disgust for her stupidity, 'Look at her—she's just about ready to have her lamb, but darned if she's not trying to corner someone else's lamb. Aren't they mad? Thomasina, do you think you could take my crook,' he jerked his head towards it, lying on the ground, 'and bring her on her side, to stop her tomfoolery. She could have it in no time that way. I'll be with you shortly.'

It was a neck crook, which they preferred there. The leg ones sometimes damaged the udders. The ewe came down easily. Thomasina bent down, felt for the little front hooves, and in a moment the wet slimy little creature was beside her. She cleared the mucus from its nostrils just as Ebenezer reached her. 'Good girl,' he said, 'you're certainly the one for here.'

She laughed. 'Nothing to that one. She needed very little help.'

53

Josh and Luke had the unfortunate one, with her lamb, up on the bank now. They came across, looked, said to Ebenezer, 'You've been busy, two to our one.'

He said, 'Not to my credit. Thomasina lambed one.'

Thomasina wouldn't have been human if she hadn't enjoyed the look on Luke's face. Josh said, 'Gosh, Luke was telling me you were from Newcastle-upon-Tyne. I thought you wouldn't be—'

Thomasina held up an indescribable hand. 'Not Newcastle. The Valley of the Tyne. Our cottage adjoined a farm which we had the run of from our toddler days on.'

They performed belated introductions. Luke said, 'Josh can manage the rest. This week'll see the end of it, anyway. Glad you've got the Rover, Uncle. Bring it over and we'll take these two to the shed. They'll be okay, I think, but better there tonight at least.'

Ebenezer had phoned the Sickle earlier because they put on an early evening meal for them in a small private room off the public dining-room, and Thomasina was glad of his solicitude—he said he didn't want the children to be worried if her arrival home was later than they expected. It was wonderful to feel so lapped around by his loving care. Thomasina had been on her own so long, she revelled in it. A little of her wariness departed.

If it hadn't been for the presence of the beetle-browed Luke she would have enjoyed it fully. She had an idea that the mere fact she was handy on a farm had only underlined for him the knowledge that Ebenezer would want her here more than ever. Oh, blast it.

But the dinner was heavenly. Drusilla Babbington waited on them herself, the steak and mushrooms were perfectly grilled, the baked jacket potatoes artistically cupped in slit foil, the vegetables obviously home-grown and flavoury. The pavlova was all a pavlova should be, crisply sugary on the outside, marshmallow-soft inside, filled with a delectable mixture of fruit and cream and tangy with the passion-fruit pulp Thomasina had become addicted to in her short stay here.

She had realized by now that Drusilla's conversation with Jacob this morning had been in approval of Ebenezer's interference in Luke's affairs, and she saw her exchange a conspiratorial glance with him, one she was sure the astute Luke didn't miss. Well, none of it need matter very seriously to her. Three weeks at the outside and she would be gone. No doubt they would

54

resolve their differences in time.

The light was fading as they crested the hill from the harbour-side at the Kiwi, the stone resting-house for hikers built by a man of vision years ago to encourage the young of his generation to tramp these magnificent hills. The city of the plains that lay below was still faintly lit by the afterglow of the spectacular sunset that had earlier painted the sky with saffron and fire before it sank below those purple, snowy-peaked mountains running like a narrow chain from north to south, sixty miles away across the plains chequered with gorse-hedges and wind-breaks of pines and blue-gums.

'It's so deceptive,' said Luke, 'that narrow-seeming line of ranges. If you fly across the Tasman from Sydney to Christ-church, the width of the Southern Alps below you is frighteningly broad. You can't help hoping you won't come down amongst them. No wonder it took time to find passes through them. It must have seemed impenetrable to them.' He laughed. 'New Zealanders like my uncle take them for granted, having always lived with them. I've been here twelve years and never cease to wonder.'

Thomasina was glad of such uncontroversial topics. 'I can imagine that. It seemed weird at first. I'd associated volcanoes with bare, arid mountainsides. I saw a plume of smoke rising out of a snow-covered gash on Ngauruhoe as we flew over, and they told us in Rotorua, you can get frost there—imagine, in a thermal area! Mr. Richmond, what part of England were you from?'

'From County Durham, so of course I know your Northumber-land well. My people lived at Whitburn on the coast. My father was an engineer, still is. My mother's very much older sister was Uncle Eb's wife. Uncle Eb and his brother Ned visited England in the thirties—after his father was gone—and tried to trace the Swainsons then, without success. Natural enough, of course, if, as you've now told us, there were no sons. He couldn't know that. He met my aunt then.'

She turned to the older man. 'Oh, do tell me how you met?'

His voice was soft as he spoke of his wife. 'My father had a picture of Hadrian's Wall hanging in the dining-room. I had a yen to try to discover what bit it was. Had no idea of how extensive the Wall is till we got there, of course. But we did find it, incredible though it seems. Not too far from Newcastle, so perhaps it was some place where he took his brother's wife

55

and child for a picnic. But we did a lot of exploring before we found it—praise be, because that was how I met Georgiana. She and her friend were exploring too. I believe it's been opened up a lot since. We weren't far from Corbridge where Georgiana lived. We were on farm land, heard squeals of pure alarm—and no wonder!

'Georgiana and Elmira were being chased by what they took for a bull but was in reality an enraged cow, recently calved, and even more dangerous. They'd got between her and her calf. We diverted it, being used to animals, of course, the girls clambered madly up the wall and by jingoes, so did we once they were safe. It was all in the best chivalrous tradition. My brother Ned married Elmira. It started quite a bit of emigration to New Zealand.'

'Ned?' Thomasina had a flake of colour in her cheeks. 'Ned for what? Edward? Or Edwin?'

'Edwin, of course. There's always been an Edwin in the descendants of Thomas. He not only loved his brother's wife, you know, but his brother. Loved him dearly. Two of my brothers had sons called Edwin to please my father. It's all in the notes he left. You'll enjoy going through them. You'll touch hands with your own past as you do. And I had a sister Adelaide. It seems terrible when they were such a united family, with Edwin going into the darkness of the pits to keep them from an orphanage, that they should have become so separated. My father evidently hadn't the faintest idea where Adelaide lived in Canada. Thomasina, can you fill in the blanks for me? What sort of life did Elizabeth and Thomas have together? Did they become prosperous?'

'For some years, yes. My grandma used to tell me. It was hearsay even to her, of course, the good years, because she was only three when her father died. But while their grandparnts lived they were quite comfortable. The little girls always had the best of kid boots made for them, the most exquisite wax dolls, and their mahogany furniture was so highly polished the children dare not leave a fingerprint on it. They used to run and get a duster and rub it off.

'Edwin petted and cosseted his Bessie. Every Saturday night she went off with the older girls to the theatre, which she loved dearly, and he bathed the younger ones and told them wonderful stories and made them the most delicious suppers. Panhaggeldy was their favourite.'

Luke interrupted. 'Panhaggeldy is a favourite of mine, though we only get it when we go to my mother's. Would you make us some?'

'Of course. There's not much to it . . . slices of bacon and potatoes and onions all simmered in a frying pan. But isn't it delicious?'

She continued : 'Edwin was a great walker. Although living right in the city, he used to get up on summer mornings on Sundays, and roam the Northumbrian fields gathering mushrooms for the ketchup he made for their suppers, blackberries for jelly, buying farm milk and butter for them. I expect he knew he needed the fresh air. He was very asthmatic. The children could never remember him without a cough. And because of his own unfortunate childhood, he had a thing about children being cooped up in schools at too young an age. He wouldn't allow any of them to go to school till they were seven. I don't know how he got away with it, and it must have driven Bessie mad, but he taught them all so painstakingly they could all count, do sums, read and write by the time they were enrolled and they were put straight into Standard One.'

Ebenezer's blue eyes were as eager as a boy's. 'Oh, child, I didn't dream you'd know so much. Go on.'

Thomasina said, 'Well, you see I come off a long line of storytellers—Great-grandfather Edwin, my grandmother Thomasina, my own father. And your father was enough of a storyteller too, to preserve this family link.'

Ebenezer said, 'My father would never go home. He deemed it best to stay away, as indeed it was, but he always hoped Bessie and Ned had enjoyed good fortune and found happiness too.'

'My grannie was told they were very devoted, so I expect they did. No fireworks perhaps, but quiet happiness. But the depression of the 1880s was very hard on them. And they never really made it up. But they managed. The older girls were at work, of course. Then in 1893 they had a black year. Elizabeth actually produced a boy that year. She'd thought my grandmother would have been the last. They called him Edward Albert, one of the fashionable royal names at the moment. He lived only a few days. Edwin's asthma had been very troublesome. The anxiety over the birth, and the loss of the longed-for son, set him back. In a few short weeks he was gone too.

'The little girls no longer wore kid boots. My grandmother never knew what it was to have a new dress, with five older sisters they were always hand-me-downs. Jane was twenty-two, though,

57

a stalwart of the family, taking on the father's responsibilities, looking after them all. The other girls helped too, of course, but in the main they married young. Jane had a long engagement, wouldn't marry till little Thomasina took her first job at thirteen.

'They were a close-knit family. They all contributed to their mother's support. They never failed to take Bessie to her Saturday night theatre, and every now and then they got up early to go to the Newcastle Market before breakfast to buy her a penny bunch of the wallflowers she loved. It's a tradition of our family to always have wallflowers in our gardens.' For a moment she caught her breath, remembering the tons of concrete that would have crushed the velvety brown and gold wallflowers in her valley garden. She continued, 'Sometimes, when they were in funds enough, they bought her a bunch of rosebuds and wondered if it recalled for her that happy laughing summer when Thomas had picked her that rose from the garden wall. Its petals, brown and shrivelled, are in the old family Bible.'

There was a long silence. Then Ebenezer said huskily, 'Thank you, Thomasina. I've always wanted to know. I'm only sorry that this branch of the family hadn't been able to do more for them. They didn't have an easy life, themselves, struggling to establish a farm here, that would pay, and that depression struck the colony badly too, but tight circumstances on a farm that could at least support a family with home-grown produce, even if very little silver was seen at times, was quite different from bringing up a fatherless family in pre-social service days in an industrial town in Victorian England. But I'm glad she had such a fine family of daughters.'

Luke's face looked grim and set. Maybe he was concentrating now they were off the hills, on driving through heavy traffic, but she wondered uneasily if he thought she had been painting the lily to play on the old man's sensibilities.

CHAPTER IV

Matthew and Edwina came rushing out as soon as they heard the car and it was quite evident by their flushed cheeks and sparkling eyes that they had had a wonderful day. Words were fairly tumbling out of them, but Thomasina checked them while she introduced their cousin and his nephew and explained that they were going over to the bay to stay for the rest of their time in New Zealand.

Thomasina was surprised, agreeably, when Luke said, grinning, 'I think they'd better have their innings now. I'm sure they're dying to tell you all they've seen. I've never forgotten what it was like when my sisters and myself were kids and the gilt vanished off the gingerbread if the grown-ups hogged all the conversation. How did you like Lake Coleridge, kids?'

They were standing on the pavement of Bealey Avenue, one of the avenues that girdled the city in its square mile. Matthew's tale was full of turbines and generators and spillways, Edwina's of fish and birds and mountains. Ebenezer watched and listened with an indulgent smile. Then they went inside to thank Mrs. Fairweather and to tell her where they were going.

Ebenezer was sweet. He thanked the landlady for being so kind to his young kinsfolk, insisted on recompensing her for the cancelled booking, said they were his long-lost relatives from Northumberland and that from now on they'd be under his wing, and he hoped she'd come over and visit them. He'd take her number and give her a ring for a definite date quite soon.

She looked up at the handsome old man. 'Indeed I'll take advantage of that. The Bay's such a gem of a spot and I've taken such a fancy to these youngsters. So did my daughter. Will you bring them back to see me some time?'

Edwina twitched her golden ponytail back over her shoulder, a sure sign she was excited. She looked up at Ebenezer with a most searching look. 'Some time? Do you mean we're staying on? You said we were your wards. Doesn't that mean—'

Thomasina said quickly, 'Uncle Ebenezer—you'd better call him that—is assuming a guardianship that isn't really his responsibility. We mustn't take advantage of his kind nature, Edwina. We're just going to have a holiday at Corrieside. But we'll certainly come back to see you, Mrs. Fairweather. It's been like a

59

home, not a boarding-house.'

They all rushed off to pack, Ebenezer following with Mrs. Fairweather. Thomasina went to follow them. Luke detained her with a hand on her arm. ' You under-estimate my uncle. He hasn't got quite as angelic a nature as you think. He's a wily old devil.'

Thomasina thought he said it laughingly, but she didn't know what to make of it.

By the time they had shared a cup of tea, packed, and headed up over the hills again, it was a clear, starlit night, with a moon high above the harbour making a moon-track right across the still waters. The children were in front with Luke. Edwina shuffled up against Luke, put a hand on his knee, said, ' It's like fairyland, isn't it? All those lights like half-bracelets where the bays are. And I love the way the roads dip up and down, don't you? Is one of the lighted bays ours?'

Ours! Thomasina caught her breath in. The children were going to fall in love with Harvest Moon Bay. It was inevitable. And with Corrieside, with their rooms, the sheep, the horses, that donkey, the hedges and fields. They were going to feel it was like their beloved Greenchester. They were going to compare it with their future in a flat in a city. There was going to be added pressure put upon her from the two people she loved best. She wasn't at all sure it would be wise to stay—too many complicated relationships here. And always she would live under the smart of knowing some people would think she was staying for what she could get out of it. One thing, Luke wouldn't press her to stay. Even if he didn't already despise her, what man would like to see his inheritance divided?

But Luke was answering Edwina. ' No, you can't see ours yet. But we will when we crest the next hill. It's tucked down into a very sheltered bay and you turn left along a long arm of land running out into the water. Corrieside is indented about halfway along it, so it lies in the sun almost all day and the hill behind the house shields it from the worst of the sou-westers. That's where our coldest weather comes from, of course, beating up from the South Pole.'

Matthew said, ' Oh, sure. It seemed so funny at first, Luke, I kept thinking the sun was going round back to front. I thought it should move from the east to the south and stay there most of the day. I lost my sense of direction.'

Luke nodded, changed gear for the pull uphill. ' I remember

thinking exactly the same when I first came out. I come from the same part as you, nearly. Whitburn, County Durham.'

'Gosh, do you, Luke? What school did you go to?'

'The Bede. In Sunderland.'

'Did you? Really, no kidding? Why, my dad was educated there. He lived in Northumberland when he was a little boy, but just before he went to High School, they moved to Sunderland. His father—my Granddad Meade—was an engineer. I'm going to be an engineer too.'

Luke said, 'So was my father. He was engaged on shipbuilding on the Wear in Sunderland. How strange! It's just possible your grandfather and my father knew each other. My dad would be younger, of course, but it could be. What years would he be there?' And they were away, trying to work it out.

Thomasina knew she ought to be grateful he was so nice to the children. It was only herself and her motives he distrusted. But it wouldn't make for harmonious living. So it was no go. She wouldn't dash the children's obvious hopes tonight, though. They'd had a big day and wouldn't be able to see reason.

Suddenly Ebenezer's big horny hand was covering hers. 'Relax, lassie. You're holding yourself rigid.' His voice was low, for which she was glad. 'Take it as it comes, girl, don't fight against the idea so much. Your pride is hurt, I know, because Luke was so rough on you, believing what he did. He'll come to accept you.'

They were talking nineteen to the dozen in the front, so she said in an answering low tone, 'But it would make me feel such a cuckoo in the nest. I've got a terrible streak of independence in me.'

'You've also got the responsibility of two children. That's a big thing. There's not just yourself and your pride to consider. When a close kinsman—I am, really, you know, your own grandmother's cousin—is ready to take over, is it really fair to them? And don't forget that while you might be able to devote yourself to them entirely just now, and support them, there may come a time when you couldn't.'

Thomasina gasped. 'Oh, don't, please! You mean if—if anything happened to me. Oh, I know so well it can, and suddenly—first Dad, then Maddy. I know, I know. I'll have to take out as big an insurance as possible to guard against that, but—'

The hand tightened on hers. 'Lassie, I meant nothing of the kind. I wouldn't be so cruel. I meant you might want to marry.. It'd be a real complication—a lot to expect of any young man

61

just starting out, to take on the keep and education of his wife's sister and brother. Could be a young man in his mid-twenties, with not much behind him. And you're the type to stay single to look after them. But if he knew they were provided for financially, it would make all the difference.'

She was silent. His words bit shrewdly. And she'd had just that experience. Oh, it hadn't gone deeply with her. No broken heart. Derry had been just a pleasant companion, no more. He'd worked on the same estate. He was more interested in the experimental side of farming, had wanted more experience and moved on. He had ambitions, hoped to have his own farm some day, but his parents weren't wealthy enough to set him up. They had been sweet to her.

He'd evidently been falling for her seriously. That had become evident, but when Maddy too had gone, leaving Thomasina responsible, he'd cooled it. She hadn't really blamed him. It simply hadn't been practical, and it hadn't been more than friendship on her side. But there was always the chance she might really fall in love and want to marry. And she would never, never let the children go.

She squeezed Ebenezer's hand, said huskily, ' I know. It's already happened. Someone cooled off. Not to blame him, he had his way to make. Look, my mind's chaotic at the moment, Ebenezer. I'll have to think it out in the cold light of day. There are all kinds of complications. I'd rather not discuss it now, with the children so near. Would you give me a few days?'

' Fair enough.' He chuckled suddenly. ' I remember asking you to make it Uncle Ebenezer too, but I think it sticks in your gizzard because you're afraid Luke will think you're trying to establish a · closer relationship, but I find I like being called Ebenezer by someone as young as you. Georgiana always called me by my full name, same as I did hers. All the old cronies round here call me Eb. So go on doing it, will you, love? It makes me feel fifty years younger.'

Thomasina felt herself relaxing. The chatter went on in the front seat. Heavens, Luke was getting the lot, all about Greenchester, their friends, the school there, Hadrian's Wall, Corbridge, Housesteads, the shards dug up in their very own garden.

Against her will she had to admit to herself he was good with them. Maybe it wouldn't be so much of an ordeal, these next few weeks, after all.

Luke said, ' That's what I find so fascinating about New Zea-

land. When you dig up something like that in England, you know
if it's Roman it goes back to somewhere about the time of Christ.
It gave me a funny feeling when I first heard my uncle talking
about early days in European civilisation here, to know it was still
almost within living memory. Uncle can remember so many of
the very first settlers—the ones who came out on the First Four
Ships, even a few from further back still. Stories by word of
mouth have a fascination none others have. It sort of bridges the
generation gap, makes you realize how short a span a lifetime
really is. Though at your age that's probably harder to grasp.'

Ebenezer chuckled out loud. 'Listen to Luke the Greybeard!
Though he's got something there.'

'No comments from the back seat,' said Luke. 'We haven't
been butting in on your conversation, which seems to have been
so mysterious you were positively whispering.'

Again uneasiness stirred in Thomasina. He wouldn't have been
pleased about that—would have suspected plotting between herself and his uncle. She had an idea that if ever she did consent to
staying at Corrieside she'd have to have it out with Luke first.

It was a relief when he said, 'Oh, look, children. We've come
back round the bend. We're almost facing the Heads at the
moment, though we'll swing back again. That furthest away
light, the solitary one, is the Winking Buoy. You'll see Godley
Head light too, guiding the shipping.'

Matthew said, 'Robert Godley was the man who had to come
out here to prepare the way for the Church of England settlement, wasn't he?'

Luke said, 'Good lad, you know a bit about us already.'

Edwina said importantly, 'We all do. When Tamsin had to
swot up all those details about New Zealand for that competition,
we all helped. We heard her homework night after night till she
was just about perfect.'

'Goodness,' said Luke. 'She *was* determined to get out here,
wasn't she?' Thomasina flinched from the irony in his tone. So
even if what Matthew had said had proved her point that they
had come out because of the competition, he wanted her to
understand he still thought it had been to feather her own nest,
to spy out the land, find out how wealthy this kinsman was.

They swept downhill into Harvest Moon Bay and Luke was
pointing out the landmarks. Under cover of it Ebenezer said
softly, 'There *was* a pattern in it, wasn't there, Thomasina? You
and your father picking up that very paper in New Zealand

63

House, you seeing that competition and winning it, even before I wrote to ask you to come out and to offer you a home. This gives you the chance of looking us over before burning any boats. Reminds me of : " There's a divinity that shapes our ends, rough-hew them how we will." Think on that, girl. But not tonight. You've had a big day and you were swept into our turbulent morning. But we don't have many like that, so sleep sweetly tonight.'

The children were delighted with what they could see of Corrieside in the dark and absolutely fascinated with the size of the house. 'How absolutely wizard for hide-and-seek,' said Edwina. They called their new relation 'Uncle Ebenezer' with every second breath, giving Thomasina a twinge. She recognized that they'd been short of relations for so long. Families dwindled and got scattered. Despite Edwin and Bessie's large family, few were left now, and even the cousins had been so much older. Most seemed to be living in the south.

Ebenezer said, 'Yes, all these little steps and stairs and odd nooks make it a paradise for wet days. We were such a large family and my mother and father practised the old-time Colonial hospitality. I feel it only comes alive when my great-nieces and nephews come. We'll get them all over bit by bit so you can get to know your new relations. Pity the spring holidays here are just over, but there'll be plenty of youngsters round to play with you after school. Now come and see your rooms. It was the old cob cottage, though it's been all enclosed now. It was just clay and tussock to begin with, you know, till they could fell the timber and pit-saw it. My father added to it when he married. I think your sister picked it thinking the further you were away from an old man the better. She'll learn that children's noise doesn't disturb me. This place has been like a tomb lately, with Louisa away. She's a woman who sings at her work. I like that.'

Yes, Louisa. Someone else to be reckoned with if she decided to stay. *If*. Two women in a kitchen always meant one too many. People were sometimes too idealistic about children in the home, starry-eyed about them in the abstract, but when it came to dealing with them in reality, the novelty might wear off. Children not only added laughter and variety to the home, but they also trekked in mud, knocked chips off furniture, made inroads on the baking, brought all sorts of problems—school, social, family problems. Bringing them up was a constant cavalcade of steering them through various phases, some comical, some disastrous,

64

many of them exhausting. This Louisa might detest them, be forever checking them, or, on the other hand, spoiling them.

Fortunately, by the time the children, excited, had explored every inch of the cottage wing, exclaimed rapturously over the models, the dolls, the games, and had been bullied through their routine of washing and teeth-cleaning and told to stop calling out to each other, Thomasina herself was so exhausted she fell fast asleep instead of, as she had dreaded, lying awake milling over the situation.

When she woke, to the sound of hens announcing the laying of eggs, and birds whistling in the spinney, she hardly knew where she was. Unfamiliar chintz curtains stirred at the old-fashioned windows and sunlight slanted in across her bed. There was a salt tang in the air.

Of course . . . she was at Corrieside and she had awakened ahead of the alarm, evidently. She must get up and find her way round that kitchen and produce a breakfast that even that superior Luke wouldn't sniff at. But first she must take a look at the harbour. It would be something to remember always, when she was pent in some high-rise flat, cut off from sea and the good earth by acres of asphalt. Longing shook her. Oh, if only that roadway hadn't gone through Greenchester! She would have managed somehow. Oh, Dad, oh, Maddy! They'd always grown their own vegetables, kept hens. Oh, stop it, Thomasina. No use in looking back.

At that moment the children burst in. 'Oh, we heard you stirring. Uncle Eb said we weren't to waken you. He's such fun. He got us to sneak in last night and switch your alarm off. You were dead to the world. He said you deserved breakfast in bed for once. I reckon that's him coming now. We've been dressed for ages. Back into bed, Tam.'

She took one look at the travelling alarm clock by her bed and yelped. It was after eight and she'd set her alarm for quarter to seven. What would Luke think?

She heard Ebenezer's voice call out, ' Is she awake? Do I hear her voice? Good, may I come in?'

Thomasina made a clutch for a blue brunch coat she'd left on the basket-chair last night and pulled it round her. Ebenezer, beaming, and bearing a large tray, entered. He stopped short, said flatly, ' Oh, you're up. Well, hop back in this moment.'

Thomasina said loudly in case Luke was within earshot, ' I just woke. I was so confident the alarm would go off at the appointed time I didn't even look at the clock. I got up to look at that dream of a harbour. I did think it was bright, but thought that was due to facing east. This is terrible, you waiting on me. Believe me, it won't happen again.'

Ebenezer said, 'Och, dinna fash yourself, lassie, as my mother used to say. I don't suppose you've been waited on since——I mean for months. And you certainly had a big day yesterday. Luke and I have managed our breakfasts ever since Louisa went into hospital. He's doing our dishes right now.'

Thomasina was horrified. 'He mustn't! We're here to do that. Edwina, run through and stop him immediately.'

Ebenezer said no. 'Let him be, it takes all the luxury out of breakfast in bed if you have to do the dishes after. Lassie, relax.'

She looked up at him. 'How come you've so many Scots sayings?'

'My mother's mother was a Scotswoman, married to a Yorkshireman. We all picked up expressions from both and retained them. The bairns have had their breakfasts. You fell asleep over your book last night. They thought it fun to sneak in and switch off the alarm.' He picked up a cushion and tucked it behind her back, then swept the children out ahead of him.

Thomasina couldn't see her tray for tears at first. It was so long since anyone had done anything for her. She subdued her feeling of guilt re Luke and resolved to enjoy it, though as soon as she finished she'd shower and start house-cleaning.

What a breakfast! But they'd be disappointed if she did less than justice to it. There was a yellow dish of rolled oats porridge, a brown pottery jug of cream with a matching bowl of sugar, a small teapot warmly cosied, the china had rosebuds on it and fluted edges, and under an inverted soup-plate was perfectly done bacon and an egg. Two triangles of toast sat in a rack. They even had an embroidered traycloth on——really, no one would have believed this came from a bachelor household! Well, she'd heard from Mrs. Fairweather (who'd been praising the way her son-in-law kept house when his wife was in the nursing-home recently) that most New Zealand men could cook a snack when needed, but this was so good it made her feel superfluous.

The meal done, she leapt out of bed with only one more quick glance at that shimmering harbour and grey-blue hills, seized some navy trews and a bright blue woven top with a turtle neck, and went down to the shower-box. She wanted no snide comments from Luke on lilies-of-the-fields who stayed in bed. She must look ready for work.

But he was nowhere to be seen. Neither were the children. Ebenezer said, ' They're round the sheep with Luke. Thought it would give you a break. I'll lend a hand here this morning. It's not one of Peggy Bancroft's days. She'll be here tomorrow to do the washing and vacuum the house through.'

Thomasina said doubtfully, ' I appreciate your thought in sending the children off, but don't you think Luke might rather be on his own? After all, as far as he's concerned, I'm here just on sufferance and children can be so distracting.'

' Luke proposed it to them. He's used to all the family being here and his own sister's children always come for the holidays. My word, it was a wild show last time, two will be nothing to him.'

Thomasina said, ' I expect he thought I'd be able to accomplish more housework—justify my existence.'

Ebenezer chuckled, ' Oh, lassie, don't get a chip on your shoulder about Luke. It was most unfortunate you stumbling into that situation yesterday—I mean unfortunate as far as you were concerned. As far as he was, that fight with Ilena was the best thing that ever happened to him. It's far too easy to drift into an alliance that's totally unsuitable.'

Thomasina looked serious. ' Ebenezer, it doesn't matter to you because no one's imputing wrong motives to you—unworthy, mercenary motives. I've not received your letter, so I don't know what was in it, but presumably you wrote offering us a home and —am I right?—a share in the estate eventually? Sorry to be so blunt, but I've got to be, so I know what Luke thinks I was rushing out to grab.'

' That was about it. What's wrong with that? You are my father's great-nephew's daughter.'

' It's hardly fair to your other relations—and they're much closer than I am. They're descendants of Thomas, direct descendants. They'll all resent me and the children. I'd hate that for Matthew and Edwina, even if I feel quite capable of fighting my own battles. If this is the home farm, they'll all expect something to be left to them. Especially as you were the youngest son. It's usually the oldest who continues on the property. So they would be justified in hating us. There's so often trouble over wills. I don't want trouble over us.'

Ebenezer's eyes had appreciation in them. ' Lassie, I'm a fair judge o' character. You've done all you could to put me off.

That's enough to convince me you aren't here with an eye to the main chance.'

'Yes, but is it enough for the others?'

'It will be, once they meet and know you. We'll have a great gathering of the clan very soon.'

She bit her lip. 'You're looking at me through rose-coloured spectacles, all carried away by the descendant of Thomas's love, named after him, at that, at last coming to his home, and some-one in need. Not desperately in need, though. We'll manage. And I feel our place is back in Northumberland, standing on our own feet. I'll look back on this as a glorious interlude. The trip alone has done something for the children . . . made them realize life isn't all sudden loss and hardship, that magical things can still happen.'

Ebenezer stood up suddenly, took her elbow, marched her through the big lounge on to the wistaria-wreathed loggia to gaze down the harbour. A big overseas ship was just swinging round into Lyttelton itself. The sun was catching the dazzling white sails of small yachts tacking to and fro off Diamond Harbour opposite the port. Lambs were baaing to their mothers, white balls of wool frisking round green hillsides. The sun was shining translucently through the daffodil petals that rimmed the edge of this hill-garden against the green waters.

'Magical things can go on happening. Would you deny your brother and sister *that*, for the sake of your own pride, your own independence? There's all this and the security of a family circle too for them. Won't you give it a try for their sakes?' He added, in a sensible, not so sentimental tone, 'I'd better put you wise to the situation re the rest of the family. You think they'll all be looking for a share instead of, as appears, just my wife's nephew, and now you three?'

She nodded. 'It could create a situation. A feeling that could last for generations and split a family up.'

'Fair enough. Look, see over there . . .' he pointed in the direction of the road that went snaking round towards Charteris Bay and the far side of the harbour. 'See that clump of trees on that rise? You can only see the chimneys of a house above them, and to the right the red roof of their woolshed. That's young Ned's property, son of my brother Ned. When his father married my parents weren't ready to move out of this house. In fact they never did. My father deeded him his share of the property. There were much bigger estates here in the old days. Now, with improving the land, we can make our living from smaller areas. He also built him the house. Daniel got interested in experimental farming, became an adviser to the Government on agricultural matters, went into politics, became a Member of Parliament and my father gave him his share in cash. His sons have adjoining farms out on the Canterbury Plains, bigger, more wealthy runs than this. My father didn't believe in his children waiting till he died to inherit. He gave the girls their share as they married. It might look as if I got the bigger share, but I didn't. Father 'treated us 'all alike. I got a certain share in the property and had to raise a mortgage for the rest. That was how Dad was able to treat the others so fairly, with cash. You see, though a farm is valuable, its assets, as you probably know, having been secretary to a farming concern, are mainly in the land itself, the plant, the stock, and you're continually ploughing profits back in. It gave me a wonderful start, though, and when Georgiana came out to me to be married, we took the wing you're in now. Mother said when we had a family they would move in there, but we never did have a family.

'Then when Georgiana's young sister and husband came out to us, about twelve years or so ago, Luke came to us. When, after a few years, I saw how he was shaping, I made over a share to him and Georgiana insisted I gave a sum of money to each of my own nieces and nephews so there could never be any family feeling. They had, of course, already benefited indirectly, through the money my father had made over to their parents. Like my father, I don't believe in waiting till I shuffle off this mortal coil. They were delighted and surprised. So you'd have no adverse reactions there. It doesn't matter to them. They've had their share and more.'

The anxiety Thomasina was experiencing lifted a little. Then she said, ' So it is only Luke who would resent me?'

Ebenezer didn't answer at once, so she knew he too felt it could be a problem. Then, ' I'm sure he won't hold it against *you* for long. He might even become grateful to you, for being the indirect cause of revealing to him how mercenary Ilena is. Had I not written you as I did, and let her know, she mightn't have come out into the open.'

Thomasina considered this, then, unconvinced, she said, ' But are we ever grateful to the people who by chance, or deliberately, destroy our illusions? I think it would only make for more resentment. Besides which Ilena may come round, she may only have

69

reacted badly at first. Don't be too hard on her. If she'd expected Luke to be the sole heir, she'd hardly have been likely to welcome the thought that a long-lost-sight-of cousin from the other side of the world was being brought into the picture as a possible co-heir. I think it'll come right and they'll reach a new understanding.'

'God forbid!' said Ebenezer.

Thomasina had another try, though why she should be so concerned to restore Luke's romance, she didn't know. 'Ebenezer, I don't quite know how to put this, but I think a lot of it may be that you don't find Ilena a kindred spirit. I mean, we click with some people and not with others. I mean, even if *you* don't like her for some reason, she could be right—for *Luke*. Your feeling might just be of the kind : " I do not like thee, Doctor Fell, the reason why I cannot tell." '

Ebenezer's frosty look softened immediately. 'You're a good lass. Not all young ones are so tolerant, and that young madam could make your position here very difficult. At least she could have, but not now. As it was she assumed too much and Luke turned aginst *her*, and serve her jolly well right. And it isn't a Doctor Fell dislike with me. I know full well why I don't like her. She's not in love with Luke, only with his prospects. I know beyond shadow of doubt that if she married Luke she'd have me out of my home in no time at all. She's devious. She'd make it so hot for me I'd be glad to go. Ever since she came to live with the Martensens she's had them by the ears—a mischief-maker. She wouldn't want an old man round even if I've always thought that if Luke married, I'd retire to the old wing with Louisa to look after me. I believe in young couples being on their own. Young 'uns need privacy for a damned good slanging match once in a while. I know from experience that makings-up are always delayed if there've been witnesses to a clash. But quite apart from anything else, I wouldn't like to see anyone like Luke teamed up with anyone as coarse in the grain as that one.'

Thomasina was surprised. She said, hesitatingly, ' She passed me in the street near the pub, flying after Luke. But she didn't look coarse, she looked—oh, what's the word? She looked patrician. Oh, it was just a flying impression in every sense of the word, but in fairness to her, I must say I thought that.'

Dear Ebenezer, he didn't mind you disagreeing with him in the least, bless him. He nodded. ' That was our first impression too. Charming voice when she's not in a temper, a beautiful seat on a horse—she's going in for show-jumping at the Christchurch

70

Show in November. And she's certainly a good-looker. Lovely features. But she has no finer feelings at all. There are more ways of being coarse than of sounding cheap and loud. Peggy, now, is a rough diamond, loud and cheerful and blatantly honest and sincere. But she'd bite her tongue out rather than hurt anyone's feelings. She can never understand the feelings of other people that she'd never experience herself. She had rather a sketchy education, but a nephew of mine who's a professor, and was writing a history of the old families of Lyttelton Harbour, vowed she was his favourite informant. Not that she had any more old-time stories to recount than the rest of us, but she speaks vividly, even if sometimes ungrammatically. And all the old-time idioms and sayings of the earlier pioneer generations have been retained in her speech. Arnold used to say his very calling made him a little pedantic. So if he thought any chapter sounded pompous or stilted, he'd go down to Peggy's quarters and after an hour or two with her, he'd get it right. No one was more surprised than Peggy when he dedicated it to her. But Ilena's no reader. She's hardly got a thought in her head beyond horses. Imagine Luke being married to a girl who didn't love books. I think it must be because of that that she has nothing of the things of the spirit in her.'

Thomasina said, 'Well, I must get on. Tell me, do you like midday dinner as so many country folk do, or just a lunch and a dinner at night?'

'Dinner at night. I find it too heavy at midday for working afterwards. I'd better show you where our store is. Although we're so handy to the village we've always bought in bulk—relic of the days when stores had to come from Lyttelton or Christchurch, I suppose. And of course the deep-freeze is well filled— Louisa saw to that before she went to hospital. Finally I had to put my foot down, thought she'd arrive there worn out. She's got a section filled with pies and biscuits and scones and things ready for us to heat up. Just remember to leave time for thawing, that's all.'

'Oh, I'll keep up with a bit of baking and leave those things for her when she takes up again, when we're gone.' She added hastily, 'No, Ebenezer, we are *not* going to discuss that again. I agreed to see what I thought when I'd been here awhile. For the present, and certainly in front of Luke, I want no one assuming we're staying on. He still thinks there's something odd about us arriving like that. I do wish I'd written from England to say we'd won the competition and would see you. It was just Matthew's idea of giving you a surprise. Which in itself sounds pretty weak now, seeing the kids let me come over on my own. In fact Luke said, "How come they didn't arrive with you, if they were so keen on surprising Ebenezer?" It was a fair question too. Everything seems to have gone against me like that. By the time we got here, it had faded a bit, that idea, and with Matthew so keen on engines and turbines and what-have-you, when Mrs. Fairweather asked if they'd like to go with her, and her son-in-law would show him over the whole thing, I couldn't have persuaded him. Added to that, there was the inducement of seeing a very new baby for Edwina. I told Luke that. I wouldn't blame him for thinking it a bit lame. I think he thinks I did get that letter, but had won the competition too. And am playing some deep game of my own, pretending the chance of a share in the estate doesn't matter to me. He probably thinks Ilena is more honest than I am, by far, over that. I wish now I'd waited till the next day, when they could both have come with me, but I thought our time was getting short.'

Ebenezer had obviously never heard that a woman likes her kitchen to herself, with no one talking while she mentally works out quantities, but she realized he'd been lonely without his wife and, lately, without Louisa. Miraculously, as he asked question after question about Bessie and Edwin, she managed to remember all ingredients. She took out her scones, well-browned, floury and large, and put them in a snowy tea-towel on a grid, to steam.

Ebenezer said, 'I told Luke to be sure to show them all the danger spots on the farm. Not that we have many, because on a hill farm, all the streams are shallow with falling down to the shore. These days, with spray-dipping instead of the old baths, there are fewer hazards, and we get so many of the young fry of the clan here in the holidays, we keep the more risky places well fenced off. The little ones aren't allowed down to the beach without an adult, either, though I expect your sister and brother are old enough to explore alone. But not when bathing. I'll tell them about it, though it's too cold yet. Bathing starts about November.'

Thomasina hid a smile. He was so transparent. He hoped by general conversation to con her into accepting the fact of staying. She'd do the same thing if she wasn't careful. Imagine if she absentmindedly said in front of Luke she was looking forward to bathing on a private beach, or to seeing the roses bloom!

Ebenezer continued, 'We've one very good bathing-pool of

72

fresh water, a small stream that comes down a gully, falls into a natural basin that we've enlarged. We've got it fenced off from the sheep and the children. There's a springboard over it—but only for jumping off, not diving. My brothers and sisters and myself made it long ago. It's safe as houses, never fuller than standing-up depth.'

'Even in winter?'

'Aye, in fact this year, after the driest spring on record, it's lower than it's ever been. Haven't seen it for a week or so. We could do with a bit of the rain the North Island's getting too much of at the moment. Mind, at the time it was good, right through lambing we've had perfect weather for once, but we need now to bring the feed away.'

At the moment they heard voices, the children's, then Luke's above the rest roaring at one of the dogs. 'Get away out of it! You've done enough damage for one morning. Don't shake yourself over us! Clear out! I'll put you in the trough after!'

They rushed to the back verandah to behold an amazing sight. Three figures, two small, one large, absolutely covered from head to foot with the blackest and slimiest of mud! They were opening the gate into the yard and were obviously making for the shed in the corner that contained a sort of utility shower.

Thomasina groaned. 'What did I tell you? It'll be Matthew. I said he was accident-prone. But how on earth did he involve the three of them?'

The three figures, side on, spun round, a fearful sight from the front. Matthew said indignantly, 'It wasn't me! It was him!'

He prodded Luke. Ebenezer gave a great shout of laughter. 'Luke! What the—what in the name of fortune have you done? You were supposed to be keeping them out of trouble!'

As more slime cascaded down Luke's face from his hair, he put up both hands and wrung it from in front of his eyes. 'I pushed them clean in the bog,' he said, 'and fell in after them.'

They both boggled. Ebenezer said faintly, 'You *pushed* them? What in tarnation do you mean?'

'Oh, that fool Shep pushed *me*! We were on the springboard. The pool's practically gone. I'd taken them on to look at it. Shut the gate behind me, of course, but Shep took the fence and bounded clean on to the springboard, too far. He took me in the back of the knees, I shot forward against the kids and we all went in. I pushed them further into it, with my weight. Uggggggh!. Good job it's got a shingle bottom. We went flat on

73

our faces and that accursed animal fell on top of us. *He* enjoyed it—positively danced on us. Gosh, I was mad! I'm afraid the kids heard a bit of language.'

Edwina, a woeful sight, said admiringly, ' Oh, we *knew* all the words, but we aren't allowed to use them. But it sort of relieved our feelings to hear Luke!'

Luke said, ' That's enough. Your sister won't be pleased with me. We daren't get back into the Land Rover. Good job it's not far. Look, we'll shower at once, with our clothes on, that'll at least get it off our hair and clothes, then take it in turns.'

Ebenezer, holding his sides, managed to sober up enough to say, ' Don't you dare go near that shower, you'd block up the drain. Stay right where you are and I'll play the hose on you.' He darted over to where a green plastic hose was attached to a garden tap. ' Now stay right there on the bricks. That step's behind you and it'll flow down on to the garden with a bit of sluicing.' He went on laughing while Thomasina clung to a clothes-post, laughing helplessly.

She said, ' I don't think Edwina's hair will ever be the same colour again.'

Ebenezer looked as mischievous as a schoolboy and really enjoyed letting the protesting Luke have it pretty full force, though he was much more gentle with the children, especially Edwina. She and Matthew could hardly stand up for laughing. Behind them a gate clicked and footfalls sounded. They swung round. Here was an elegant figure in a blue trouser suit with a blue-and-white striped top advancing towards them.

Thomasina breathed a prayer of thanks that it was not Ilena. This woman would be a little older, with high-cut cheekbones and a tender curving mouth. Curving was right, because it was breaking into laughter too. Luke rushed across and turned off the tap.

The newcomer said, ' Oh, *aren't* you having fun! Really, I never knew such a family for accidents! What on earth has happened now? And how come, in the driest September on record, you can be in such a pickle, Luke?

There was no time for introductions. Luke began a spluttering explanation, but his uncle beat him to it. ' Elizabeth, believe it or not, but Shep pushed the lot of them into what's left of the swimming-hole, off the springboard. Luke was taking the children to show them the danger-spots on the farm! Look at them! Elizabeth, I'll see to you when I've got enough off them to let them get into the shower-box.'

She said, waving a pad and pencil at them, 'It's okay, no hurry. I've plenty of time. I left the children with Innis. Drusilla told us your long-lost relations had arrived and Jeremy said to come on down this morning and he'll send a photographer over this afternoon, if possible.'

Thomasina stared in horror. That could set Ilena off again !

Elizabeth didn't notice the look, or recognize it. She said, 'My husband, Jeremy Ffoulkes, is the editor of the paper the original article you saw was in. I used to be the lady editor. But we live here for the children's sake. It's no distance to Christchurch.' She collapsed again as more moans and groans burst forth from Luke. 'If only that photographer was here this moment, he'd qualify for the Picture of the Year Award !'

Luke said threateningly, 'If you let as much as a whisper about this get into that article, Elizabeth, I'll murder you. Uncle Eb, for heaven's sake get cracking on that hosing again.'

Under cover of it Elizabeth said to Thomasina, 'This is just marvellous. Look at Ebenezer, it's given him a new lease of life. It's wonderful to see him like this again. What an introduction ! So you're Thomasina, named for Eb's father. Oh, how sorry Jeremy will be to have missed all this !'

Most of the slime had gone, but the three looked such wrecks, clothes plastered to them, hair streaming. Luke said, ' Right, ladies first, Edwina, but don't be too long.' Thomasina stepped forward quickly, said, ' No, Edwina, you're going to make a mess in there even now. Turn your back to everyone and slip your clothes off. You haven't got much on and it will save a lot. Matt, when she's done you can do the same.'

'But not me,' said Luke hastily, ' I've got my limits. You'll have to put up with my mud in there.'

Thomasina said, ' Are there towels in there?'

'Yes, good hard khaki linen ones. That'll induce a glow, and boy, will we need one !'

Thomasina turned to her cousin. ' Ebenezer, would you go into Edwina's room and find some clothes? Just anything you can find—panties and a top and some trews. And if you can snatch up something for Matt it would save time. I'm sure Luke won't want to stand there looking like a drowned rat for longer than he need.'

Luke said, ' Horrible description. She's doing nothing for my ego. Matt, while they're busy in there, we'd better do running exercises all on the one spot to keep warm. It might be sunny, but that bog was ice-cold and that water from the hose comes from fathoms deep. What's more, that old so-and-so enjoyed hosing us with it. Now, one-two-three—off!'

Thomasina disappeared with a naked Edwina carefully keeping her back to everyone and soon the child was revelling in the warm water. When there wasn't a trace of mud left in the golden hair, Thomasina enveloped her in a towel and carried her into the outer room and called Matthew. Elizabeth brought in the child's clothes and soon she was looking more normal. As they began to emerge Luke rushed in, chivvying Matthew to hurry, and he began peeling off his soaking shirt. Thomasina looked back over her shoulder as they left. 'Hot scones are ready and the kettle's boiling.'

Elizabeth said fondly, 'You're just like a happy family already!'

Thomasina caught Luke's eye. For once the eyebrows weren't beetling. They had flown up in an expression of comical surprise. But he just said, 'Well, that may be. But scram. I'm about to take my trousers off. I'm freezing. Right, Matt, out you come.'

Suddenly Thomasina felt their stay mightn't be all enmity as far as Luke Richmond was concerned. At least he had a sense of humour!

Encounters like that didn't make for formality and Thomasina felt she'd known Elizabeth Ffoulkes for years, especially as she'd read two of her novels in England and last night had started the first chapter of her third before sleep engulfed her.

By the time the tea was made and Elizabeth had spread the scones with raspberry jam, Thomasina found herself saying: 'You're younger, of course, but you do remind me of Madeline, my stepmother. I miss her so much. We were more like sisters. She was only ten years older than I.'

Elizabeth chuckled. 'I must be the stepmother type. Perhaps it gives us a certain look or something. I've a stepson, Roddy, who's almost seventeen. He and I are great pals. He likes all the things I do—birds, tramping, exploring rock pools, collecting wild plants, studying all wild life. I'm sure he'll become a famous botanist in time. And Jeremy and I have a twin son and daughter. We could hardly have done anything else. Jeremy was dead set on having a girl, and I wanted a boy for Roderick. They're only six, but the greatest friends with their half-brother. How Rod has the patience, I don't know, because in the holidays

76

they're just his shadows. They're such toughies. Rosamond lives in jeans or shorts, same as Tony.'

'You don't follow the local custom of Biblical names, then?'

'In second names we do. It's Rosamond Mary and Anthony Daniel. But we weren't descended from people here. A very old English friend of mine was left Cherrington Lodge by Miss Janet Cherrington. She was Rebecca Janet. My friend went to England to live with his daughter there and left me the Lodge on condition I gave up work on the *Argus* and devoted myself to writing novels while I was still young. Jeremy was a widower and I nursed Roderick for him when he had some trouble with his leg. So when I married my editor, we stayed on here. Once you've lived at Harvest Moon Bay you get bewitched and never want to leave. That's what happened to Cousin Louisa.'

Ebenezer said, 'Cousin Louisa is really no relation to us, she's Elizabeth's cousin by marriage. She kept house for Elizabeth for a while, went back to town but couldn't settle. But when Georgiana died, she came here.'

Elizabeth said, one eye on Thomasina's interested expression and reading it aright, 'She's wonderful with children, a sort of universal grannie. Not too old, either. She did wonders for our Roddy who was a very withdrawn sort of child to start with. Roddy and Louisa still take long walks together every holiday.'

More of her inner tension left Thomasina. Elizabeth was a disinterested party. Ebenezer had said something the same, but he had his reasons, of course, for trying to reassure her on that score.

The others trooped in, vowing that nothing so sharpened the appetite as being sluiced down with icy-cold water from the hillside. Elizabeth was an excellent interviewer, not too obtrusive with her ballpoint and pad. She drew them out skilfully, only jotting when certain details must be absolutely correct.

'I've been mentally writing this for weeks, ever since Ebenezer told me he was sending for you, but Drusilla told me that according to what she was told last night, you won an airline competition and arrived here as a complete surprise to Ebenezer and Luke. Give me a few details about the actual meeting.'

That struck Luke, Ebenezer and Thomasina completely dumb. Matthew gazed at them, a little surprised, and said, 'Yes, Sis. You never got round to telling us how it went. We had the chance to go to Lake Coleridge to look over the power-house, you see, so we couldn't turn down a chance like that. But I'm sorry we

77

missed it because I was the one who thought of it. How did it go? Did Uncle Eb guess? Did you have to tell him who you were? Or—' He stopped and said, 'What are you looking like that for, Tam?'

They all looked at her and to her horror Thomasina felt her colour rise. Then Luke's voice fell into the gap and mercifully switched their eyes back to him. 'She came up by the short cut and was halfway up the steps in the bank when I spied her. I was in the stables. So I bounded over to this glamorous-looking stranger, and was most surprised to find she was my cousin-by-marriage twice removed. Or is it three times? I took her back to the stable where Uncle Eb was hunting for Sukey's nest in the loft, so he'd heard enough of what was going on to guess who she was. We lost no time then running out the red carpet, believe me! It was a very delightful encounter, I can assure you!'

His eyes, those unexpectedly brown eyes in a fair man, met hers and they had the same look of devilment his uncle's blue ones often wore. Thomasina checked a rising giggle.

Elizabeth said, 'This is really a wonderful climax to that series the *Argus* ran. To actually have you here as a result, Thomasina, is the sort of happy ending that will delight editor and staff alike. Especially the editor. He thought it up, and to think it actually found a relation for a neighbour of his makes him positively smirk. Especially when Ebenezer went to England so long ago, and failed to find trace. Of course he'd nothing to go on, really. How strange that you won that competition even before you knew Ebenezer was going to ask you to come here to live. We can take pictures of Corrieside too—oh, of course, we have some from the first article—and can end with three orphaned descendants of the original heroine now living on the estate.'

Thomasina said quickly, 'Not living, just visiting. We'll be going home.'

Elizabeth said, deep disappointment in her tones, 'But I thought your home at Greenchester was to be demolished for a motorway. I thought this such a happy solution. Ebenezer came over with your letter, saying what was going to happen. He was as excited as a sandboy. Oh, forgive me. It's not my concern. It's my journalistic love of a neat ending. Not everyone wants to leave their own country, and even if your cottage is demolished, England is still the land of your birth. Anyway, ending the

78

article with your visit here will make a very good climax.'

Again Thomasina's bluey-green eyes met Luke's brown ones, but this time there was no mischief in Luke's. His gaze was unreadable. Thomasina transferred hers to the children. They were sitting unnaturally still and all expression had been wiped from their faces. Unchildlike both faces looked. Masks, like adults' faces were when feelings must be concealed.

Matthew rose, said, 'Excuse us, please, there are things we'd like to do outside. Come on, Edwina.' They went out, not eagerly as this morning, but dejectedly, shoulders drooping.

Thomasina felt beset with conflicting emotions. Anger had to be fought down. If it hadn't been for this beetling-browed man here, she would have stayed, gladly.

She noticed Elizabeth Ffoulkes and Luke had a long conversation down near the stables. Maybe he was telling her it wasn't as idyllic as it had seemed . . . not roses, roses, roses all the way, this visit!

CHAPTER V

Elizabeth rang an hour later to say the photographer couldn't get over that afternoon, probably not this week even. 'It won't matter. A feature article like this doesn't have to be hustled.'

That suited Thomasina all right. She had plenty to do. It wasn't easy, suddenly being pitchforked into someone else's household, without any knowledge of their likes and dislikes, beyond the fact that from what he'd said at first, Luke Richmond didn't like what he'd called later studio-type meals—snacks held on one's knee in a midst of a litter of reference books, typewriters and carbons were probably what he'd imagined them having at Greenchester. Perhaps he imagined their father as having lived in a sort of chaos, oblivious to what was going on round him, typing into the early hours, being less than a father, disregarding mealtimes and bedtimes alike.

Oh, no, Dad had been tied to a nine-to-five routine for so long he found he worked best that way. And Maddy had loved the smooth rhythm of the daily round, though never put out if occasion demanded a different timetable. But Thomasina felt as if she were on trial as far as Luke was concerned.

Peggy Bancroft proved a gem. She talked a blue streak as she put it, but didn't let it interfere with good, solid work. She liked the extra money she earned, she said. ' I'm no dressmaker, so I make a bit so I can buy things off the hook. That way I don't feel so extravagant. I admire people who can run up a dress out of a remnant. Saves their husbands a mint of money. But Josh is so funny. He's actually pleased I can't dressmake. He had a mother and four sisters who were wizards with the sewing-machine. I envied them when we were engaged and said most pathetically that he'd be wedding someone useless in that line. " Praise the Lord," said my Josh. "There's no peace in our household when a man comes home at night. That blasted machine never stops whirring. It makes interference lines on T.V. It's just a madhouse, all dummies and paper patterns and clippings all over the carpet and pins everywhere. You can't get round in bare feet. And when there's a wedding on, they're always in a flap at the last trying to finish something." Oh, yes, he's a very satisfying sort of man, my Josh. Not one of your inarticulate ones. Mind you, I know plenty of women who are very tidy

80

dressmakers, but I'm more than grateful Josh's sisters weren't tidy. It lets me out. Still and all, I'm glad these days of high prices I can earn the money for my own clothes. And I love coming up here, anyway. It's the atmosphere.'

'Do you, Peggy? What do you like best? The architecture? The age of the place? Its history? Its mellowness? The pictures?'

'Those too, but most of all the books. Because they're shabby, well-read. They've always been readers here. They ornament the house so. I mind a girl who once read that books are the best ornament for a house, so she bought a yard of them, beautifully bound, and never as much as opened one. As if it meant that! Books are supposed to furnish the mind, not ornament the shelves. Eb, he doesn't mind me staying on an hour or two when I'm finished my work and dipping into them. He's bought me a lot too, and I use a bit of my money every month to buy more. Especially the kind I know I'll read over and over. I love it when I find bits underlined. I ask Eb if he has any idea who's done the underlining. Sometimes he knows, sometimes not, because some were bought secondhand. Anna had a lot of the books from Cherrington House. I can pick old Obadiah's markings, and hers. Look, there's a poem here she had underlined. I love it too.'

Peggy went across to a shelf, flicked a few pages over, came back to the table. 'It's called *Immortality*.

This loveliness that stirs my bounding heart
    To songs of praise has always blossomed here;
When Earth was young, unscarred by war and hate,
    These self-same streams went singing, crystal-clear;
These mountains caught and held within their folds
    Cloud-shadows, dappled grey and indigo;
Someone, held spellbound on this emerald hill,
    The same delight in God's sweet world would know.
So, when this pasture knows my feet no more,
    When all my earthly gipsyings are done,
There will be other eyes to watch with awe
    The timeless magic of the setting sun.
I would bequeath to all who follow on
    My rare delight in leaf and bloom and tree,
For in their worship of the world I loved
    My soul shall find true immortality.'

Thomasina's eyes were shining. 'Oh, Peggy, you've made my day! I've so missed Dad sharing those things with me and

Maddy. Anna must have been a kindred spirit.'

Peggy said slowly, watching her face, 'Then you've come to the right place. Both Mr. Eb and his nephew like reading aloud. When I come across things like that, read and loved by people who are dead, I get the strangest feeling. As if death didn't matter quite as much. As if I knew them. Do you ever feel that way, Thomasina? As if you knew people who lived long before you were born?'

'I do indeed. And especially since being here, though I used to get it when I walked on Hadrian's Wall. Dad had to have a lot of gen on that. I helped him get it, and I did a lot of his typing too, because we just had to get books out as quickly as possible that year he gave up his regular job. We had to be so careful with money, you see.

'And he met an archaeologist at one of the digs, who said he was so identifying himself with the Roman legionaries who were exiled there that on days of bitter rain and sleet, and weather moods of terrible dourness, he kept thinking nostalgically of the Italy he'd never seen, the blue skies, the olive trees, the cypresses. So he upped and offed and lived there for three months, and came back and felt that the whole life they lived there came more vividly alive for him.'

Peggy took another piece of shortbread, said, 'And do you ever find yourself wondering since you came here what it might have been like if Elizabeth Temple Watson had met Thomas first and came out here? What differences it might have made?'

Thomasina was silent, considering that, then she said, rather astonished at herself, 'Do you know, Peggy, I haven't. It's the maddest thing—I keep looking at Anna Swainson. It's the strength in her face that attracts me, I think. It's a much stronger one than my own great-grandmother's. Though she's just as beautiful. Every time I look at her picture I think *she* wouldn't have been afraid to go out to Canada. She'd have joined her young husband and perhaps Edwin's asthma mightn't have taken him off at forty-four. And I keep on hoping that Anna never felt as if she was only second-best with Thomas. That Elizabeth was the one he couldn't have, and Anna the one he could! It's stupid, it's almost becoming an obsession with me.

'Anna was so sturdy-spirited. Physically too. I've seen the churn she used to use. It must have taken some muscle. Especially the hot days when the butter wouldn't come. There are all the rag mats she made, the knitted quilts, the trees she planted.

There's that old recipe book—only she'd written: " Anna's Receipt Book " across it. They used to call them that, didn't they? In with the recipes she has other entries like, " Set the eggs under Brownie today " and " Prissy calved when Thomas was away. The calf was wrong way round, so I had to turn it myself. Thomas said I did well. A fine heifer," and other things like " Planted fifty eucalypts today and seventy-five raspberry canes. Berries are fetching good prices in Christchurch." And she salted great tubs of beef when they killed a bullock and she made all their clothes and papered rooms and whitewashed the dairy times without number. I just hope Thomas appreciated it all.'

A voice joined in from the passageway. ' Don't fash yourself, Thomasina. He appreciated it all right.' Luke's!

They swung round from the afternoon tea-table in great surprise. ' How could *you* know?' demanded Peggy.

Luke said, but it was Thomasina he was looking at, ' Seeing you care so much, I'll get Uncle Eb to show you her real diaries, note the recipe book entries. They're just full of their happiness together. I expect Uncle didn't show you because he was sort of fostering for you the old love story of your great-grandmother and his father. He might have thought it would brush some of the romance off to have Thomas so happily married.

' Anna Cherrington was one of the most sought-after girls of the district. Thomas was lucky to get her. She had half a dozen dangling after her. And she was a Cherrington, which says volumes. None of old Obadiah's offspring could be anything but high-spirited. Thomas may have had one calf-love episode in his youth, but Anna's conquests were legion. Thomas did think he was too old for her, but Anna gave up the most eligible young man in the district to marry him. She liked mature men, she said.'

Peggy heaved a satisfied sigh. ' So it's not just in books there are happy endings. I must be gone or my own man will love me much less that he did yesterday! See you the day after tomorrow, Thomasina, and for goodness' sake leave me something to do. It seems to me you try too hard to justify you staying here. It's daft and all, that it is. Mr. Eb doesn't expect it. You're supposed to be on holiday.'

That left Thomasina alone with Luke. She poured him some tea, then looked up to find him regarding her from under those brows.

She said, a little defiantly, ' What it is, Luke? You have the look of a man wanting to say something and not knowing quite

how to begin. Don't give yourself any inhibitions—out with it!
I can take it!

He smiled a little. 'Just that I was wondering how to say it.
I—I rather liked you caring about Anna, that's all. I found it
rather . . . endearing.'

Thomasina blinked. It was so unexpected. Colour ran up into
her cheeks, making her self-conscious. Then she managed a
laugh. 'I'm tongue-tied too. The trouble is we're more used to
acrid exchanges, aren't we? Of course I care about Anna. The
other was just one summer's idyll. But Thomas and Anna lived
together for fifty years and more and they must have been pretty
fine people to produce and mould a son like Ebenezer and a
grandson like young Ned. I haven't met the rest yet, but they
seem a close-knit family. From what Ebenezer tells me the next
generation are the same—all the cousins. Never jealous.'

She stopped dead, aware she had been led into opinions she
couldn't justify without—

Luke said sharply, 'Why should they be jealous? Exactly who
do you mean?'

'I mean Ebenezer's nieces and nephews and their children.'
He still looked questioning, so she added hastily and feebly, 'I
mean, they all get on well together, coming over here in the
holidays and so on.'

He said, lips tight, brows down, 'I don't think you meant that
at all. You said jealous. Or not jealous. Come on, what do you
mean? How could you know?'

It was obvious she was picking her words carefully, and that it
was making him downright suspicious. 'Just that Ebenezer said
they weren't looking for a share of this property. I thought they
might have. I mean, old Thomas was *their* forebear—'

He stood up. 'Say no more. I know exactly what you mean.
You've been probing. You've been hinting to my uncle, who is, I
know, only an uncle-by-marriage to me, that they have more
rights here than I have! I'm glad I had this chat with you. It's
most revealing. I was in danger of respecting you a little. What a
sucker I am, a sentimental sucker! Just because you showed some
regard for Anna, I thought there might be more to you than I'd
thought at first. Pah! You and Ilena are certainly tarred with
the same brush, only you're more cunning, not so blatant. From
there it would be only a step to hint that even you are more
relation to old Thomas Swainson that I am. True enough. I'm
just related by marriage, well down the scale. Good grief, I've

had you!

'You've been disarming old Eb by cooking him all the old-fashioned dishes that are traditional in his family . . . Yorkshire puddings, leek dumplings, treacle tarts, steak-and-kidney puddings!' He uttered one of his indescribable sounds and marched off, slamming the door behind him.

Thomasina waited no more than thirty seconds till she followed him. It had taken only that long for the full understanding of the insult to seep in. She flew along the passage after him and up the stairs, turning the corner just as he reached his room and strode in banging that door behind him too.

Not for an instant did she hesitate. She went in like a small tornado, flinging the door so wide it knocked a chair over. She stood there arms akimbo, eyes flashing, breast heaving, the mouth a straight line for once, struggling for the right choice of words with which to wither him. He'd swung round as she barged in.

He said, 'How dare you come into my room! Have you no respect for my privacy? A shut door is a door shut to keep people out! What a nerve!'

So the wrong words tumbled out. She said contemptuously, 'Stop acting like an outraged Victorian spinster with her privacy stormed! You sound like your own great-aunt Tabitha!'

'What the devil are you talking about? I haven't got a great-aunt Tabitha!'

'No? But if you *had* a great-aunt, I'm *sure* she'd be called Tabitha. It sounds like whalebone stays and high necks and reticules. All stuffiness and primness and prudery! How dare I come in to your room? I'll tell you why! Because firing unjust accusations at a person and not giving them a chance to reply by flying off and banging doors in their faces is as good as imprisoning them. As shutting them up without a trial. No one's going to say that sort of thing to *me*, or *do* that sort of thing! *Most* Englishmen have a keen sense of justice. They know everyone's entitled to be heard. Of all the unsportsmanlike things to do! Say your piece and stride off and give me no chance to refute it!'

He looked a little dazed from the force of her fury and shook his head a little as if coming up for air. Then he said, 'Refute? But can you refute it?'

'Yes, I can. I'm not one of your meek and mild people suffering things in silence and being a martyr. If you don't listen to me here and now I'll tell Ebenezer I won't spend another

85

night under this roof till *he* tells you exactly how our conversation took place. And when I've told you I don't expect just an apology like he insisted upon last time, I expect you to grovel! Do you hear me . . . grovel?'

'Like hell I'll grovel! It would take some explaining, believe me. Asking if the rest of the family aren't jealous of me, the nephew-by-marriage only, inheriting! What else—'

'I'll tell you what else if you'll only stop talking long enough for me to give you the context. And I'd very much like to get it out without interruption and in a lower tone of voice.'

'Oh, so you don't intend to go on shouting? That's a relief!'

She said, between her teeth and in a low intense tone, her cheeks scarlet with rage, 'Thank your lucky stars I did shout. If I hadn't I'd probably have burst a blood vessel over the injustice of it all. I'm not one for bottling things up—and if I get attacked as you attacked me, I let fly! Now listen!'

She flung the tawny hair back out of her eyes and said, 'I did *not* ask weren't the rest of Ebenezer's nieces and nephews jealous of *you*! Ebenezer was putting pressure on me to stay. I said I didn't feel it would be fair to his other young relations if I did and if Ebenezer willed the other half of the estate to me. I felt it would be fairer to have that half divided among the others, not given to *me*. You've got to believe that. *You* seem to have the idea that anyone offered such a thing would leap at it. But not me. I don't want to live here expecting to step into a dead man's shoes. I'd hate the thought of it. Your uncle is singularly une-motional when he talks of his own life ending. He's sort of philosophical and natural, and he doesn't know what it does to me. I don't want to be anyone's heir, thank you. I value my independence too much. I won't be beholden to anyone. I couldn't even begin to be natural under those circumstances.

'I could love Ebenezer very dearly, given a chance, and on an equality. As a young woman liking a sort of grandfather-figure, not a benefactor and a recipient. Oh, no, not for me. The Meades just don't work that way. My own father could have inherited a mill had he been willing to give up his own work to manage one —my own mother's father's mill. There was a terrific row and my grandfather cut us right out, but we never cared. The old man was an absolute autocrat, a despot. Ebenezer certainly isn't, but I still like to meet people on equal terms.

'If I were able to give services for our keep, say if Louisa hadn't been well enough to come back, I'd willingly have taken on the housekeeping, but for *less* than he paid her, because there'd be three of us to keep, but to be more or less adopted into the family and be dependent on its bounty—oh, I couldn't. It would stick in my crop. I don't want the children to grow up under those conditions. Rather than have them burdened with a duty to be grateful, I'll take them back where we belong, even though it means changing the country for the city and a lower standard of living than we had in Greenchester. But it would be better for them, eventually, than growing up here being continually sneered at by you because you think their sister is trying to feather a nest. I was trying to resist Ebenezer's insistence by saying I thought the others might resent—justifiably—a stranger from over the sea coming in and scooping half the estate. Divided things never work, anyway. We'll get a flat in Newcastle, among some of the most warm-hearted people in the world, and I'll get a new job and there'll be a bit from time to time from Dad's royalties, bless him, and we'll stand on our own feet and be as free as air. This will be just an unpleasant memory. I'll never have to see you again. I hate to disappoint darling old Ebenezer, but I couldn't take what I'd have to take—from you—if we stayed. Does *that* convince you, Luke Richmond?'

Into the silence fell a sound—of a door opening and closing but some distance off. They both stiffened. Then footsteps came upstairs and Ebenezer's voice was calling out, 'Thomasina, where are you?'

There was just no time to dart out. Luke's room was so near the head of the stairs. They both remained rooted to the floor. Then Luke called out, 'We're in my room, Uncle Eb.'

They were both glad the door was wide open, but even so Ebenezer's face showed surprise. There was something in their attitudes that puzzled him—the way they were facing each other. He looked from one to the other, a line between his brows.

Thomasina said, weakly, she thought, 'How did you find Louisa?'

Ebenezer said, 'Well enough, but—'

Luke said anxiously, 'No setback, I hope?' Thomasina knew he was extremely fond of Mrs. Stirling, though tied in with it, possibly, was the idea that the sooner Louisa returned, the sooner Thomasina would go. He needn't worry. She'd see to it that they stuck to their return bookings. This was a lovely corner of the world, but the relationships and undercurrents made it anything but idyllic.

87

'Not physical complications. Just that her daughter from Auckland has flown down and doesn't want her mother back here too soon. Says it's too much for her. And so, of course, it is. She wants to take her up to Auckland with her. She went off to the Ward Sister to ask when she could return for her, and Louisa whispered to me she didn't want to go. The daughter said she mustn't take on this house again for at least three months. That would mean she'd be in Auckland in midsummer, and Louisa can't take all that heat—too humid. Elizabeth and Jeremy are off to the States and Canada for that business trip in November, so she can't come to them, but just before I left Elizabeth's sister came in and said she could go to them. Josie's very handy to the hospital too. But as far as we're concerned it's a poser.'

Thomasina kept quiet. This was between the two men of the household. Then Luke spoke. He looked across at Thomasina and actually grinned, his brown eyes dancing. 'I've got the perfect solution for you, Uncle, all sewn up just a few moments ago. I thought you weren't handling this business very well yourself, so I've taken a hand and Thomasina has just promised me she won't return to England. She'll make Corrieside their home.'

It was just as well that this remarkable statement made Ebenezer stare very hard at his nephew, because Thomasina felt and looked exactly as if someone had chopped at her clean in her midriff. Then she sensed that Ebenezer was going to swing round on her, so she wiped the expression off her face, swallowed and became more or less in control of herself again.

He came across to her, hands outstretched, cupped her face in them, and kissed her. 'Sensible lass . . .' he swung round again to look at his nephew. 'And clever you, Luke. I hadn't realized you could be so persuasive—or that my own powers were so much less than yours. You've always been such a one for bull-at-a-gate tactics. It beats me.'

His nephew said modestly and solemnly, 'Oh, those were the sort of tactics I used, Uncle, with such success. I sort of bull-dozed her into this. You can see she's still looking a little dazed. You have to be masterful with some women, I find.'

His uncle gave him an apprehensive look. 'Well, don't push your luck too far, son. If Thomasina was a spitfire like that Ilena, she'd be flaring up right now.' At that moment all three of them recalled that at their first meeting Thomasina had smacked Luke's face and they all broke down.

Thomasina sobered up first, said, 'I know exactly what you're thinking. I'll never live that down. But there's one thing I must make plain. I want no share of the estate, *now or ever*! I just don't approve. I'll take a wage, slightly less than Louisa's because there are three of us to keep. And it's not even permanent at that. I'll stay here till Louisa is well. You must tell her that, or she might feel she's being pushed out. That will give us a breathing space. By the time she comes back they'll surely have settled the compensation rates in England, and if the children want to stay in New Zealand, I'll get a job in Christchurch and take a flat there. Actually, Mrs. Fairweather says when she's tired of keeping a boarding house she's going to divide that place into flats. She might let us have one. We could visit here often, even spend school holidays here, but that way I'd keep my independence and no one could think I was here on the make.'

There wasn't the glimmer of a smile on Luke's face as he said admiringly, 'I've always liked independence in a woman. I do wish my great-aunt Tabitha could have known you. You'd have been a woman after her own heart.'

Ebenezer stared. 'Your great-aunt Tabitha? I've never heard of her.'

Luke said, 'She died long ago, God rest her soul. A remarkable woman. She was a Richmond—Dad's side of the family. No relation to Aunt Georgie, you see.'

Thomasina crushed down the laughter rising in her. Ebenezer said, 'I'll just go and tell the kids. Do let me do it. They were so good. I left them at the Museum while I went to the hospital. They're playing on the swing.'

Just as he turned to leave the room Luke said easily and naturally, 'Oh, you were after that jacket of mine with the button off, weren't you, Thomasina? I'll get it for you,' and he added, ' I must remember to shut this door when I come out. That's twice it's knocked that chair over.'

When Ebenezer was out of earshot he said, mock meekly, 'You see I'm not really very good at grovelling. Was it an acceptable substitute?'

Thomasina took the coat from him, and her eyes met his. Her look was reflective. 'I guess it was, because I *think* it means you believed me. I'd not have stayed otherwise. But one hint from you that I'm biding my time so I can worm my way in and you won't see me for dust! So if you want a housekeeper for the next few weeks, you've got to behave. I don't mind staying if I'm needed, not otherwise. I want no jobs created for me. So I warn you, Luke Richmond, watch your step.'

She preferred to keep it that way rather than to thank him or even to let him guess that her heart was flooded with relief at the thought she wouldn't have to leave Corrieside yet.

Purely for the children's sake, of course.

Nevertheless, Thomasina found it an almost intolerable situation. She felt anything but natural. Money had never been a predominant factor in her life. Not that she scorned it. Oh, no, you had to have a certain amount, to pay your way, to be able to afford simple pleasures, to have the felicity of buying gifts for one's dear ones, to support pet charities, but as a family they hadn't yearned for the fleshpots, for exciting continental holidays, fabulous clothing, or eating out at expensive places. They'd been happy, as times improved, when they could afford new bicycles for the youngsters, replace one secondhand car with another, buy books without feeling the money should have been spent on housekeeping.

But now, for the first time, Thomasina longed to have just enough to have built a new home in Greenchester and to have continued their existence much as it had been before that dark day when they had first known their father had less than a year to live. Even if one didn't love money for its own sake, the independence it gave was magnificent.

Here, at Corrieside, she would always feel that Luke and Ilena, and many others, would look on her as a poor relation. Yet was it fair to deprive the children of the lovely quality of life as lived here at the Bay of the Harvest Moon? Already they weren't looking back any more. Of course children lived in the present and they were certainly revelling in this, going round the sheep with Uncle Eb or Luke, exploring the glorious rock shore, seeking out the nests of the sea-birds just to watch them, fishing, rambling round the tussock-covered hills, making friends with Peggy's children, growing tanned already, and filling out, losing that look of care and loss that had marked them this last horrible year.

What a carefree existence—for them—it could be. The blessings and advantages were so great Thomasina knew she must bear her inward resentment that she was taking charity. You couldn't afford unreasonable pride when your pockets were empty.

However, on the matter of wages she made her own terms. Ebenezer was cunning. He discussed it with her in the farm office, feeling, she was pretty sure, that it might lull her into thinking it less of a family matter and more of a business one.

When Ebenezer told her what he paid Louisa, Thomasina regarded him suspiciously, her bright head on one side. 'Ebenezer, please! I'm not an innocent. You're stating a wage like that because you're a perfect darling and want to give me more than I'm prepared to take. I want merely an ordinary housekeeping wage, less an amount for the children's keep.'

His lips twitched. 'I can knock that suspicion into a cocked hat. Here you are, lassie.' He reached into his top drawer and drew out his cheque-book, flicking the butts over. 'There you are, made out to Louisa Stirling.'

She gazed unbelievingly at the amount. 'I didn't think wages would be as high at that.'

'Heavens, girl, housekeepers are as scarce as ice on the Equator. One has to pay to get them, but Louisa is worth twice that much and so are you. Both you and she are not just house-keepers, you're homemakers. There's a world of difference.'

She said slowly, 'Well, I'll accept that, as long as you take off a reasonable amount for the children's keep. Otherwise, it's off.'

She found it hard to meet Ebenezer's eyes. They held a hurt look. She bit her lip. 'Ebenezer darling, I know you want to do this for us, but—well, I hardly know how to put it. You see, I don't think you've ever known what it is to be short of money. It makes you fiercely independent, determined to work your own way. You've always had the security of Corrieside behind you, had plenty and to spare, so you can't even begin to know what it means to—'

He had held up his hand. 'Correction there. Girl, don't you realize men of my age came through the Depression? You look at these smiling acres now and feel it's a land flowing with milk and honey . . . and fleeces and frozen lamb and good beef steers. You should have seen it in the early 1930s. That wasn't very long after I brought Georgiana here. They were the lean years. Dad had gone, Mother was still with us, an old lady. We were mortgaged up to the hilt, living on borrowed money, haunted by the nightmare of knowing we might have to walk off the place as so many others had. I can remember when we had to kill sheep because it wasn't worth taking them over to Addington Sale

Yards. Farmers all over the district were on relief work.

'We managed to hang on, but do you know why? Because we had a benefactor. He too was a pioneer's son, his father had lived here, had built the cob cottage, in fact. He had a sentimental feeling for the old place and thought we'd worked damned hard to stay on it. He made the estate a gift of five hundred pounds. It paid the interest on the place till the tide turned. Only just. He would on no account allow the money to be returned to him.

'He said his life was nearly over and that Corrieside would, in future years, find some way of helping someone else. That there would always be fluctuations in the price of wool, of meat, and that he was sure that some day, we would help someone else stay on their farm. Well, it didn't quite work out that way, but when farms were so hard to get after the war and competition so keen, Corrieside was able to help one or two young men purchase farms. Can't I be permitted, in view of that long ago generosity, to help my own kin? My father's brother's descendant? Surely we don't need all this pride within the family circle!'

Thomasina said unhappily, 'If it were just you, I'd take it gladly, Ebenezer. But there are others to be considered. Especially Luke and Ilena. I was the cause of their quarrel. Before Luke even knew I was in the country, I made trouble between them.'

Another voice cut in from the doorway—Luke's. It said, 'You can forget about Ilena. She doesn't count. That's all washed up.'

Ebenezer didn't look half as surprised as Thomasina. He was facing that way. Luke said, 'The lamb buyer is here, he wants a preliminary look. Can you and Thomasina finish this interesting discussion later, or must it be clinched now? Matthew and Edwina are doing the honours.'

Thomasina said, 'Luke, I think you're wrong. It may have seemed all washed up, the day of the quarrel, but I doubt it. I think it was natural of Ilena to be perturbed. She's bound to come round.'

Luke's eyes were colder than she'd ever dreamed sherry-brown eyes could look. 'Oh, she'll come round all right. I know Ilena. She's waiting for me to make the approach first, that's all. Well, she'll wait for ever.'

Thomasina said, 'Then in that case I feel she'll make the overture herself when she realizes you won't.'

His voice was sarcastic with a hateful inflection that indicated what he thought of women. 'I'm sure she will. But that doesn't have to add up to a reconciliation. It takes two. I'm finished

I'm even grateful to you for that, Thomasina. The
posed revealed to me what she was really like. Not

when she knows I've no intention of sharing in the

'Thomasina, don't be tiresome! You're maddeningly persistent. Look, if it's on your conscience you were unwittingly the cause of that row, forget it. You go on as if you thought it *was* an engagement. It was nothing of the kind. Why worry about Ilena?'

Thomasina gave a sigh. 'You seem incapable of putting yourself in my place. Here am I, an English girl, coming out here and busting up a promising romance. Most of the people round here, though they naturally had English pioneer forebears, are third and fourth generation New Zealanders. The whole community will look on me as the cuckoo in the nest who spoiled things for a New Zealand girl.'

She was amazed when both men burst out laughing. She said indignantly, 'What's so fu—' but got no further.

Luke managed to get in first. 'She's not a New Zealander, you nit. She's the English niece of the Martensens. Mrs. Martensen asked me to look up her sister in Surrey. I think I painted too glowing a picture of life here. Ilena was a stable-maid there. So she came out on a visit, and has stayed on.'

Thomasina knew in an instant it wasn't the life here that had attracted Ilena. Surrey was one of the most beautiful of English counties with an unspoiled sweep of countryside, and a richness and charm and history beyond improving. Ilena had come here because she wanted Luke. A wave of pity swept over her for the girl.

Luke said, 'I thought you'd have picked it from her voice. Still, you didn't mine, did you?'

Thomasina said impatiently, 'Don't you understand? English voices I've lived with always, so I don't notice them. I do notice New Zealand ones. And I was so embarrassed by the quarrel I was forced to hear I wasn't thinking about accents, believe me.'

Luke said, nodding, 'Fair enough, but no one will regard you as the cuckoo in the nest. I might as well confess I heard your whole conversation with Uncle Eb. Oh, I know I was eavesdropping, purposely, but it seemed to me I could butt in at a wrong moment. Thomasina, I know it's laudable to be so independent, but you've made your point and I think it's time you thought of someone else's feelings other than your own.'

93

Thomasina felt rage flame up in her. Sparks were shoot... her eyes. 'Luke Richmond! You put the most extraordin... interpretations on things! First you think I'm a gold-digger, no... when I've made it plain I like to be independent, you accuse me of what amounts to selfishness. It's beyond me!' She flung out her hands in a despairing gesture.

He remained maddeningly calm. 'Look at Uncle Eb. He's so wistful. He wants so much to help you with the children. You're denying him that pleasure. It's downright cruel. Take your wage on the same terms as Louisa—you'll probably work harder, because she's past the outside work, but you could be handy there. Look at the way you lambed that ewe. But do let Uncle Eb keep the children. If you're too full of sticky pride to let him give you an allowance for their clothes and other expenses—well, I daresay he'd let you provide these things for them. If you decide to stay you'll get the child allowance anyway—we have a reciprocal agreement with Britain—so how about it? I don't care to see my uncle getting so frustrated.'

Thomasina was stumped and knew it. She cast her eyes down, then looked up quickly and caught a strange look in those brown eyes. What was it? Concern for his uncle? Had Ebenezer been really worrying? So she must be concerned only with her own feelings, because she hadn't noticed it.

Suddenly she was less tense. She said quietly, 'All right, Luke. If I can make my own terms about keeping the children in clothes and so on, I'll accept their keep. Maybe I *was* too proud. But it's only now when you've assured me you'll no longer regard me as on the make that I can concede this much. I'll take that wage and our board.

'If you'll let me help outside I'll feel I'm returning a bit. And as my work in England was with farm accounts, perhaps you'd let me help there. And when Louisa comes back, perhaps I could take over the garden and more of the outside work.'

This time she thought Luke looked at her with true respect. He said, 'That's fair enough, isn't it, Uncle Eb?'

Ebenezer agreed quickly. 'It would be ideal. Louisa's family are always thinking she does too much. Actually, I can't hold her back, but after this operation she may be very glad to take things just a bit easier. And I loathe the book work. Luke's not bad at it, but he often finds it hard to fit in the time. Then that's settled. You stay. You'd better get cracking and cancel that return trip and send for your own treasures. The old wing is yours to do what you like with it.'

CHAPTER VI

Ebenezer decided it warranted a celebration. 'I didn't feel completely sure of you till now; until I had you on the payroll and knew you no longer had to pinch and scrape, I couldn't feel that old story of long ago was really rounded off. We'll go off to the Sickle tomorrow night for dinner. I'd like Jeremy and Elizabeth to join us as it was Jeremy's idea for that series that brought us together.'

He was like a boy planning it. Doctor Andrew Carmichael and his wife Innis were coming too. Thomasina felt relaxed. After all the doubts and hostilities of the immediate past, it was heaven to be planning something that was pure pleasure. Thomasina woke the next morning in a blaze of sunlight in her darling room and lay there blissfully anticipating it. She would slough off all the cares of the last twelve months and be young and frivolous again tonight.

She met Elizabeth in the village on the same errand as herself . . . visiting the hairdresser. Elizabeth said, 'I love meals out and being all festive, don't you? And Roderick, my stepson, is getting to the age where he likes it too. So I'm glad Matthew and Edwina are coming. The twins are going over to the Dower House—that's where the doctor lives, you know. Old Obadiah did everything in the old tradition! He did well when he formed his almost feudal type village here. Oh, Jeremy would pick me up on that—he edited it out of an article of mine once—not feudal, because every man owned his own land or house, but he sort of welded it into a lasting society where each one recognized that he needed the help of his neighbour. I'm glad they made Cherrington House into the hospital. It preserves it for all time. That's why I'm glad you've come to Corrieside. It was just becoming a huge, outdated old house where two bachelors and Cousin Louisa rattled round. It needed children to help fill it up. I foresee a lovely future now for Corrieside. It's come alive again.

'My twins are wildly excited, they're going over to the doctor's place to stay the night. Innis's two are a little bit younger, not by much in the case of the eldest, and they'll have a wonderful time, I'm sure. Whether Matron will or not is another thing. She's going to babysit. How are you having your hair done, Thomasina? With that length you could have it almost any style. I wish you'd have it caught up on top with curls hanging down behind. Ebenezer showed me that picture of your great-grandmother the other day; you could look just like her.'

Thomasina burst out laughing. 'That's wishful thinking. She was a gipsy type. Her complexion was more Spanish, whereas I get my reddish colouring from my mother.'

Elizabeth studied her. 'Yes, it's sort of Viking. Norse blood?'

'I expect so. My mother was a Stanger and they originated from Orkney, though they'd lived in England for generations.'

'Nevertheless, it's just the colouring. In your high cheekbones and your mouth, you're like Bessie. What an interesting mixture you must be—Viking and Spanish and gipsy.'

Thomasina's laugh was rueful. 'Yes . . . but it doesn't add up to a placid nature, though—spitfires the lot.'

'But too much placidity isn't always a virtue—it can be bovine. You don't get reformers and explorers and crusaders from them, and if you *are* a spitfire, you've learned discipline. You're anything but quick-tempered with the children.'

Thomasina shrugged. 'I learned control from my stepmother, but if you doubt I have a temper, ask Luke.'

Elizabeth's blue eyes widened, but in delight. 'Oh, do you strike sparks from each other? What fun!'

'Fun? We've been dreadful.'

Elizabeth giggled reminiscently. 'It doesn't mean a thing. You ought to have heard Jeremy and me during what was—in a very peculiar way—our courting days.'

Thomasina said dryly, 'It's hardly a similar situation.'

'Isn't it?' Elizabeth's tone was more amused than surprised.

'It certainly isn't. He only tolerates me because I'm useful in a twinfold way. I keep house and make his uncle happy.'

'I can't believe that. I think everyone you meet will like you from that moment.'

Thomasina collapsed into laughter. 'Oh, Elizabeth, you ought to ask Luke his opinion on that!'

'Well, I will,' said Elizabeth seriously.

Thomasina stopped dead in the middle of crossing the street and clutched her. 'Elizabeth, you won't? Oh, I oughtn't to have said that.'

The blue eyes were shrewd and amused. 'All right, I won't ask him as long as you satisfy my curiosity a little. Are you sure you aren't exaggerating? Surely you didn't have words the moment you met?'

'Have words? Elizabeth, within five minutes of meeting him I smacked his face!' She paused, said in bewilderment, 'You don't even look shocked!'

'No. Many a time I longed to smack Jeremy's. But it was all a misunderstanding. Time took care of it. But I wish I'd been a fly on the wall. Oh dear, it's time we were there for our appointments. By the way, I realize you wouldn't be likely to tell everyone, so it's safe with me.'

Thomasina suddenly looked lighthearted. And felt it. Perhaps confession was good for the soul.

Luke was late in that night. He'd gone to a homestead at Purau Bay. Thomasina, having dressed Edwina and supervised Matthew's appearance, was getting dressed herself and was surprised at the relief she knew when finally she heard the car drive in and Luke's footsteps bound across the courtyard.

She heard him call out to his uncle, 'I thought I was going to miss that dinner. I came on an accident near Charteris Bay. Car over the side, but no one seriously hurt, only shaken. But they were upside-down and couldn't get out. By the time it was sorted out it was too late to ring you, so I thought I'd better just hurry home. I'll shower and be with you very shortly.'

He'd certainly wasted no time. He was standing in the big hall with Ebenezer when Thomasina and Edwina came down. Luke gave an involuntary whistle as he saw Thomasina. Her colour deepened and she thought Ebenezer looked amused. She pushed Edwina ahead of her as they reached the foot. 'Don't you think my little tomboy sister looks sweet?'

Edwina did. This was one of the dresses that had been given them for the trip and she was hardly recognizable as the urchin in jeans who mucked out the stables.

Thomasina had brushed out her hair till it shone palely gold like silver-gilt almost, and her ponytail was tied high with a stiff bow of gauze and the ends curled softly and naturally down her back. She was wearing a blue blouse with full bishop sleeves heavily embroidered in white and the silk pinafore dress over it, laced at the waist with black velvet, was in a bright coral. She wore black patent court shoes.

'I think I look pretty good myself,' she announced naïvely. 'It'd be a frightful bind to wear these sort of things all the time, but I reckon I can stand it once in a while.'

'Your sister looks pretty good too,' said Luke.

T Y—D

97

The dress suited the hairstyle Elizabeth had suggested. It had an old-fashioned simplicity. It was a blue and white floral cotton with a high Empire waistline and a square neck edged with white embroidery threaded through with a black ribbon, and the long skirt was edged with embroidery. Wide flowing cuffs fell from the elbow and gave it almost a medieval look. The hairdresser had swept her hair back from her temples and the curls cascaded from a circle of forget-me-nots clipped round it. She carried something in her hand and held it out to Ebenezer. 'I couldn't manage this clasp. Neither could Edwina. It's very old.'

He looked down on it. It was metal and was a pendant with a sort of iridescent surface, in blues and purples and greens. It had strange Eastern designs carved upon it. He looked up and his eyes met hers. 'It's Indian. Was it—'

She nodded. 'It was Bessie's. Gran said Thomas brought it for his young sister-in-law on that leave. From a bazaar.'

'I thought so. Dad had a stud-box exactly the same. Look, Luke's eyes are younger than mine. That's a very intricate catch.'

Luke managed it, though he took time over it. Thomasina, to her surprise, was acutely aware of his fingers at the nape of her neck. He turned her round, adjusted it dead centre over her bodice, said, 'Were her eyes bluey-green like yours? If so it must have matched—'

'Sorry. According to Gran, her mother's eyes were as black as sloes. I'm afraid I'm not her replica. I wish I was, for Ebenezer's sake.'

'I doubt if he'd change you,' said Luke, and their eyes, close together, met.

'Very nicely said,' said Ebenezer on a note of satisfaction.

Thomasina glanced down at herself. 'I feel a bit like a dairy-maid in a dimity gown. But my only other two long dresses clash abominably with Edwina's coral. One is purple and one is orange.'

Ebenezer said, 'They may be more sophisticated, but that one pleased an old man very much. I like simplicity.'

She grimaced. 'But it doesn't really express my personality. I'm too much of a spitfire. Never mind, it may have a good effect on me. I won't go round slapping people's faces tonight.'

Matthew was shocked. 'Tamsin! You never have. You never would. Dad wouldn't have allowed it.'

Luke burst out laughing. 'She only means she sometimes feels like it when people rile her. Tamsin, don't sound such a savage.'

Tamsin, her family pet name for her. Certainly he was thawing.

They stopped at the mail-box and took out the evening paper. Ebenezer opened it and spread it out for all to see. Headlines. STORYBOOK ENDING TO A REAL-LIFE HAPPENING. THE *ARGUS* PLAYS FAIRY GODMOTHER AND BRINGS MEMBERS OF A FAMILY TOGETHER GENERATIONS LATER. Jeremy and Elizabeth had really spread themselves. The pictures of Corrieside, the ones of Thomas and Bessie and Edwin had been well reproduced. Ebenezer, of course, was remarkably photogenic and the children, both on ponies, looked the perfect picture of happy emigrants. There was one of them all together with Luke, of course, and another one that made Thomasina blink. Where had they got that? There hadn't been one taken of just her and Luke. Ebenezer saved her the necessity of asking. He tapped it with his finger. ' I'm glad they made something of that. Jeremy told me the rest of us hadn't come out too well on it. We all talked or moved at the wrong time except you and Luke. But he thought it a very good one of you two.'

It was. Luke hadn't been aware the photographer was ready either, and he was looking down on Thomasina, who was looking up at him from her careless perch on the wistaria-wreathed verandah rail. She groaned inwardly. That exchange of glances, seemingly affectionate, was merely freakish. It hadn't meant a thing. It looked like love's young dream and at the time they'd been on very stiff terms. That picture would hurt Ilena, she thought.

They all arrived in the inn courtyard at once. Doctor Andrew Carmichael said without apology, ' Now don't let's linger indefinitely over the pre-dinner drinks, or for sure I'll be called out before I can sample the main course, let alone those super desserts Drusilla is putting on for us.'

His wife, Innis, dramatically beautiful in oyster crêpe and black, said suspiciously, ' How do you know?'

' Well, I dropped in to see if she'd heard how her daughter's getting on in Picton Hospital and had a preview.'

Innis said accusingly, ' Andrew Carmichael! No wonder you didn't want tea and scones at four! My guess is you sampled every one of them.'

He was quite unrepentant. ' Well, it's an awful waste to order something under a fancy name and find out you've only got a glorified bread pudding!'

99

Elizabeth said, 'Sh, Andrew! If Drusilla hears you she'll put arsenic in your entrée. Bread pudding!'

Ebenezer said to her, 'Elizabeth, I'm glad you wore that dress. It's my favourite.'

She burst out laughing, turned to Jeremy, said, 'What did I tell you?' And to the others, 'Jeremy too always liked my old blue velvet and persuaded me to have another made almost identical. I told him what would happen. And it cost me more than twice as much as the old.'

Thomasina said, 'Jeremy, I applaud your taste. You look ravishing, Elizabeth, with that soft white fur round the neck and elbow cuffs.'

'Indeed, I think so,' said Jeremy, and there was that in his eyes as he looked at his wife that made Thomasina fiercely envious. She thought any woman would/like to be loved like that.

Roderick said, 'Do we have to talk clothes . . . can't we eat? I'm starving, and I reckon Edwina and Matthew are too.'

They went in laughing. The atmosphere of the Harvest Sickle was a good mixture of the old and the new. Things the pioneers had brought out from the northern hemisphere, and greenstone weapons and tools only to be found here. Horse-brasses hung on the walls, pictures of local agricultural shows, views of the harbour with the First Four Ships at anchor, a picture of Edward the Eighth, as a boyish Prince of Wales, stepping ashore, the beginning of the rail tunnel, so early after colonisation, the Summit Road, women, cloaked and bonneted, climbing the Bridle Track to the plains, a picture of the Yorkshire inn the Sickle had been named for, and fine portraits of that superb Yorkshireman, Captain James Cook, and his botanist, Joseph Banks, for whom the Peninsula had been named, way back in 1769.

Drusilla, a perfect hostess, with the confidence of knowing she had an excellent cook and staff in her kitchen, was at her endearing best. 'We've a small party here of overseas business men, in Christchurch for a conference. One of them was reading the article—I couldn't resist telling them you were all celebrating here tonight—editor and all.'

It was the greatest fun. Thomasina had only one misgiving. She said to Luke, under cover of the chatter. 'I'm sorry about that photo, Luke. I wish they hadn't used it—of the two of us.'

The beetling brows beetled. 'Why?'

'Well, it looked just a little too-too.'

'Too-too what? I'm not fond of these catchy expressions. I never know what they're supposed to mean. I like my i's dotted and my t's crossed. Too what?'

'Too romantic. Newspapers can't resist dramatising such things.'

'Oh, bosh! Besides, who cares?'

'Well, Ilena might. I should, in her place.'

Luke said as intensely as a whisper could sound, 'Thomasina, I could slit your throat. You're the most maddening girl. What if she does? In any case she's not likely to see it unless her relations save it for her return. She went off to Queenstown, down South, after our fight.'

Thomasina looked sober. 'Perhaps she thought a change of scene would help her. It—'

His sigh checked her. She changed it to, 'How did you know, Luke?'

'I rang. The Martensens told me.'

He'd rung. So he *had* wanted to make it up. Then no doubt feeling so ill-used she'd gone off in a huff, he made up his mind she could make the next approach. Oddly enough she'd thought Luke more the type to flare up quickly but to subside and be sorry just as swiftly. She'd not dreamed he'd sulk. Still, she was probably wrong about him on all counts. His uncle had deemed him too placid. That would be it. Placid people were so unused to feeling stirred up they didn't get over it so quickly.

But they were two of a dinner-party and this was no time for the give-and-take of a controversial subject.

The Sickle had moved with the times and was dine-and-dance on certain nights. This was one of them. Matthew was horrified. 'Why didn't we come on one of the other nights, then? Who wants to stop eating to dance?'

Roderick burst out laughing. 'I'm with you there, Matt. Dad says wait till I fall for a girl and then I'll like the dancing better than the dining, but I can't imagine it. Especially with food like this! Dad,' as Jeremy said something to Elizabeth and they began to rise, 'couldn't you fix it with Drusilla to serve us three kids straight through? We'll be just about drooling by the time you get back to the table. I've ordered honey-glazed duckling with orange balls, and Matt and Ed are having venison with almonds and cherries and I have a feeling if this fills up any more we mightn't get a full choice of sweets.'

Jeremy chuckled, 'Please yourselves. I doubt if I'd have

danced between courses at your age.'

Andrew gave a satisfied grunt, and looked at Innis, eyes twinkling. 'Darling, mind if I follow suit? I'll dance with you non-stop once I've eaten if I don't get called out. Our spring rush with babies is still on, you know. I think a doctor could be forgiven for breaking the rules, don't you?'

Innis looked at him saucily. 'I do. Besides which, it will give me a much better dancer as a partner. There's no one here foots it as featly as Ebenezer.'

Ebenezer rose with alacrity. He looked ten years younger and the compliment put a sparkle in his eye. Thomasina felt a wave of affection for him come up and swamp her. 'Oh, I do love him,' she said involuntarily to Luke.

Luke had already risen. 'Both Elizabeth and Innis think nobody dances like my uncle, but I hope you'll find me not too bad.' In actual fact he was a beautiful dancer, and the band, a local one, played delightfully. Thomasina herself felt she had never danced as well.

Luke said into her ear, 'Did you mind my doing that, back at the house?'

'Mind? Mind what?'

'Calling you Tamsin? I realize it's just a pet name, a family name. It just slipped out. I remember once Elizabeth saying her father called her Lindy-Lu—her second name is Lucinda—and that she didn't like anybody else except Jeremy to use it.'

No, she hadn't minded. She said so.

'Is that just politeness? Because I was sincere about asking. I wouldn't be huffed.'

This time she looked up, her turquoise eyes meeting his sherry-brown ones candidly, though she was suddenly a little shy. She said, 'It wasn't just that I didn't mind, Luke. I liked it. It sounded so natural. I did think of asking Ebenezer to use it, then I realized it gave him a great pleasure to say Thomasina, because of his father.'

'Thanks, Tamsin. You've done so much for Uncle Eb. He was so lost. He used to get up, after Aunt Georgie died, with the air of someone who has still another day to get through, get through somehow. We've been such pals, he and I. I was such a greenhorn when I came here. I know at his age I can't expect him to last for ever, but please God, a few more years yet.'

Thomasina experienced a feeling that made her tingle to her very fingertips. He didn't want his uncle to die even if it meant

102

Corrieside would be all his.

This night had an enchantment about it. The twilight had faded now and little lights glimmered out among the trees in the side garden, and in a gap between them was the starlit pale expanse of the harbour waters and round the over-harbour side, cars with amber lights like cats'-eyes, went purring round. In all those bays window-lights shone out marking homes, some of them ones where, in pioneer days, lamps had been placed to guide the men of the house home, because in the days of rough access tracks, small boats were often used to cross the waters with their produce. What a charm this had. You felt it wasn't a case of the past and the present linking, but of a continuity that had never been broken, families continuing on the same traditions.

The music stopped as they reached a window. She pushed aside the rich burgundy brocade curtain and looked out at the bays, putting her thoughts into words. Luke put up a higher hand and held it back.

'That's what makes it sad my uncle and aunt had no children. Apparently there was no reason why they shouldn't, so they kept on hoping till it was too late to adopt. There ought to have been another Swainson to carry on, to give him grandchildren, provide future generations.'

Thomasina said, 'But there's you.'

'It's not quite the same. I'm just his wife's young sister's son.'

'But, Luke, he'd never think of it that way. He looks on you as a son. If he hadn't, I'm sure he would have brought pressure on his own nephews or their children to farm Corrieside.'

'Not Uncle Ebenezer. He's no autocrat. And it didn't mean as much to them because mostly they grew up on their own parents' farms. It was different with me. Even in Whitburn our house was a rented one. I seemed to put my roots down here from the time I first set foot on Corrieside soil. But I still feel it's second-best for Uncle. My ties are of affection and marriage, not blood.'

They turned to look at the table Innis and Ebenezer had returned to. Ebenezer felt their eyes on him and looked up. For a moment sheer pleasure beamed out of his eyes. Instinctively, and as one, slightly embarrassed, Thomasina and Luke moved away from the window and returned to their seats.

Jeremy gazed at their dinner orders with great respect. 'My goodness . . . steak and oysters with a suet topping! That's substantial fare! Old Obadiah Cherrington wouldn't half have approved of you two. Just as well you danced first!'

But they did dance again, though not always with each other. The business men came over, asked if they might add their congratulations, and said they'd enjoy taking copies of the paper home to be able to tell their wives they'd met the principal characters, including the editor, and the children. Thomasina found herself in demand. Innis and Elizabeth too. Andrew was pleased. He managed to get through all the courses undisturbed.

The band struck up again and Luke acted quickly, getting Thomasina on to the floor again. She was filled with a new happiness, one she didn't dare believe in. She felt as one does when a child, sometimes, and a day is so idyllic it is never to be forgotten. These were such dear, dear people, all of them at the table, especially Ebenezer, her own loved kinsman. She thought of the devastation that had swept over her when she knew first that the cottage at Greenchester was to be demolished and she shivered suddenly and violently.

Luke's arm tightened about her. 'Someone walking over your grave? Isn't that what it's supposed to mean?'

'I was suddenly aware of how happy I am, at this very moment, surrounded by such lovely people, one of them of my very own blood. And how alone I felt last year, just coming to the surface after losing Dad and Maddy, suddenly terrified because our home too was to be swallowed up. Shows one doesn't realize what can lie round the next corner.'

Suddenly the craggy brows came down, but not angrily, more as if to hide his feelings from her. 'And you came here and got swept into one of my worst moments! When because of Ilena I bawled you out too. You ordered me not long ago to grovel. I hadn't time, Uncle came in then. So I had to improvise because we didn't want to upset him again. But I'll grovel right now.' He laughed. 'Recall Gordon Johnston's sermon on Sunday? It hit me amidships.'

Her brows had a line between them. 'How? I mean how did it apply to anything between you and me?'

'It was in the first part. What Jeremy would call the intro. Talking about the regrets we know because if we'd been in full possession of the facts we mightn't have sat in judgement on someone, or acted so hastily. I just leapt to the conclusion you'd got Uncle's letter, and had come out post-haste to see what there was in it for you. I was raw, of course, from what Ilena had said, and classed all women as such. The injustice of it must've burned clean into you. It could have given you a complex.'

Thomasina's eyes were shining, but suddenly she burst into a peal of genuine merriment, so much so she had to stop dancing. He steered her over to a window. 'What is it?'

'It's only when things go underground that complexes develop, you chump. I got rid of mine by smacking you, smacking you hard, across the face, remember?'

'Remember? Do I what?' His eyes were alight with laughter, and his hand came up to caress his cheek reminiscently.

She said, 'So I grovel too. We're quits. Right, Luke?'

'Right, Tamsin,' he said, and it was a pact, signed and sealed.

Then Ebenezer claimed her for a dance. He looked down into her happy face and said, 'I think it's been a very successful celebration, eh? You and Luke have at last forgotten your differences?'

She nodded, eyes alight. 'Yes, we've each apologized to the other, in fact, grovelled.'

The old man's eyes swept her face searchingly, flickered to Luke, dancing now with Innis, and said softly, 'I think Georgiana would have been pleased.'

Thomasina had a moment of panic. He mustn't read too much into their cessation of hostilities. It was too soon. But she dared not say so.

It was almost as if he sensed it. He said, 'We've always had harmony at Corrieside.'

She looked rueful. 'Till I came.'

Ebenezer shook his silver mane of hair. 'Till Ilena came. I was very afraid for Luke when I saw what was happening. So were Drusilla and Elizabeth and Innis. We're all much happier now.'

CHAPTER VII

In October the lilacs and wistaria were full out, pluming the old house and the contoured hill garden with lavender and purple. The guelder roses were hung with snowballs amid their delicate green; behind the house a whole row of hawthorns, grown from the saplings pioneers had brought out on their long voyages, crusted their boughs with rose and ivory. Ixias girdled the dark-foliaged prunus trees with scarlet, and azaleas set the whole hillside aglow with coral and yellow and flame-coloured branches. Thomasina was so glad that the flowers she had loved all her life bloomed so abundantly here.

She loved to run out on the verandah after breakfast and breathe the scented air . . . lily-of-the-valley from the cooler patches of shade, wallflowers in browns and yellows in full sun, spicy stocks, flowering rosemary.

She came in one morning with her hands full of the wall-flowers, her bright head silhouetted against the sun, its tawny locks swinging free, her eyes astar. 'Look, Ebenezer,' she said, holding them towards him as he read the morning paper.

He looked up, smiled. 'I know what you're thinking. You're remembering your great-grandmother. I like to think Bessie's girls got up early to get her wallflowers, dewy-fresh, from New-castle Market. Imagine, a penny a bunch!'

She nodded, 'And Edwin too brought her offerings. I can just see him, rising at five on Sunday mornings, and getting right out into the fields to pick her the button mushrooms she loved. Gran said her sister Jane used to think it was sweet the way he would bring her back a little posy, tied with a bit of wool, of field daisies and clover.'

She suddenly noticed Luke was there too, sitting on the arm of a chair busy with something. Then she put down her flowers and went across to him. 'You've cut yourself! Let me see.' He was trying to wind a large and clumsy bandage round it and as fast as he did the blood was seeping through.

For once when she spoke to the older man her tone was sharp. 'Ebenezer, didn't you realize he'd cut himself badly?'

He dropped his paper and came over, 'Sorry, Luke, you sounded so matter-of-fact. Oh, look out, he's keeling over!'

But Thomasina had seen it first and she pushed Luke right off the arm into the deep chair. Then she forced his head down below his knees. It was only momentary. Luke lifted his head and looked sheepish. Thomasina slipped out and returned with something in a glass. Luke sipped it, coughed and pulled a face. ' I thought I was getting brandy. That's sal volatile!'

Thomasina said severely, ' No talking.' She went across to the sideboard, whipped out a clean table-napkin, clapped it round his hand and exerted pressure. ' I'll look at it in a moment. You've lost a lot of blood.'

Ebenezer said, ' He did it on his slasher. He was attacking gorse away down at Donovan's Head.'

Thomasina looked horrified. ' All that distance away! And all uphill. Luke, why didn't you tell your uncle it was bad and he'd have called me? No, stay put. The chair doesn't matter. I'll bring in some proper dressings and disinfectant, and do it here.'

Ebenezer was exerting pressure on the pad. Luke's colour was coming back. Thomasina sped back. When they uncovered it her eyes met Ebenezer's. Then she said briskly, ' Well, you must know it will have to be stitched. But first I'll clean it a little, and jam the new dressing on quickly, then I'll drive you up to Cherrington House.'

Ebenezer said, ' Andy will be there right now on his rounds. I'll come with you too.'

Luke protested, ' It'll make me a proper sissy. Two of you!'

Thomasina said, as she would have to Matthew, ' Don't be stupid. If you pass out again when I'm driving, you might slump against me and put me over the bank. I'll bring the car right to the door.'

He was very groggy on his legs. Country hospitals were so delightful, such a homely atmosphere despite their clinical aseptic efficiency.

Matron and Andrew left their rounds immediately. Ebenezer and Thomasina stayed to watch. Andrew whistled when he saw it. ' Lucky you didn't pass out before you reached the house. That'll take seven stitches at least. You've had tetanus immunity, of course. But you won't be using this for at least a week.'

Luke was horrified. ' At this time of year that's a disaster.'

Andrew grunted. ' Not in my dictionary. This is only a small setback. A bit further and deeper and you'd have been in Christchurch having a very tricky repair job done. Besides, you've got Thomasina—she and Peggy can neglect the dusting, and pitch in.'

'Callous lot, doctors,' said Luke.

Andrew looked at Thomasina. 'You made a good job of this. When Louisa returns would you like a job as a nurse-aide here?'

Luke said hastily, 'She's needed at Corrieside. We aren't going to let Louisa do as much when she gets home.'

The doctor grinned. 'That's what *you* think. Gallstones isn't such a major operation. Once she's well you'll never hold Louisa back. Good thing not to. When she thinks old age is creeping up on her the rot will set in. So watch it.' He turned to Thomasina again. 'Think about it. So many girls don't want to come so far from town anyone living here is a godsend.'

'At the moment,' said Luke grumpily, 'she's a godsend to us, so hold your horses. Louisa won't be on deck till Christmas. She's staying with Josie first, then with Elizabeth when they get back from Canada.'

It was so unexpected Thomasina had a warm feeling inside. Luke wasn't resenting her at all now. He'd made that point at the Sickle, but now he didn't even want her working in the village.

Luke refused to go to bed, but they made him lie on the couch in the dining-room. Like the master bedroom above it, it looked right down the harbour through its French windows. Thomasina removed the lunch dishes and Luke's tray, then brought him some medicine in a glass. 'Antibiotic to ward off infection, I suppose,' grumbled Luke. But he took it. 'Thomasina, I get awfully bored when I'm sick, could you—'

She said disapprovingly, 'Do you? I didn't think readers ever did. When I was a kid and had to have a day in bed, I just revelled in being free to read and read.'

'Well, I don't feel like reading. I've got a headache. But I thought you might take pity on me and catch me up with some of your family history. You and Uncle Eb have retired to the sitting-room so often to go through it after the kids are in bed that I've missed out a lot on it.'

Thomasina said carelessly, 'Well, it's all been on the Swainson side, I didn't think you'd be interested. Besides, most nights you were on farm accounts.'

'I'm interested in all history. You don't have to belong to one particular branch of the family to be keen. Look at Elizabeth Ffoulkes, for instance. She's swotting up miles of stuff about Oxford, all the milling of the bush there and so on.'

'Yes, I know. She came down yesterday and borrowed a book on it, but then that's the setting of her next novel.'

He sounded peeved. 'Well, I don't care. After all, I come from County Durham and know Northumberland well and you were telling Uncle about some of your Temple-Watson relatives who are interested in the digs round the Roman Wall. I'd like to hear about it. After all, I'm an invalid!'

She chuckled. 'You sound like a peeved child. You aren't going to do anything but sleep this afternoon. I'll entertain you tomorrow if I can find the time. That wasn't an antibiotic. What would you need one in medicine form for? Andrew gave you a penicillin injection. That was a sedative.'

Luke was asleep almost before he finished protesting, and before Ebenezer's rich chuckle had died away.

The children loved Marama School. It had much the same atmosphere as the Greenchester one, apart from the natural geographic emphases. Matthew chose to learn Maori as an extra and Edwina was delighting Ebenezer with the natural rhythmical way she was learning *poi* dances and action songs. Edwina had, miraculously, managed to stay out of trouble, and when Thomasina saw how she had attached herself like a shadow to Luke, she realized how much the child had missed her father. She quite automatically sat on his knee every night when they watched television and quoted him as an authority on every possible occasion.

Thomasina had to admit he was good with Matthew. He stood no nonsense from either child, but Matthew naturally gravitated to him for advice on all things, whether it was maths, geography, conjuring tricks, how to build a model plane, the lot.

He gave both children extra jobs outside while he was disabled. Edwina took over the poultry which was more a personal supply venture here than a money-making extra, but the surplus eggs went into town, and Edwina could have the proceeds from that.

They all fed difficult or motherless lambs, though they were fewer every day now, but Matthew was responsible for the calves and had been given two of his own, plus some lambs. Their pocket-money devolved from household chores for Edwina, and chopping wood for Matthew; and keeping the stables clean, something they both loved, was shared.

When Thomasina was made aware of how much he was paying them, she demurred. At first she accused Ebenezer of getting round her firm refusal to let him buy their clothes, but he grinned and said it was all from Luke. 'He's my partner, you know, and about as independent as you. Said as he too was benefiting from your keeping house for us, he'd pay the kids for the extra help if they worked well and consistently.'

She swung round on Luke doing a crossword with his left hand, but before she could say anything he said hastily, ' And they do work well. They're well brought up. Matthew loves it. He told me the other day he's changed his mind about being an engineer. He'll make a great farmer. I told him it wouldn't be just a case of staying on here after High School, though, that he'd have to go to Lincoln College and learn the scientific side too. Look, Thomasina, take that frown off your face. They earn every penny, and they aren't likely to squander it. I'm taking them over to Christchurch when I can drive again, to open savings accounts for them. They have to put a certain percentage in. Otherwise they'll spend up to the limit on rubbish. They can buy their own clothes then, instead of you having to.'

Thomasina was touched almost to tears. Here was her one-time enemy—or was that too strong a word?—her one-time antagonist, making the way before her much easier. She looked across at him. He'd just come back from the hospital, walking, after a change of dressing. He was wearing an orange shirt, with short sleeves and an open neck, against which his throat was so bronzed, his hair looked bleached, and, as the eyebrows weren't beetling down, the sunlight struck almost amber lights from his eyes. She liked his line of chin, the firm cut of his lips, the whiteness of his teeth in his brown face.

The light in the room suddenly changed, as it often did in that room open to the four winds of the harbour. It was a trick of the sunlight, the moving clouds, the glinting of the green waters, and the light being reflected back on the ceiling.

It always reminded Thomasina of a searchlight sweeping the room and revealing every corner. It had once even shown up to her unwilling gaze a fine festoon of cobwebs in every corner. Today it revealed more than that. As it passed over Luke, sitting with his bandaged hand supported on the dining-table, and lit up those brown eyes, she knew with startling suddenness her feelings for Luke had gone from absolute destestation at their first meeting, to unwilling respect, to a companionable association, right on beyond friendship now, to something she would rather not admit.

It hit her amidships and she wanted to wheel out of the room and run, to hide it. She had never before felt as if her feelings had been stripped naked before others. She made the most tremendous effort to appear ordinary, managed to say, not quite looking at him, ' I appreciate that, Luke. I think you've done it very nicely. I don't approve of children having too generous an allowance if allowed to spend it all. Matthew, for instance, would spend the lot on books, bicycles, or accessories, and Edwina would buy nothing but saddlery. Neither would spend it on clothes. But it looks as if you've impressed it on them what their earnings are for. I'm grateful. It's not easy being a much older sister and having to be forever saying no, even though they were used to doing with less. But their long apprenticeship in being careful could have made them very free spenders, now things aren't so tight. So thanks a lot.'

Luke nodded. ' Fair enough. It'd be the very devil, I'd say, if you had to pursue a certain course with kids, then other people spoiled them. Not only that, but they could have resented the authority of a sister. They take it better from parents. You seem to have managed that hurdle very well indeed. It's been as tough for you as for any solo parent. It's a job better done in double harness.'

Thomasina felt a glow of pleasure positively spreading through her. Ebenezer said, satisfaction purring in his voice, ' Well, we may have got off to a stormy start, but we weathered it, and even if it mightn't be Harmony Hall every hour of every day, I think things are turning out even better than I'd hoped.'

There was such a warmth in his voice that Luke turned and looked sharply at him. He was matchmaking, the old man! Thomasina turned, said, ' I think I hear the phone,' and sped from the scene.

She gained the sanctuary of her room, rushed across to her mirror and anxiously surveyed her reflection to see if her colour had betrayed her. But if she had flushed, it must have subsided very quickly. Her eyes looked a little apprehensive, that's all. But that was only because, gazing in the mirror like this, she was forcing herself, in the knowledge looking back at her from her imaged eyes, to admit her feelings. She was conscious of as much alarm as joy, because she knew Luke was only being friendly. He looked on her now as a cousin-by-marriage. There was nothing loverlike about him and old Ebenezer, impatient as old men often were to realize dreams, could make things embarrassing. To him it would seem as if Thomas and Bessie's romance had come to a belated flowering, here in this idyllic corner of the southern hemisphere.

Thomasina had said to him just the other day that these days three-score and ten wasn't a life-span, eighty was, and more. He'd said, 'Probably not, but at this age, one never knows. It wouldn't worry me at all now, since Georgiana died, if any night at ebb-tide, my spirit drifted out through the Heads to join hers.'

So, thinking his time might be short, he could be impatient. It would create a hideously embarrassing situation for her and Luke. So she must bury her feelings deep. It was no time since he had doubted her motives. Ilena's outlook had made him cynical about women. Who could blame him? He must never think that she, Thomasina, was taking this way of inheriting Corrieside. Not marrying for money, perhaps, but certainly marrying where money was! What a horrible label!

She would be glad when Luke's hand was healed because she had so much to do for him. He was clumsy with buttons, couldn't manage a tie. She played checkers and Scrabble with him at night. It had forced them too close at the very time she was far too conscious of her own recently awakened feelings.

She was glad when they needed her outside. In fact she did much more of it than she had needed. Peggy helped more in the house, but even so, since she also had her own home to look after, things fell behind inside. Thomasina was glad of Louisa's store of deep-frozen cookies and only hoped she'd be able to restock for her before Louisa's return. Once they were all used up it was so hard to keep up with the daily demands. Thomasina quite liked cooking, except for the fact that there was far too much of it and it disappeared too fast.

But one day Ebenezer decreed a rest. 'It would be a splendid opportunity to pay a visit to the Martensens just now.'

Luke said sharply, 'You mean while Ilena is still away?'

Ebenezer never avoided an issue, but his voice was mild. 'Well, that too, but I really meant while you can't manage outside work. And I'd like Thomasina to have a meal cooked for her for a change, and to get her off this property. Yes, come to think of it, I'd rather take her over there when that one's still in Queenstown. She's making rather a long stay of it, isn't she?'

'Why not? She's not seen anything of the Lake District till now. Queenstown's only her base. She's had several trips away from it. To Te Anau, Manapouri, Milford Sound, to Lake Wanaka and even over to the Haast.'

'Oh, you've been talking to the Martensens, have you?'

Luke's voice was nonchalant, an achieved nonchalance, Thomasina suspected. 'No, I'd a letter from her last week.'

Not even Ebenezer had the nerve to ask what sort of a letter. He just said dryly, 'Oh, I don't remember you mentioning it.'

Luke's voice was dry too. 'I didn't. You'd only have waxed sarcastic. I thought I'd let sleeping dogs lie. The whole thing's dying down and better that way.'

The whole thing. Did he mean the quarrel, or their association, Ilena's and Luke's? Hard to know. Would he have answered that letter?

There was a silence between the two men, then Luke laughed. 'You're dying to ask, you old so-and-so! It was a perfectly ordinary letter. It didn't mention the bone of contention at all. Best that way. After all, we're so friendly with the Martensens, it saves embarrassment.'

'That's a nice label,' said Thomasina tartly. 'I just love being called a bone of contention. Ah, you left yourself open to that one, Luke,' and she smartly removed one of his pieces from the checkerboard between them.

Luke grimaced. 'I'd better keep my mind on my game. You're getting better at this.'

'So I ought. I've wasted too much time on it. But for not much longer. That hand's nearly right again. And do me a favour . . . when Ilena comes back and finds us here, will you inform her immediately that I did not come in response to Ebenezer's offer? That his letter hasn't reached me even yet. That I won a competition and came out under our own steam and that I'm merely a wage-earner here and am going to remain that way.'

'Not much use, she wouldn't believe it.'

Thomasina felt rage rise in her. 'Don't be so maddeningly casual about it. You wouldn't like that sort of thing said or thought about you.'

Ebenezer cut in. 'He means Ilena couldn't even begin to understand an independent girl like you, Thomasina.'

Luke made an impatient movement. 'Oh, leave Ilena alone. I can't keep my mind on the game.'

It was obvious his resentment against Ilena was fading. Well, that was healthy. Enough bad feelings existed in this world without wanting anyone to cherish some. Only—Thomasina flinched from that qualifying word. What a coward she was! Why didn't she just admit to herself that she'd rather Luke remained hard towards Ilena? For the first time in her life she experienced jealousy. She remembered he'd been writing in Ebenezer's study last week.

His uncle had remarked. 'My word, you must have developed writer's cramp after that lot.' Luke had shrugged, 'Well, it takes longer with one's left hand.'

Thomasina remembered now she'd said, 'Any good at dictating? After all, I'm a shorthand-typist. I've my portable with me.'

Luke had replied, 'Oh, it was personal mail, not business.' He hadn't said letters in the plural. So it must have been one very long one. What a fool she was!

They finished the game now, and Thomasina brought her portable out. Luke said, 'Aren't you tired? Can't you take a rest? I think Uncle's right, we'd better make a day soon with the Martensens to get you away from work. You've scrubbed and done the washing today, and made fresh scones for lunch and that lambswool duster was hardly out of your hand the rest of the time. You'll wear yourself out.'

'Oh, I'm just in the mood to write a bit of fiction, to lose myself in it.'

Ebenezer went out to answer the phone and put his head back in to say, 'I had a drink of chocolate when I was out there and a piece of your sultana cake. I'm going up to bed to read. You'll be making yourself and Luke some supper, I know, but I don't want any more.'

Thomasina knew by now that when New Zealanders said supper, they only meant their last snack and cuppa before bedtime, not a meal.

She was gladder than ever that she was typing, if they were to be left alone. It was true enough that one lost oneself in writing. All cares fell from one, and to a time one moved in a world of the imagination, peopled by creatures of one's own invention. She didn't hear Luke go out of the room, or come back in again.

It was little short of midnight when she typed the last page and drew it out of the machine with a satisfied sigh. She turned round. Luke was sitting in one of the big winged armchairs by the dying fire, doing nothing. Beside him on a low table was a tray with sandwiches, slices of the sultana cake, and some nutty cookies Peggy had made yesterday. A vacuum jug was beside it and proved to contain hot chocolate.

Luke smiled, a rather nice smile that softened the craggy features. 'I didn't dare disturb the muse, Thomasina. I thought if I put our hot drink in this, we could have it the moment you decided to break off. How did it go?'

She came across to the opposite chair. 'Oh, cucumber sandwiches—I love them. As much for texture as for taste, they're so crisp and cool. Oh, it went very well. First short story I've tried with a New Zealand setting. It's been fizzing inside me all day. Dad warned me I wasn't to keep thinking there'd always be plenty of time to make a success of writing. That was when he first knew his life wouldn't be a long one. It was so poignant, that just as he tasted real success, his career was cut short, yet now that I've got over the first sense of loss, I feel thankful it at least gave him a year devoting his whole time to what he liked doing best, and he had the comfort of knowing a small income would result for the children.'

'You mean for the three of you?'

'Well, no. For the two of them and Maddy. I was an adult, earning. And for two or three years I'd been supplementing my money with a few articles and poems for magazines. Sometimes I just can't believe Maddy's gone, Luke. She was so lovely. So full of fun, and loved Dad so much. He was lucky in both his wives, though with him and Maddy, it was idyllic from the start. With my own mother there was her old battleaxe of a father to deal with, a man who thought money could buy any allegiance. Dad was very fond of his own kind of office job, though writing was dearest of all to his heart. But my grandfather actually thought Dad should give up his own work and be a mill manager. So the old boy cut Dad out of his will. Me too, of course. Mother was gone by then, so it didn't hurt her.'

She sighed a little. 'But Dad was so happy-natured money didn't matter. Oh, I shouldn't say that. He plugged away night after night when he came home from the office, at his first couple of novels. But that was only partly for money for his family, mostly because he was a born writer. If he'd gone into the mill it would have demanded all his time, and he'd never have made it. Anyway, it taught us all there are things that matter more. Freedom, for instance. Freedom to express oneself.'

He handed her the chocolate. 'But how free are you at this moment? You're bound to this place through the very ties of your affection for Uncle Eb. By your sense of duty to the children. You think this is the best life for them. And your house duties leave you very little time for writing.'

Thomasina bent to pick up another sandwich and her loose

hair swung over her cheeks, hiding her expression. Her voice was casual. 'Oh, it has its compensations. I feel part of a family. Ebenezer makes me feel so wanted.'

They ate in silence after that, a companionable silence.

Thomasina had a feeling she wouldn't sleep easily. Her mind was full of the characters she had brought to life on the restricted canvas of her short story. She felt she'd like to have known them longer. Would like to have kept them for a basis of a novel. But she had no time for longer writing at the moment. And this last half-hour sitting opposite Luke by this lovely old fireplace built of the warm golden Charteris Bay stone had set all sorts of longings astir.

She stood up. 'I think for once I'll leave those dishes till morning. I'm going for a turn round the garden before bed. My mind's rather active. I'll be sure to lock the windows when I come back in. Goodnight, Luke.'

She unlatched the French windows, stepped off the verandah on to the old flagged path and lifted her face to the gentle breeze that came off the harbour. Nothing could compare with these little wandering winds because they carried with them the salt tang of the ocean and the myriad scents of the garden that Anna and Thomas had so loved and cherished.

Summer was just round the corner and a patch of night-scented stock spiced the air. The first roses, old-fashioned creamy cluster ones, and big pink cabbage-roses, were beginning to bloom. But the charm of this garden at night was its white flowers. In the day they were paled to insignificance beside the tangerines and purples and scarlets of the other flowers. At night the others couldn't be seen, but the white marguerites and alyssum and snow-in-summer, came into their own and glimmered like stars in the darkness.

She heard the door and knew Luke was coming after her. He said, quite diffidently for him, 'Care for company? I feel restless, too.'

She would have preferred solitude, because she was afraid of herself, but it would be ungracious. They paced the uneven garden paths where, long ago, children in sailor suits and white embroidered pinafores had played hide-and-seek and chasing on hot summer afternoons while the grown-ups sat on deck chairs or played croquet, pausing now and then, no doubt, to exclaim excitedly that another ship under sail was entering the Heads. Luke said so.

She nodded, 'And the ladies would wonder what word of new fashions the ships would bring, whether crinolines were giving place to bustles now, what designs the bolts of cloth in the hold would show. In a world not dominated by the news media we know today, radio and television pictures transmitted so swiftly by satellite, the only news of the Northern Hemisphere would come to them on those sailing ships. They would pore over the London illustrated papers, lap up snippets about the Queen and the Royal Family, read the letters from Home over and over again.'

They paused at the old rail fence, in a gap between two tall lombardy poplars and saw below them, the stars reflected in the still waters.

Luke said, 'Do I detect a note of homesickness? Don't be afraid to confess it, Thomasina. One doesn't relinquish all ties without a pang. It's not as if you are in your teens, as I was, when I left County Durham. At twenty-five your life could have settled into a certain pattern. There would be people you would miss. My own mother was dreadfully homesick for a while. She said she used to look at the ring of the Cashmere Hills that shut away the port from Christchurch, and hated them because they stood for her as a barrier between herself and all that was loved and familiar. Not that she ever said a word till one day she said how much she had grown to love their outline against the sky. Dad took her Home not so long ago. She loved it, but said she knew now her roots were here. I must take you over to meet my parents soon, Tamsin.'

He moved nearer. She could feel the warmth of his arm through his sleeve. She didn't speak because her heart was full. She wanted nothing more than to turn to him, but she dared not because another girl had sickened him with her mercenary motives. And he could suspect hers. But these thoughts of his were kindly ones.

He slipped an arm about her shoulders, said, 'I'm a clumsy oaf, I suppose. That was different. Mother came here with a family and a husband. You're here on your own, apart from your guardianship of two children. No one of your own age and blood to companion you. Sometimes you look like a little girl lost, Tamsin, wistful. It makes me wonder if—'

She prompted him, 'Makes you wonder what, Luke?'

'If staying here, for the children's sake, you may have made a personal sacrifice of your own? If there was someone you cared for and had to leave? Though I can't imagine any chap letting you get away from him.'

It was a compliment she appreciated, but she mustn't read too much into it. He and Ilena were writing each other. All those angry words mightn't have meant much.

She said slowly, 'It wasn't as definite as that. There was someone before Dad took ill, and even after that, but then Maddy died and I was left with the two children.'

There was a pause. The arm round her shoulders tightened, in a brotherly fashion. He said, 'You can't mean any chap would expect you to give them up—to put them in a Home? Why, that would have been monstrous! What sort of a chap would—'

She stopped him. 'Luke, you're a very black-and-white sort of person. I like it. I used to be, too. Rather too idealistic, though, always getting hurt. Derry and I weren't engaged. He had his way to make. He worked with me and we went round together, that's all. I suppose if he'd been staying in that office job it might have been different, but he was ambitious. Wanted his own farm some day, and was trying to save towards that. And he wasn't very good at saving. So he opted out.'

Luke uttered one of his indescribable sounds. Thomasina, feeling a little laughter might lighten the situation, giggled. 'Luke, you're so funny. You're so articulate, except when you get angry and you snort and grunt and get all beetle-browed!'

He peered at her in the starlight, realized indeed his brows were drawn right down and said, 'What an insult, you're a cheeky brat! But spunky, and very understanding and tolerant.'

She said, a little breathlessly, due to his nearness. 'Oh, thank you, Luke. Considering I behaved like a termagant when first we met, I appreciate your like tolerance.' He came closer still, smiling. She said, with a minor panic within her, 'But try to extend that tolerance towards Ilena too. I think you were all the more furious with her because she jumped the gun. Perhaps she and Derry too, are more practical than either you or me. Although you hadn't declared yourself, I expect she knew it was just a matter of time, and even if she did me an injustice in thinking I'd rush out here, she was right to fear this possible usurper from England who looked like inheriting half of Corrie-side. A divided inheritance always makes for trouble, Luke.

'So being of a practical turn of mind, she tried to check it while there was time. Some girls do dream dreams before actually being asked. It's still a lot easier to be a man, you know. He knows exactly where he's going, emotionally, and when he'll be ready to ask. A girl has to wait. Ilena's written you, as you said, a perfectly ordinary letter. I think it's in the nature of an olive-branch, and that you ought to take it.'

The arm fell away from her shoulders. She felt him stiffen, then he moved away.

His voice was rough. 'What do you think you're doing? Running a lonely hearts club? Was this short story you've just written a love-story?'

She was startled. 'Yes, why—?'

'Because I think like all writers you want to play God and tie the ends up. Well, leave *my* life alone. I'm more than capable of running it myself. Oh, go inside! Most of the time I like and admire you, but at other times, Thomasina Meade, I could cheerfully throttle you!'

She turned and walked over the grass, not quickly, not slowly, even though she felt like bolting from him and slamming that door. She wouldn't even allow herself the luxury of a display of temper this time.

She knew what it meant. It meant that the breach with Ilena had gone far more deeply than Luke Richmond would admit. He couldn't bear it to be talked about. She mustn't do it again.

CHAPTER VIII

Thomasina felt she ought to be grateful for the presence of the children. Otherwise, no doubt, she and Luke would have been extremely stiff with each other next morning, but she granted him that, he wouldn't allow any hint of disharmony in front of the children. No doubt it was also in consideration for his uncle.

The men were outside all day, as Luke's hand seemed better, and Peggy's bright chatter kept Thomasina from brooding and regretting. Peggy did a lot for Thomasina's ego. ' I like the way you pitch in to any job at all. Though you needn't think because there are three extra in the house, you've got to do some of the scrubbing and washing. You're looking a bit peaky.'

Ebenezer said at lunchtime, returning from the phone, ' We've been invited to Martensens tomorrow. I reckon Josh could do without us for one day. It's a long time since I had a good crack with Conrad Martensen.' He grinned. ' I thought it wiser to stay away. The less I saw of Ilena the better, and Conrad was so fed up with her he used to get a lot off his chest. Ruth begged him to say nothing, but just play it along. He was trying, but it got his goat to see Ilena imposing on his wife. It's the devil of a coil really. Evidently Ruth and Ilena's mother were distant cousins, but bosom friends in their youth. Ruth was delighted when her daughter decided on a visit here. But it's been such a long one. Ilena says nothing about returning. Well, she had her reasons, of course. Perhaps she'll pack it in soon.'

Thomasina found herself inwardly wincing for Luke's sake. She noticed his brows were down, but he said nothing.

' However, this Queenstown business has me hopeful. I think she's working in as much sightseeing as possible before returning. Having got her come-uppance and knowing Luke's prospects aren't quite what she imagined, she may sling her hook. That was behind her trip, of course. Pity Luke ever visited their place in Surrey when he was in England. It was just before he discovered you, Thomasina, and she was here six weeks after he got home. It's been a mighty long stay. And she's certainly worn out her welcome out there.'

Thomasina felt she'd like to scream. She couldn't think of a thing to say. Obviously Luke *wouldn't*. He'd be too enraged at being talked over like this. Who wouldn't be? And after her gaffe last night, it would be the last straw for him. Ebenezer, out of wishful thinking, surmised the scene in the stable had washed things up completely. Thomasina had doubts . . . things said in temper were rarely conclusive.

Ebenezer went on, 'So we'll go over tomorrow and enjoy ourselves like we used to. Maybe Conrad will let fall a few things. What she's planning. In fact, I might ask him outright is there any hope of her going back.'

At that Luke said, 'Oh, no, you don't, Uncle. Nothing of the kind. You trade far too much on your friendship with the Martensens. You'll let well alone!'

'Well?' ejaculated Ebenezer. 'There's nothing well about it, and won't be for us or for them till that mischief-maker packs her bags!'

Thomasina had to hand it to Luke, he was very patient with his uncle. He said, 'Come on, you old fire-eater, let's go round the sheep. Nothing like hard labour to work your spleen off! I've got the horses saddled. I can use the tips of my fingers quite well now.' As they went out of the door he looked back, said,

'Thomasina, how about us riding over for lunch tomorrow? You're coming on pretty well now. It'd be longer than you've had, but I reckon you could manage it. Good practice.'

Thomasina had a sudden vision of that other girl's superb horsemanship and shrank from appearing a novice at the Martensens. The whole family was noted for show-jumping. That ought to have added up to finding Ilena a kindred spirit, but evidently not. But she would appear much less, herself, than at her best. And after lunch, wanting to show her the farm, they'd probably insist on her riding round the sheep over unfamiliar territory, over which she'd have to pick her way so carefully, she'd hold them up. So she said, hastily, 'No, thanks, I'd much rather not.'

She thought Luke looked disappointed, and knowing how he loved riding knew, not for the first time, a pang that she was such a duffer at it. She'd had little opportunity till now. Still, neither had Edwina, but by now that small girl could ride her pony bareback in such a fearless way that Thomasina admired her fiercely. Especially when she herself was still so inwardly nervous of horses that even when they came nudging round she was a bit scared, and was frankly terrified when astride one. It seemed such an enormous height off the ground. Perhaps if the Bruces had had horses she'd have grown used to them. Even the sight of their ironclad hooves filled her with apprehension.

Luke just said now, 'Well, plenty other opportunities for practising. We'll take the car, and if Conrad wants us to go round the place, mounted, he's always got spare hacks.'

Yes, and from what Thomasina had heard, mettlesome ones at that. She made up her mind she would wear a dress tomorrow, Not trews. Then no one would persuade her into riding one of their horses. Better by far just to take short rides here, on old Ambler, well named. Even he gave her the sensation of being astride a warhorse!

But she looked forward to the outing. She had been tied to the place rather much, even though she so loved Corrieside. Thomasina took great pains in selecting what she would wear, which was absurd when Ilena wasn't going to be there. She looped her hair back in a high, more sophisticated version of the ponytail, and tied it with a bright green gauzy bow, and combed out the ends she had set with rollers the night before, so that curls fell softly at the back over the hair that belled sideways round her face.

She slipped into a dress that contrived in clever fashion to look like a pinafore dress, but was really a marigold one-piece with full bishop sleeves of a silk material paisley-patterned in brown and tangerine and green. Above it her eyes looked more green than blue today, and the colour was picked up in the chunky green necklace she had twisted twice round her neck. She slipped her feet into green slingbacks with open toes. Not the best for visiting a farm, but not too absurd either, and they were fairly flat.

She came out on to the back verandah to find the men waiting for her and the Holden estate car parked near the steps. Peggy came out.

'Oh, Thomasina, you look a million dollars! I wish I had your colouring. I wonder if Romola could put a few sort of chestnut glints in my hair, I'd like it a bit brighter than it is at the moment.'

Thomasina said, 'I don't see why not. Do make an appointment. It would suit you. But just highlights. Your hair is so glossily dark, I like the way the sun catches it. Peggy, don't let the youngsters go down to the shore, will you?'

'For sure I won't. Unless when they come home, I take mine and yours too. You don't mind if they have supervision, do you? Now, off you go. You worry far too much about them. Bye-bye.'

Martensens was a homestead very like Corrieside, though a little smaller, and with just as lovely a garden each side of its long curving drive edged with rhododendrons that were masses of colour, from the pearliest of pinks to the deepest of cerise.

Thomasina said, ' I just love these old Peninsula homesteads. I can positively see them peopled with lovely women in long sweeping gowns, pushing little balls through their croquet hoops, or gathering for their parties. In the days of large families, there was always so much music and pretty fair talent, and with all the friends of the young people, it would be so gay and friendly.'

Luke took it up. ' Conrad's very keen on family history. You ought to get him going some time. Perhaps a little later when the outside work eases off. He's quite a romantic, knows the history of almost every courtship that took place at Marama, and certainly every single one that had this romantic garden for its setting. Can't you just imagine it?—Those secluded shrubbery paths, the little winding one that dips down into the fernery, that rose-covered summerhouse. I defy anyone, however, hard-boiled, to remain absolutely prosaic in this setting.'

Again Thomasina experienced that new, painful emotion—jealousy. Evidently Ilena was the practical type. Luke wasn't. He was a dreamer as well as a worker, but could it have been that even Ilena had been less prosaic here, in this garden, on lovely summer afternoons last December, or on autumn evenings in April and May, with the twilight folding purple wings over the harbour waters and the sunset staining the sky with incredible colour behind the Seven Sisters to the west?

They swept up to the front door and it swung open and Ruth Martensen was running out to meet them. In spite of her fifty-odd years, she had an eager girlishness that captivated Thomasina immediately and a little of the reserve she felt about this visit disappeared.

She was demonstrative, kissed Ebenezer and Luke, and before they had a chance to introduce her, kissed Thomasina too. ' I feel I know you already. I've been dying to meet you, but quite honestly, ever since you arrived, I've been flat out. It's always like this at this time, of course, all you think of all day is feeding lambs or men ! And with Ilena away it was a golden opportunity to catch up with things. The time I spend tidying up after her ! I give her her due, she's marvellous in the stables, but in the house—oh dear, I made a resolution last night not to criticise her and I'm doing it already ! It's becoming an obsession with me. Nothing less like her mother could be imagined. But I'll stop. It's bad form. Come away in. The boys are out with Conrad, but they'll be in soon.'

The interior was like Corrieside, mellow, panelled, and modernized to blend with the charm and graciousness of the old. The midday dinner was ready, the table beautifully set, yet nothing too formal. The roast beef was done to perfection, the Yorkshire pudding was crisp and curled, and the baked apple dumplings with butterscotch sauce so delicious Thomasina was inspired to ask for the recipe.

They had coffee out on the verandah facing the harbour, on wrought iron tables that had been brought out by the first Martensen who had arrived on the earliest of the First Four Ships, the *Charlotte Jane*.

'That was about all the furniture they had for a start,' said Conrad, 'plus their beds and a chest of drawers and a cradle. They lived in barracks at Port first of all, then a lean-to in Lyttelton, then, after going over with the others to view the plains, they came back over to the Head of the Harbour, turned sods and built a cottage. We've preserved it in the old orchard. I'll show it to you after, Thomasina. Then, as conditions improved, after the hungry maw of the land for improvement had been satisfied, they built the first two rooms of this house, and kept on adding.' He laughed at Thomasina's rapt face. 'My, but it's grand to have a fresh audience! It's an obsession with me, family history, stop me when I start to bore you.'

That just wasn't possible. The tales of the adventurous life lived here in mid-Victorian days thrilled Thomasina. In a way, she now felt she had always known them. It seemed quite incredible that there had ever been a time when New Zealand had barely existed for her. When she hadn't known that such a place as Lyttelton Harbour was so closely associated with her own forebears. It was part of her very life now. She loved every hill, every peak, every bay of these green waters.

Most of all she loved Corrieside, the worn steps trodden by pioneer feet even years before Thomas Swainson had arrived in New Zealand, each odd little addition, each treasure, each bit of china and furniture, valuable or not. Just for its associations. Ebenezer had said one day, stroking the panelling in the hall in a gesture that was caressing, 'These walls are impregnated with love.'

Conrad told her that long ago, his uncle and Ebenezer's oldest sister, Jane Temple Swainson, had done their courting in this garden and later married. Their descendants lived on in a Gebbie's Pass homestead. Conrad said dreamily, 'Theirs was a true romance and it endured. Thomasina, Eb tells me you write too. I'd love their story to be written some day, linking Corrieside and Harbourage. Not a plague on both their houses, like in *Romeo and Juliet,* but a blessing on both their houses, as it was. Would you give it a go?'

Thomasina clasped her hands together at her breast. 'Oh, how I would love to . . . if you think I could do it justice.'

Ebenezer and Conrad and Ruth all urged her to try. Suddenly Thomasina was conscious of a singing within her, a hope not known before . . . that all the tangles of emotions and discords over the inheritance might disappear. The attitude of the Martensens had fostered this, the fact that they too thought Ilena was at last returning to England.

It was so evident they had done all that they could to welcome her. Thomasina knew from things Ebenezer had let fall from time to time. She had fiercely criticised their way of life. She had no feeling at all for the old homestead, had said, 'I can't think why you don't pull it down instead of spending so much on it for maintenance. You could have a farmhouse like the Kinmonts with every possible convenience. It's like a ranch-house. Fabulous. That striking decor.'

Ruth Martensen had started. 'I'd have thought, coming from the beautiful part of Surrey I knew so well when I used to spend my school holidays with your mother, you'd have liked this homestead—it's like a bit of England here in the southern hemisphere. I remember we visited there when Conrad was courting me, during Battle of Britain days when he was there with the Second Echelon from New Zealand. He looked at those glorious old houses round Godalming and Farnham, and said he could understand, seeing their beauty, why his forebears had wanted to create the same architectural styles here.'

Ilena had shrugged. 'One grows so tired of antiquity. I prefer houses that have rebelled against conventional styles. The unusual. And bold, splashing colours and designs. Up-to-the-minute.'

Ruth had said, 'Well, we all have our likes and dislikes. But these lines have stood the test of time. And what is up-to-the-minute today is apt to be thought old-fashioned and ugly in a very few years. Fashions in clothes don't matter so much. But you're stuck with a house for generations. However, what matter? This suits old-fashioned me!

She'd said to Conrad later, 'She looked at me with positive pity and said, "But of course, it mightn't rest with you. When Finlay marries, his wife might have other ideas".'

Conrad had told Ebenezer, 'Ruth almost panicked. The relationship isn't a close one, and when Finlay was left that legacy from my aunt, she lost interest in Luke for a bit and really rushed our son. Finlay is so quiet we were just afraid she might bowl him over. We hadn't realized how shrewd he is beneath it all. He saw through her. He said nothing to any of us, but when the chance of a travelling scholarship for studying Australian sheep-breeding came along, he upped and offed. And he's decided to stay there for a bit. So there was only Luke left. But now it looks as if he's got wise to her too. She's so cold and calculating. No warmth to her at all, except when she's trying to impress.'

But that was in the recent past. Today they wanted to forget Ilena. Conrad went on telling her the family stories.

'They must have been tough days with access so rough,' said Thomasina. 'We take the trip to Christchurch as a matter of half an hour or so, but in those days it would be all tramping and horseback. It made for wonderful stories and great bravery—not so much scope nowadays for heroism, both masculine and feminine breeds!'

'I don't know,' said Conrad. 'Ruth featured as a heroine not three months after coming out from England after the war finished. She was scanning the bays at the far side of the harbour one day with the binoculars, when she saw a dinghy turn turtle between Four Winds Headland and that tiny island that's almost covered at high tide. There were two youngsters in it, so she—' he waved his wife's protests down—'flung herself on my horse that was saddled, fortunately. There was no one else home. And she off down to the shore. One child was hanging on to the dinghy, the other was in a bad way, almost done. She got him ashore first and went back for the other, somehow pumped the water out of the first, got them both on the horse, led them back up to the house and got the doctor. I can tell you I had nightmares for weeks thinking of what might have happened to her.'

Thomasina said wistfully, 'It must be wonderful to be a born rider like that. If you hadn't been, two lives would have been lost. I think I'd better persevere with my riding lessons. I expect there are still times when a horse might be the only means of transport.'

They all burst out laughing. Thomasina looked amazed. Conrad sobered up. 'That was the real heroism. She was terrified of horses. I'd been giving her lessons for the last month and just the day before she'd lost her temper with me and said it was no use, she was just plain yellow where horses were concerned and I could forget all about them. But when the emergency cropped up, she was in the saddle before she could think, but it was blamed lucky our track to the sea was clear right through. No fences.'

Thomasina looked at Ruth Martensen. 'And now? Are you still afraid?'

She knew what the answer would be. Ruth shook her head. 'Never again. I knew I had what it takes then to master and control an animal.'

Thomasina nodded. 'It must be wonderful to feel like that,' she said wistfully. 'I keep thinking if only those reins were like the wheel of a car, responsive to one's slightest touch. If I could be sure that when I did a certain thing, what I wanted to happen *would* happen! I tell myself I'll be all right, but as soon as the horse takes one step forward, I find a sort of shivering panic comes over me and I think how terrifying it is to be perched up on a great huge beast with a mind of its own, and that *any-thing* might happen!'

Luke took his elbow off the table to swing round and stare at her. 'Fair go? I mean is that really true? That you've been scared stiff?'

She nodded, looking ashamed.

Luke said slowly, 'Well, hats off to you. I'd never have known. I thought you were just not a natural, that's all. I mean not everyone can be, but practice makes it come easier. Well, you've been pretty game. And you don't have to force yourself to please us. It's handy but not essential. The Land Rover goes most places these days.'

Thomasina felt warm pleasure suffuse her veins. Then she said slowly, 'No, thanks, all the same. I'll stick it till I master it. You see, now I know Mrs. Martensen felt like that too, I feel okay. I thought I was the only ninny round here, to be just plain scared.'

Luke said, 'Confession's good for the soul. You'll probably never be scared again. I've known it happen before.'

'Do you mean to say lots of people know fear?'

'Of course. Why not? Especially those who aren't trained to it in infancy. Did you think you were the only one?'

'Well, the only one round here. I feel good now.'

He smiled at her in a fashion that seemed to make her heart turn over. It wiped out the other night's regrettable words, she thought.

Conrad lifted his head. 'I thought I heard a car.'

The next moment they heard one being driven away and the footfalls coming through the house. Then turned to the French windows behind them. Ilena stepped through on to the verandah, superbly groomed, in a cream trouser suit, braided in sailor blue, dark smooth hair flowing, creamy matt skin, eyes of deepest blue, longly-lashed.

Thomasina was glad Ruth Martensen acted so spontaneously, even if it must have cost her an effort, in welcoming her back. Because it would be terrible to feel one wasn't wanted.

Ruth said, after the first greeting, 'How on earth did you get here? There's no bus at this hour?'

Ilena's eyes flickered to Luke, then she smiled at everyone, said, 'I'd not intended coming up from Queenstown till tomorrow by plane, and I was going to ring Luke to collect me. But there was a conference on at my hotel. You'll know about it—agricultural, some from all over the world. Not just farmers—experts, mainly men, a few wives. They were awfully good to me, insisted on my joining them on some of the expeditions laid on for them. Some of them had hired cars and drove through the passes to Mount Cook. They offered me a seat. We stayed at the Hermitage two nights. One of them offered to come through Gebbie's Pass, drop me here, and go on to their quarters in Christchurch.'

Thomasina was ashamed of the naked thought that leapt into her mind: 'I wonder how the *wives* liked Ilena joining the party?'

Ruth said, 'Oh, you should have brought the driver in for lunch.'

Ilena said, with the faintest hint of disparagement in her tone, 'Oh, no. We had a dinner at the Sickle.'

Ruth said, 'This is Thomasina Meade, Ebenezer's young relation from Northumberland. She arrived just after you—'

'Yes, I know. Just after I went south. Luke wrote and told me. Hullo, Thomasina. Enjoying this lovely bay? Much better than the industrial north, eh?'

Thomasina managed to say evenly, though conscious of a surge of outraged loyalty to the North of England leaping to life within her, 'Oh, we lived in the lovely valley of the Tyne. Greenchester—a village. But the Bay is glorious. I've certainly lost my heart to it.'

She rather expected a cynical curl of the lips, with Ilena thinking it was more likely she'd lost her heart to the propects, but the girl just nodded, said, 'Yes, parts of England are quite unspoiled, my own Surrey, for instance. Do you happen to know it?'

Thomasina was glad she could respond warmly. 'I do indeed. I loved Surrey. I accompanied my father there. He wanted to write a thriller about Guildford Castle, modern, but with a background of history. We stayed in Guildford and Godalming and Chiddingfold, tracing the activities of the Plantagenets, Richard the Lionheart, Bad King John, their mother, the princesses. They lived a good deal of their time at Guildford, as you probably know. I'll never forget those beech woods just greening and arching over the roads, and the bluebells, so blue you kept thinking it was the shimmer of a lake under the trees.'

Ilena's eyes kindled a little. 'My home's not far from there. Hazelmere—wonderful country for riding.'

Thomasina felt a little disarmed. Perhaps this was the true Ilena. You couldn't judge a person properly if, on your first glimpse of her, she was consumed by anger. No one was at their best in a temper.

Conrad made an effort. 'This coffee's still hot, care for some?'

'Yes, don't mind if I do.' Small talk became easy because the subject became the beauty of the Lake District and Fiordland. Just as well, considering the circumstances under which Luke and Ilena had parted. But of course there had been that letter. No doubt that had smoothed the way for a resumption of a less hostile relationship.

Ilena, oddly enough in spite of her sophisticated appearance, talked knowledgeably then of the conference. 'That side of farming is far more fascinating than I thought. The marketing under world conditions, the financial aspects, the sense one has of how terrifically dependent upon each other the countries of the world are, in the matter of imports and exports and balances of trade.'

Against her will Thomasina was impressed. There was more to this insolent beauty than one would have guessed. What a grasp she seemed to have of these things! Despite themselves Conrad and Ebenezer began to be extremely intrested as Ilena covered various aspects of the conference she had gleaned from her close contact with its members. Conrad said, 'We've heard some of it on TV, of course, but it's interesting you managed to pick up so much. You seem to understand it too.'

Luke drawled, 'Oh, Ilena has a greater grasp of things financial than most women.'

If there was a hidden barb she gave no indication of its having found its mark. 'Well, as a secretary to a big combine in Surrey was a close friend, I picked up a certain amount, familiarity with terms and so on, and knew what they were talking about.'

The men decided to ride out to the boundary of the property to inspect some culverts that were important to Corrieside too as the creek that flowed through them watered Corrieside also. Ilena sprang up. 'I'm dying to feel a horse under me again. I'll change. How about you, Thomasina? Do you ride? I could rustle you up some slacks if you'd like to.'

'I'm just learning and I've a long way to go. I jolt up and down like a sack of potatoes. I'll wander round the garden with Mrs. Martensen. She's promised to give me some slips for the garden, plus a lot of advice. In a topsy-turvey hemisphere I'm not sure what to plant and when. I'd like to get annuals in, this coming week, but if I'm told what perennials to get it would help for next season.'

There was a slight glint in Ilena's eyes, there one moment, gone the next. Perhaps it did sound as if she were well entrenched.

Thomasina would have enjoyed the stroll more had her thoughts not been over the hills and far away with the riders. Ilena, as before, had looked no less than magnificent mounted; Luke as at home in the saddle as walking. Mightn't that amount to kinship? Interests shared? Perhaps she and Ebenezer were being intellectually snobbish about her not being a reader.

They came back for a late afternoon tea, glowing with the time spent in the saddle. Luke and Ilena were cantering well behind the others. They seemed easy, relaxed.

When they were leaving Luke said carelessly, 'You drive, Tamsin.'

Surprised, Ilena said, 'Good grief, changed a bit, haven't you? I thought you couldn't bear anyone at the wheel of your beloved vehicle! Oh, is it your hand? But it's nearly better, isn't it?'

Luke grinned aggravatingly. 'That depends. She may jiggle

round, as she said, like a sack of spuds in the saddle, but as a driver she's unsurpassed. She was secretary to a farm concern in Northumberland, but did duty as a chauffeuse too, to her chief, Sir Guy Crowsey. You can't fault her.'

Thomasina said, groaning, 'Don't say it! I'll probably chip the bodywork going through the gates. I hate people saying things like that.'

But she knew a pleasure out of all proportion. Ilena said, 'Well, I wish you luck—you'll need it after a compliment like that. By the way, Luke, I'll ride over tomorrow, about eleven. I daresay Thomasina won't mind an extra for lunch—Luke tells me you're quite domesticated, Thomasina.' She made it sound a dull virtue.

But Luke answered for Thomasina. 'She's not cooking lunch for anyone tomorrow. Make it the day after if you want to come. We're having the day off tomorrow.'

It was the first Thomasina had heard about it. She turned to ask Ebenezer where they were going, but before she could, Luke said, 'I'm taking Thomasina to Akaroa. Time she saw our French settlement.'

Thomasina re-composed her face immediately. She wiped the look of query off and replaced it with the expression of one who is anticipating a promised treat and said, 'I'd no idea till I came here that there was anything but British pioneering here.'

Ruth said, 'It's an example of a well-integrated community. All New Zealanders now. Used to be whalers from all parts, the English, the French, and a few Germans. But it gives the little harbour town the air of a Normandy village. The architecture in many cases is decidedly French—steep little gables, even the way the houses huddle together. And the gardens have a subtly different continental air. You'll love it, Thomasina.'

Thomasina slid in behind the wheel, Luke beside her, and Ebenezer on the far side. Ilena came to the open window, leaned her arm on it, bent down said, 'Oh, Thomasina, I nearly forgot to tell you. The talk of the Conference ought to have jogged my mind, of course. I was to give you regards from Derwent Ford. He was coming up to Christchurch a day after the others.'

'Good heavens,' said Luke flippantly. 'Derwent Ford. Sounds like river crossing in Cumberland.' He added, 'One of these chaps at the Conference? Some bigwig pal of your former boss, Thomasina?'

Ilena replied for her. 'No, nice chap, but small fry. Young.'

Thomasina's thoughts were racing. Derry? Here? How surprising. Now why on earth did she wish he hadn't met Ilena? She decided not to rouse Ilena's interest, said, 'Derwent Ford. Well, fancy him being in New Zealand!'

Ilena positively stared at her. 'Did you say fancy? But you knew he was here!'

It was a statement, not a query. And suddenly Thomasina felt and looked hot—and uneasy. But how stupid. She pulled herself together, said smoothly, 'I'd no idea at all. I think you must have picked him up wrongly.'

She felt as if everyone else's eyes too were riveted on Ilena, who had a puzzled crease between her brows. She sounded completely bewildered. 'Why, I'd no doubts you knew he was here. I mean, the way he talked—He even said—' suddenly she checked, as if thinking better of what she was going to say. She finished, instead with, 'But if you say you didn't know, then you didn't.' Another hesitation, then, 'But he even said—' she broke off, said, 'Oh, what does it matter? I've passed the message on, anyway.'

Thomasina pressed the self-starter, never was such a lovely sound at it purred to life, cutting off further conversation. Everyone waved and she went off to a smooth start.

They were no sooner on the road before Ebenezer began to chuckle, 'Well, that was smart thinking, Luke, it saved us the infliction of a visit. And you'll enjoy Akaroa, Thomasina.'

She said hastily, 'It was rather a shock to me. I could have given the show away. Can you really spare the time, Luke?'

He sounded surprised. 'Would I really have proposed it otherwise?'

She had to accept that, but she doubted his motives. Ebenezer, of course, thought it a joke, but she herself had rather thought Luke was fighting an attraction. Seeing Ilena again could have set up all sorts of emotions once more. He might have sounded definite when she'd played eavesdropper, but that had been in the heat of battle. No doubt he hadn't wanted to make the first move, but it could be he was being deliberately tantalizing. Ilena had a strong personality, so had Luke. He hadn't liked it being assumed they were on the point of an engagement. So his apparent interest in Thomasina was a declaration of his freedom. Luke wasn't the type to be run by any woman, even if his feelings were involved. Thomasina had an idea she was being used and she didn't like it.

And she felt extraordinarily uneasy about Derry. Why should she? But Ilena had seemed to make a mystery of it. How stupid! He'd been down south working since just after Maddy died, and she hadn't even seen his mother after that one visit Mrs. Ford had paid her. Mrs. Ford was sweet.

But when they headed for Gebbie's Pass next morning, leaving behind them a harbour that was like a sheet of glass, and drove through valley roads sweet with blooming orchards and emerald hills, away from the small and rather complex world of Harvest Moon Bay, gladness invaded her heart and she gave herself up to the loveliness of the day. It was marvellous having that prize wardrobe.

Her suit had white trousers, a tunic top of vivid green with a long fringed scarf of white tossed over her shoulder, and there was a white jacket with gold buttons like a sailor's reefer to put on if it became colder. She had gilt thonged slip-ons on her feet and a long strip of green nylon spangled with gilt tied her hair back. For the first time for months she felt carefree and young, and said so.

Luke laughed and his hand left the wheel to pat her knee in what could have been a brotherly gesture. 'Good for you! I feel like a day right off the chain too. Let's forget such things as demolition road gangs in England and complicated situations in New Zealand exist at all. Let's just think those lambs gambolling there on the hillsides are sheer delight, a picture of pastoral beauty. That they never had difficult births with a male midwife assisting them into the world; that none of them had to be coaxed back to life and force-fed; that every single ewe was endowed with the instinct of motherhood and wasn't stupid or as stubborn as a mule. That there are no vagaries in overseas markets or local ones, that currency doesn't get devalued or revalued, and that the word inflation hasn't been even invented!'

Thomasina laughed, falling in with his mood, 'Let's pretend I've just arrived from England and you're showing me round. We've never shouted each other down or smacked each other's faces or—'

'Here, cut it out! The smacking wasn't reciprocated. But I get the idea. All is sweet harmony. No one has to explain any animosity, any motives. The slate, from this moment, is clean.'

Idyllic was the only word for the day. The road snaked through the Pass and every valley running back into the hills was smiling. When they came out on to the Canterbury Plains, Lake Ellesmere lay with pewter-grey rippled waters, thick with black swans, and the tang of the open sea beyond came through the windows.

'But we'll turn away from the Pacific soon,' said Luke. 'Not that you could call it a pacific stretch of water this side of the Peninsula! On the Christchurch side, reaching away up north, you get the long sand-dune beaches. Here you have great flung-up stretches of jumbo-sized shingle, brought down from the mountains across the plains, and the sea roars up on to it, tossing up driftwood of matching size, sometimes whole trees stripped of bark till they're as smooth and white as bleached bones. The sea sucks away steeply—they say there are great cliffs beneath the waves like those above Birdling's Flat over there. The waves seem to surge back into them with a sort of relentless and evil pull, to discourage swimmers. But our landscape will be more gentle today. We turn back into the hills about Akaroa Harbour. There you get sheltered and tranquil bays with little French houses nestling amid walnuts and vines and trellised arbours.'

He laughed, suddenly self-conscious. 'I'm waxing lyrical! If you get tired of it, stop me in mid-flow. I love Akaroa.'

'But surely it can't be more beautiful than Harvest Moon Bay?' She thought he looked at her sideways, quickly, and she said, intercepting the tail end of the look, 'I'm entirely sincere in saying that, so please don't look at me askance. I—'

He put out a hand again, this time touching her in an admonitory fashion. 'Tamsin, don't be touchy. Want to know why I looked at you then?'

She looked candidly, the turquoise eyes meeting the brown ones, as he glanced momentarily from the road, demanding frankness.

There was the gleam of white teeth in a tanned face as he smiled. 'Because I like enthusiasm not only in a voice, but in the expression. So many people these days have inhibitions. Are too sophisticated, too afraid of sounding naïve if they express pleasure in simple things. They'd rather sound wearily worldly-wise, cynical. Oh, help, I'm sounding pedantic. It's a fault of mine.'

Her gaze had returned to the road too, but there was a smile in her voice. 'I like it, Luke. You're an articulate man, and your choice of words is so good it marks you as a reader. My father always recognized that and told me to watch for it.'

Perhaps he didn't know how to answer a compliment like that, because he said suddenly, instead, 'Tell me, do you have another dimple to match the one this side? I can only see the one on your right cheek.'

She laughed. 'I don't. It makes me feel lopsided. There's nothing regular about my features, I'm afraid.'

'But far more fascinating. Who was the woman the poet wrote of? "Icily regular, splendidly null." Or was it the other way round? But you know what I mean! I like the very unevenness of your teeth, Thomasina, it gives you a crooked smile.'

She had to hide her pleasure in the compliment by saying, 'Do let's get off the personal. Oh, Luke, what a view!'

While they had talked they had passed the sleepy hollow of the Little River township, the miles had slipped by and they came up the crest where the Hilltop Hotel crowned the summit and the whole stretch of Akaroa Harbour lay below.

Luke drew in, leaned across to open the door for her. 'The only way to view it is from the outside, with the sea-winds in your face.'

They came to the wall, looked over and there was silence between them, the greatest possible tribute to the scene below.

She lifted her face to the caress of that sea-wind, then said wonderingly, 'How come the water is so different from Lyttelton Harbour? You said this was another drowned volcanic crater. But this one is a sort of milky turquoise. What makes that?'

'I've no idea. Maybe it's taken a stranger to waken us to that fact. I'll try to find out. Perhaps different mineral action.' The curves and hollows of the hills and bays seemed as if sculpted out by a leisurely hand that had spent aeons of time smoothing out the rough places. 'Oh, how Dad would have loved this!' cried Thomasina, and for the first time she could speak of him without the fierce pain that always hushed her to silence after the first spontaneous utterance. She turned to Luke and found his gaze upon her. 'Dad was so keen I should follow in his footsteps. When we came upon a scene we hadn't know before, he used to get me to jot down all the separate words or short phrases I felt would fit the view. He said if I jotted down a full description I'd be chained to those words, almost, when I wanted to use them in a story. But if I put words down on their own, later on I would marry them to full description that would blossom out into something much richer because I wouldn't be rushing it.'

Luke swung round, went back to the car, put his hand through the window and brought up a notebook with a pencil dangling from it. 'Write,' he commanded.

Under some notes of his that said, 'Sheep-dip, drench, eartags, after-shave lotion,' she wrote 'Iridescent . . . turquoise . . . hills the colour of Blue Diamond plums . . . abiding . . . cradled in the lee of storms . . . peace . . . plenty . . . salt-tanged . . . cherished . . . but the keyword is peace.' He read over her shoulder, nodded.

They dipped down to Barry's Bay, then uphill and down to the first of the French names, Duvauchelles. Luke went on recounting the history, as he knew it, of each feature. Suddenly she said, 'And what about that little peninsula, with its tiny isthmus? It looks like a haven from the rest of the world. I could imagine building a house there, and making it a kingdom of one's own, almost an island, but with access whatever tide or storm.'

He quirked a brow. 'Do you really want to know the Onawe history?'

'Yes, why not?'

'Because you'll find it so deflating. The last thing you wrote was: "the keyword is peace." And of course it is, *now*, but its history isn't one of peace. It's thought that the Peninsula has been occupied for about five hundred years—I mean Banks, not Onawe. A lot of it is lost in antiquity, of course, because the people had no written language, but in later times a fierce feud raged here because of some terrible insult. So the war of "eat relation" sprang up and persisted, till the numbers were so reduced that eventually those who could recount the stories and genealogies of the centuries became very few. That feud was wiped out when the ferocious Te Rauparaha came down and attacked Onawe, the fortress, in one of the tribal wars. So the scene of peace was once the venue for almost unparalleled ferocity. Does it spoil it for you, Tamsin?'

'Only in regret for the suffering of those times. As a contrast, it deepens the atmosphere now prevailing. Peace achieved as an aftermath, and I hope kept that way for evermore.'

It was a day she would ever remember. No matter what motive had prompted Luke in the first place, they had found here a rare kinship of mind.

Akaroa itself enchanted her, with its narrow little *rues* of gabled French houses, smothered in vines and creepers, with fences rioting over with Bourbon roses that were bearing fat buds already, and wached over by tall Normandy poplars that would be flaming torches come autumn, and sheltered by mulberry and walnut trees.

Luke ran the car right through the dreaming town with its rock shore and wading birds on the right, and up to where the road petered out against cliffs and only walking tracks went on. He took the picnic hamper, helped her over a locked five-barred gate, and they climbed a rolling hill with sheep-nibbled turf. Under a gnarled ngaio tree, low and spreading, they put the rug and set out their viands. Curls of lettuce, chicken joints, early tomatoes, crisp rolls, butter. Luke produced a bottle of cider. He laughed. ' I always want to drink cider here, though I suppose it ought to be Bourbon or champagne. This could make you think you were in Devon. I expect you know it? I just paid my first visit there when I had my trip Home.'

' Dad and I had a short holiday there, and in Dorset. I can see Dad now, drinking cider in a beautiful old pub in Devon. We did a lot of rambling round the lanes, sweet with primroses and violets.' Again only the sweetness, not the pain.

' I was there in spring too, about a year and a half ago. I was almost on my way back to New Zealand.'

She blinked. ' That was when I was there. April not this year but the year before—the time of English spring. We stayed in Lynmouth for the Easter.'

' What?' He was staring at her. ' Not really? I spent that Easter in Lynmouth too. How extraordinary! We might have passed each other in the street, perhaps even leaned over the rail on that bridge that spans the torrent, at the same moment!'

She nodded. ' And watched the darting flight of the swallows over the water.' Then an odd ache touched Thomasina's heart fleetingly. Oh, if only, if only Dad had known Luke!

She shook off that pang, said, ' I'd like to write this up as a tourist attraction for the airline that sponsored my trip out here.'

' Then you'll want to see as much as possible, though if you're in no hurry, we can come back again. Uncle Eb will be tickled pink if you do things like this about his beloved Peninsula.'

' Yes, we can come back, but I'd like to capture the mood of today.'

Because one never knew. Some days couldn't be recaptured.

They wandered round the little French museum, looking at treasures long-loved, brought from France, which had survived longer than the ones who had brought them here on the *Comte de Paris*, old pistols that had featured in duels, snuff-boxes, patch-boxes, miniatures; then Luke took her up the hill to a sloping cemetery where in the dreamy tranquillity of God's acre, the people who had mended their *seines* on that beach, who had built those gabled houses, embroidered those shifts and wedding-dresses and baptismal robes, slept above the harbour they had learned to love after the hardships of the first few years.

The names were so fascinating—Le Lievre, Rousselot, Malmanche . . . François, Etienne, Justine, Victorine . . . They sat down on the rim of a grave shaded by a tall poplar and festooned with ivy, and Luke waited in silence while Thomasina scribbled furiously the outline of her article when it was still fresh in her mind.

When she had finished and gave him his notebook to stow in his pocket, he said, 'Thomasina, how much success have you had?'

'A number of poems in magazines. Some were included in an anthology. I was very thrilled about it. People keep anthologies to dip into for years. There's not much money in poetry, however. But I've done a score or so of articles, mostly about the valley of the Tyne, and the Roman occupation. And about a dozen short stories have been accepted. They pay well. Not a big total, but it's a foundation on which to build.'

'M'm, sounds very promising to me. Life at Corrieside doesn't leave much time for it, does it? Don't you feel frustrated?'

'Not particularly. Even before Dad and Maddy left us, I was working all day. I only had weekends and nights. Dad did say not to lose sight of the fact that it can be later than we think, but he also thought most writers write better from maturity and experience even if imagination must be prèsent too. One enriches the other, he said.'

'So you really don't mind devoting your time to Uncle Eb and the house?'

'Mind? I'm grateful for it. I love Ebenezer. He's someone of my own. He's created an atmosphere similar to our little cottage atmosphere in Greenchester. The children feel loved and wanted. Not just by Ebenezer either, you've made them feel that way too, Luke. They're far more important to me than any career. I couldn't give it up entirely, but doing an article or story now and then will satisfy me just now. I'd not have done more had I stayed in England. Possibly less, in fact. And I'd not have had half the inspiration in a tiny flat. '

He rose, put down a hand to her, pulled her to her feet. 'Well, be fair to your own interests too. I'm sure neither my uncle nor myself would worry if you skimped a bit on the housework or let

Peggy do more. I'll ask her myself if she could give us an extra day to free you for more time at a desk.' Great happiness was surging in on Thomasina. Who could have dreamed, at their first meeting, this would happen? She felt cherished. No longer a cuckoo in the nest, but belonging to Corrieside.

Luke said, 'Life's been very hectic—our busiest time of year, but it will even out soon. We go over the hill quite a lot to the theatres in Christchurch. There's a Shakespearean company coming soon. You love Shakespeare, don't you? And there are Gilbert and Sullivan operas, world reputation singers and musicians. Life can wear a different complexion soon.'

By the time they left the little town, dusk was deepening the shadows and long before they came to the narrowing of the hills where the road went through Gebbie's Pass, a huge moon was rising over Harvest Moon Bay. The great orange ball lit the silhouette of the hills against its light, and it had laid a golden track across the waters from Diamond Harbour to Quail Island. They came up over the cattle-grids and through the tree-shadowed drive dappled with a mosaic of moonlight and leaf-shadow.

Luke drove into the big garage near the stables, switched off his engine, said, 'I'll come back for the hamper later, I'll see you to the house first.'

Thomasina said, 'Oh, I'll help carry in the things. It would save you coming back.'

He laughed. 'Oh, Tamsin, don't be such a spoilsport, you goose! I have my reasons.'

He took her arm, crossed the stable courtyard with her and up the narrow stone steps cut in the bank. He stopped exactly where, that day of furious anger, he had seized her and marched her into the stable. He turned her to face him. In the mooonlight they could see the gleam of the tiny pear-blossoms as they floated down from the great old tree Thomas had planted for Anna. He laughed a rather confident laugh. 'This is why I wanted my hands free, simpleton,' he said. 'I wanted our first kiss to take place where we first met so dramatically.'

Their *first* kiss. Magic ran tinglingly along Thomasina's veins. That statement held a whole future. Lavender grew in the broken pockets of the wall here and the first few buds were just breaking. They were crushing them, and the pungent aroma rose to them.

It wasn't a hard, demanding kiss. It was a kiss that sought a response and found it, but had all of a gentle enchantment in it.

139

How strange it was that in that very moment of exchange and surrender and delight, Thomasina found herself thinking how different kisses could be. She had been annoyed with herself the first time Derry had kissed her because she had found it a disappointingly prosaic experience. Had wondered afterwards was kissing overrated. Now she knew it wasn't.

They drew apart a little, both reluctant. Suddenly she felt a little shy and said, to cover it, ' Let me come back and help you carry the things in. With all we bought for them, they'll wonder why I didn't help.'

' True enough, so okay, pal. I knew I could never manage *that* satisfactorily burdened with so much paraphernalia.'

Satisfactory. He, too, had found it that. Thomasina checked her racing thoughts.

They collected the gear, came up the steps again, and into the house. By the lit windows they could see, the children would be reading in bed. But Uncle Eb, judging by what they could hear, had company. Perhaps Jeremy, or Andrew. Luke pushed open the dining-room door, and in they went, having dropped their burdens in the hall.

The visitor was a stranger to Luke but not to Thomasina. She made a terrific effort and managed to sound reasonably welcoming, ' Oh, hullo, Derry,' she said, ' long time no see.'

CHAPTER IX

Afterwards she realized that was the precise moment Luke changed towards her. At the time she was just overcome with surprise—but it would be her use of the diminutive of Derwent's name. It would be then that he realized this Derwent Ford Ilena had spoken of was no less than the Derry she had unguardedly spoken of in the garden that night as the man who had let her down.

Ebenezer was beaming. Pleased, no doubt, that a friend from the other side of the world had been able to visit her. He was so transparent. So anxious she should put permanent roots down here. Anything to make her feel the land of her birth wasn't too far away was welcome.

She managed to sound moderately pleased herself, but wondered if it was really necessary for Derry to step forward, take her hands, and bend his head to kiss her. Instinctively and swiftly she turned her face sideways so he had to kiss her cheek. She was amazed at her inward flinching, but again, later, analysed it as distaste and resentment that soon after the sweetness of Luke's first kiss, someone else had kissed her.

She found herself murmuring the usual things, small world, and what a surprise. Well, certainly the greatest surprise had been hearing from Ilena that he was in this part of the world at all, the second that he'd managed to find time on a business trip to actually come here, so far off the beaten track.

She was amazed to see Derry look rather taken aback. 'But—but you knew I was coming!'

She looked stupefied. 'I *knew* you were coming? How could I? Oh, did you give Ilena a message to that effect? Then she didn't pass it on, did she, Luke? She only mentioned you when we were leaving the other day and Ebenezer and Luke were both in the car with me.' She turned to the other two for confirmation, but before she got more than two words out, Derry said, 'I didn't give Ilena a message to that effect. I just sent my regards. I wrote to you. Surely you got my letter?'

'I didn't get any letter from you. I haven't heard since I left England. I didn't expect to. But how would you know where to write? Before you met Ilena you hadn't known my address. You were away from Northumberland long before I left there. Oh, you must mean you wrote from Queenstown after you met her. But where is it?'

Derry had a peculiar look on his face. Thomasina was aware that Luke was glancing sharply from one to the other and that the brows were down. She felt distinctly uneasy, and was annoyed she should, because what did it matter?

Derry sounded so puzzled, so open. 'No, of course not. I wrote from England to say what marvellous luck that I'd been chosen to accompany Wilfred Steenson and that of all places in the world—or in the Commonwealth, rather—the Commission was coming to New Zealand and I could see you.'

Thomasina swallowed. 'But you wouldn't have an address, or know I was staying here.'

'Mrs. Bruce gave me your address. You were bound to turn up here.'

Thomasina said thinly, 'I didn't get your letter. Mail seems to be remarkably unreliable of late. It seems odd.' She turned a little to Luke. 'I haven't had that letter, have I, Luke?'

It was natural enough because Luke was nearly always the one who collected the mail from the box at the main gateway, not at the short-cut entrance from the village.

There was a hint of reluctance or stiffness or something in his reply. 'Well, it wasn't among any I've collected for you.' That meant a slight doubt. He seemed to hesitate, then said, 'There does appear to be a hoodoo on our mail. My uncle, not knowing Thomasina had won this competition, wrote asking her to come out to us. But the letter must have missed her by just a day or so. Matthew, meanwhile, proposed that they just arrived on our doorstep as a great surprise. But oddly enough, although Thomasina left a re-direction order at Greenchester Post Office, and all other mail has been sent on—first to Christchurch Post Office as directed and then to here—that particular letter never turned up.'

Derry said, 'Mrs. Bruce didn't mention the competition. Just that you'd come out to see your uncle. She gave me this address, not the Christchurch one.'

It was so absurd to feel on the defensive. 'Well, she would. By then I'd have written to her from here.'

He appeared to be considering something. He finally said slowly, in the most puzzled tone, 'But I wrote two letters. Surely both of them couldn't have gone astray! The first one was just to tell you I had the chance of coming. The second one gave the

142

dates and said you could expect to see me some time this week.'

'Then you must have got the address wrong. Both of them wouldn't have gone astray otherwise.'

Luke didn't think so. 'It's easy to get a street number wrong, but coming to a country estate like this, not so easy. I mean even if you got the rural mail delivery run number wrong, Derwent, care of E. Swainson, Corrieside, Ngahuru-Marama, would get us. You did have that on?'

'Yes, I even added Banks Peninsula before the rural mail number.'

'So it ought to have come,' said Luke.

Thomasina was immensely grateful when Ebenezer said easily, 'Well, it'll probably turn up after you're safely in Britain, lad. There'll be some piffling reason why. One we can't think of at the moment.'

But it was strange two letters could have gone astray. They all knew it.

Ebenezer went on, 'I was so sorry you were away today, Thomasina, when Derwent came. Had you got the letter you'd have stayed home. I felt the time would be very short for him, so I've asked him to stay the night, in fact till he leaves from Christchurch airport.'

Even while Thomasina expressed polite pleasure at the prospect, she was thinking what a nuisance. She couldn't be bothered with Derry. Their association was something that belonged to a seemingly long-ago existence that didn't matter any more in the light of this new life that had brought her Luke. Her friendship with Derry had never been an ardent one. She'd known more of a cynical amusement when he'd faded out than disillusionment. And having a visitor here would overlay the delight of this day when she and Luke were on the brink of falling in love.

It was so frail a thing at the moment, she felt, gauzy and insubstantial, that anything might shatter it, like a rough hand disturbing a newly-spun spider's web. Luke had just begun to trust her. It was ridiculous, but from his expression this very moment, she could imagine he was thinking she just might have concealed the fact that Derry was coming to New Zealand. He might be thinking it would have been natural for her to say, when she had mentioned Derry that night in the garden, that he was in New Zealand right now. It would also have been natural for Derry to have been in contact with her. Even a casual acquaintance coming this distance would have done so.

Ebenezer said, ' I'm quite proud of myself. I've put fresh sheets and pillowcases on the bed in the spare room next to mine, and switched on the blanket to air it. I put towels out too.'

Thomasina thought wistfully that she'd have loved to have written her travel article on Akaroa tomorrow, while it was fresh in her mind and not overlaid with prosaic housekeeping duties. Now she'd have to entertain Derry and liven up the meals. And she had an idea she was going to find it boring.

She was glad when it was time for bed, though she felt it was going to be a tossing-and-turning night. It should have been one when she could have lain awake for a while in a dreamy drowsiness, reliving the little happinesses of the day.

She undressed, slipped into a shortie nightgown in apricot dacron, sat down in front of her mirror and began brushing her hair. How relaxing that was! Tension began to go, and presently she put the brush down, rested her elbows on the dressing-table, cupped her chin in her hands and, gazing almost unseeingly at her own reflection, began to weave dreams. Gradually the enchantment of the day came back to her. Derry ceased to matter. He was only an interruption in this state of happiness and expectancy.

Finally she rose, then thought how she would love to read that book Luke had said would assist her in getting her facts straight for her article, and give her some dramatic stories about the early days on Akaroa. He'd said it was in the dining-room and had been put out to mark the Centennial, by the local newspaper.

She went to scoop up her blue brunch coat, then, smiling a little, thought she'd use the apricot negligée that went with this nightgown. It was a foolish little thought, because Luke had probably gone to his room by now, but if it so happened he was just coming upstairs she had no objection to his seeing her in so glamorous a garment.

She didn't tip-toe. No one would be asleep yet. And she used the main staircase. It took her some time to find. It always did when you didn't know how big a book was, or what colour.

She had just spied it, on a lower shelf, when she heard the door open. It would be Luke. He had heard her and come down. How felicitous! She would say to him she wished Derry hadn't turned up, that she hadn't seen him since just after Maddy died, and she would be jolly glad when he took himself off.

She turned her head, smiling. It was Derry.

The smile died an instant death. He must have noticed. But

144

he disregarded it and smiled. 'I heard someone go down and hoped it might be you. Too many people round earlier for my liking.'

She said coldly, 'If you want a yarn, Derry, I've had a long day and I came down for a book to read. We've got plenty of time for a gossip.'

'Have we really? It doesn't seem half long enough to me.'

Oh, dear. Seeing her must have revived some of his earlier feelings for her, but they didn't matter now, couldn't, mustn't. He would be back in the northern hemisphere soon. She looked at him reflectively, thought of Maddy's comment when she'd first met him. 'Tall, dark, handsome, eh? The answer to most maidenly prayers.'

But not to Thomasina's prayer. Oh, no. How could this too-perfect regularity of features compare with Luke's rough-hewn face, the over-emphasis of certain features, the overhung brows, the grooved lines each side of his mouth, the jutting chin, the rather wiry bleached hair? Endearingly rugged was his description, not classically handsome.

Derry was still regarding her smilingly. Heavens, he probably thought she was gazing her fill at someone in whom she'd once been romantically interested and now was suddenly restored to her. He said admiringly, 'That's the most gorgeous outfit. You really look something all dressed up, Thomasina. That trouser suit today was really something. I always felt you'd be capable of knocking everyone else out if only you'd spent a bit more of your money on yourself.'

It jarred. Thomasina knew that in those hand-to-mouth happy days beyond recall she hadn't been able to afford clothes like these.

She shrugged. 'These were part of the perks for the competition. When they're worn out I shan't be able to afford clothes like these.'

He looked surprised. 'What, with wool prices soaring again? I'd think—'

Her voice was curt. 'Wool prices have nothing to do with me. I'm well paid, yes, but it's a housekeeper's wage. But I'm much better off than in Britain because here Matthew and Edwina are provided for. I wanted their keep taken off my wages, but Ebenezer wouldn't hear of it. But I won't let him buy their clothes. That's over to me.'

Derry said, 'I think you under-estimate the regard Mr.

Swainson has for you. From what he said I think he's looking on you and the kids as his heirs. He said it was like a miracle, you cropping up, a descendant of his Uncle Edwin's, to him. Must have been wonderful for him when he had only his wife's nephew to carry on.'

Thomasina tossed back her loose hair with an angry gesture. 'He did think that way, yes. But it's not for me, Derry. I'd feel like the cuckoo in the nest pushing out the others who have more right to it. To be quite candid, though Ebenezer has plenty of great-nephews and nieces of his own, if anyone deserves the lot, it's Luke. He's worked on this property for years, worked hard. Ebenezer's pretty fit for his age, but Luke has borne the heaviest load and saved the farm a mighty lot of hired work.

'If I was a close relative it might be different, but someone unknown to this branch of the family till a year or so ago, coming in to feather her nest at the expense of the rest of the family— oh, no, it's not for me. I've a good wage and I like the life. The children adore it and they love Ebenezer and Luke. I can manage their clothes and insurance and other expenses fine out of my wages, and it means I can put away the royalties from Dad's books as they come in every six months, for later years, in case they want university.'

Derry made a deprecating gesture. 'Oh, Thomasina, don't be so naïve! Your father's books are hardly likely to become best-sellers. Had he lived he'd probably have made a comfortable living out of them—no more. But he was just getting known. What had he written? Three, four thrillers? But with no new books coming on—'

The turquoise eyes flashed. 'He'd written five, and I finished the sixth from his draft. They're written for sheer entertainment, yes, escapism if you like, but what's wrong with escapism? We all need to escape and relax these days of tension and mental stress. I've been amazed at the letters that have come from readers through Dad's publishers. From men in all walks of life saying they've enjoyed them. Even to a couple of professors and no less than three politicians! Grateful for relaxation they were. But you're no reader, so you can't judge—I know that. So don't be patronising about my father's books. *You* couldn't write anything more than a factual report!'

Derry stared and burst out laughing. 'I'm finding out things about you I never knew before. And I like it. There's more go in you than I dreamed. You were so even-tempered. Was it control? I find this interesting. Fire under the respectability, not ice!' He took a step towards her, and another. His intention was obvious. The bookcase behind her cut off her retreat, though she backed up against it. She held up a warding-off hand, a gesture he completely disregarded.

He caught her, bent his head, laughing. The next moment she was twisting out of his grip, having avoided the kiss, and turned at a noise to see the French windows opening and Luke himself framed in the aperture. She felt completely dismayed, knowing what it would look like. It would appear as if she had twisted out of Derry's embrace merely because she heard the door opening. And because she'd brushed out her hair and got into this wretchedly glamorous garment, any interpretation could be put upon it.

Guilt sat heavily upon her.

Luke had a sardonic twist to his lip. 'Oh, I'm sorry. I'd no idea anyone was here. I was taking a turn round the garden before locking up. Don't let me disturb you. Take all the time you wish.'

He turned, locked the windows, came across the room, outwardly nonchalant, inwardly furious, she knew.

She said desperately, 'Luke, I came down to get that book you mentioned about Akaroa. I though it would help me with the article. Then Derry came down. Were you looking for a book too, Derry?'

She had a wild hope he might back her up.

He laughed. 'As you've just told me, I'm no reader!'

Thomasina's colour flamed. It was the colour of anger, but Luke would read it as guilt. She turned and grabbed the book from the shelf, said in a voice that threatened to break, 'Here it is. Goodnight,' and went swiftly between the two men to the door.

When she regained the solitude and blessed privacy of her own room she flung herself down on the bed and gave way to tears, tears of chagrin, anger, and, at the last, desolation. All the tears she hadn't shed for months. Oh, she had cried when Dad died, and then for Maddy, but not afterwards, because children couldn't take long-term grieving, and she had made herself create an atmosphere as happy as was possible even when their home had first been threatened with demolition. But now she cried for herself, for the fragile dream that had been destroyed by Derry before it had scarcely begun.

147

She awoke hating the day, even one like this that began in beauty, with the sun rising in splendour of rose and gold in an azure sky beyond the Heads, and tinting even the green waters with iridescent colours.

She didn't sing this morning as she prepared breakfast, cut the lunches for the children. Miraculously everything went right, but she did it all mechanically, responding to the small talk in a way that sounded natural enough for Ebenezer to notice nothing.

Luke seemed irritatingly cheerful. She'd heard him out in the stables before breakfast whistling tunes with a real lilt to them. Even *Funiculi, Funicula* which she couldn't imagine anyone whistling without a light heart! And he couldn't have been more friendly towards Derry. He'd dropped the Derwent this morning.

He said, 'We'll all help with the dishes. I made my bed. Peggy will be down at ten. Then we can all go round together. Uncle is determined you're to come too, Thomasina. We're not as busy now, anyway, with lambing and tailing behind us.'

He began to explain that they used the rubber ring method, because they thought docking carried more risk of infection. 'Lambs are frisking round the paddock in no time after they're put on—half an hour or so. Then they just drop off. Makes for clean sheep, of course, and saves them from fly-strike to a good extent. But of course, you'll have seen this on the farms round Queenstown—you were having field days, weren't you?'

Thomasina cut in, 'Ebenezer, do excuse me from coming round with you. After all, I'm no expert on New Zealand farming and you could take the horses if I wasn't with you. Derry's quite a rider. If Peggy's coming today I could shut myself up with my typewriter and get my article on Akaroa done while it's hot in my mind.'

Ebenezer shook his head. 'No fear, lass. We want you with us. There's no hurry for it.'

'In fact,' said Luke with an undertone of sarcasm that Thomasina couldn't miss, 'you might know more about it if you wait. You could even read from cover to cover that quite hefty tome you came down for last night. I'm quite sure you didn't read right through the night. As Uncle said, what's the hurry?'

She said hastily, 'Well, Dad always believed in striking while the iron was hot and I don't want that airline to forget me. I want to keep them up with a regular supply of material on tourist attractions here. Especially the less-known ones.'

Derry said, 'Not much cash in it, is there?'

'Mightn't seem much, but every little helps towards my fund for the children's higher education.'

Ebenezer sighed. 'She's distressingly independent. There's no need for it now.'

Derry looked at Thomasina. 'See! Your uncle thinks you carry independence too far too.' He turned to the others. 'So did my mother. She begged her not to be so stiff with pride. When the village was saved by taking the road through Thomasina's cottage, the people there felt so badly about it, they were organising a public subscription for Thomasina. Well, for the children really. A fund to be invested for them. But she wouldn't come at it. That could have made all the difference to—to them.'

Thomasina saw a peculiar look flash into Luke's eyes. She found herself biting her lip. Now Luke would think that but for that, she and Derry might have married. She had given him to understand that Derry, poor-spirited, had faded away. Now he would think they had quarrelled about her refusing to take the village people's money. Or, worst of all, he would think she had turned the offer down because there was the bigger hope of inheriting some of the Corrieside money. Oh, yes, that would be the train of his thoughts. He would think her particularly cunning, in view of what had happened the day of her arrival, in refusing, this far, anything more than a wage. And would assume that in due time when all their suspicions were lulled, she would allow her objections to be overruled.

She said, 'It wasn't like accepting a subscription from a lot of wealthy land-owners as might happen here. Most of those villagers were just mill-workers, or land-workers. It would have been a terrific sacrifice. I couldn't have done it.'

Ebenezer saved the day. 'Well, I can admire a spirit of independence as long as it's not carried too far. I can admit I myself under those circumstances wouldn't want to be beholden to people who weren't well off themselves, but it's another kettle of fish entirely to refuse help from a kinsman who has very few of his own to spend his money on. Thomasina, you look heavy-eyed. You're not going to stew over that machine today. You're a bit young for such a sedentary occupation anyway. We weren't going to ride—too much mounting and dismounting. We'll take the Rover, and Peggy will cook our lunch. Josh can come here for his.'

If a shadow hadn't lain over Thomasina's heart she could have enjoyed it tremendously, and Ebenezer entered wholeheartedly into showing someone very knowledgeable of the technical side of farming the extent of and methods use at Corrieside.

It was all so normal, Thomasina eventually felt a little of the tension slip from her, though Luke never caught her eye or drew her into the conversation. Perhaps it was natural—Derry was a fresh audience.

Derry said, 'You've got mostly Romney and Southdown. Before I came here I'd no idea Corrieside might have been the place where Corriedales were first bred. But Ilena said no.'

Luke nodded. 'Yes, we've been asked that before. No, the place the Corriedale breed was named for was in North Otago, a run of that name, owned by a Doctor Webster. In the early sixties James Little, the founder of the breed, arrived from Scotland to manage the run. He brought with him twenty-two Romney rams which were rather scornfully regarded by the other farmers who ran Merinos.

'Little found the Romneys not ideal for the conditions and decided to cross the two breeds. He managed to produce sheep with the fine wool of the Merino and the good meat qualities of the Romney, but before long, when Doctor Webster died, the flock was scattered, so the Corriedales as we know them today weren't produced there, but Little moved to North Canterbury in 1878 and this time he bought Lincoln rams to cross with the Merino ewes " to go into breeding Corriedales neck and crop ", as he put it. This was so successful that by the turn of the century there were nine Corriedale flocks.'

Some things made her uneasy, the way in which Derry slipped in leading questions about prices for stock, for frozen meat, for the fresh market for local consumption, what they thought the later developments of the Common Market might have on the New Zealand economy, their chances for other markets, the effects of inflation, the versatility of this farm for changing to other productions if one particular market dropped. It was the way he kept forsaking the general for the particular concerning Corrieside that made Thomasina uneasy. As if it mattered to him how things stood. She saw Luke glance at him quickly once or twice, then at her.

But the exercise of walking from each stop of the Rover did her good, tired her so physically that she'd sleep better tonight. At the most it would be only two or three days and he would be gone, so it was stupid to feel afraid. What harm could he possibly do her in that time? She and Luke would soon revert to a more trusting relationship. She would seek Luke out when he was gone and explain, without sounding as if she was excusing herself, that she had been resisting Derry when he came in. Oh, if only she were more sure of Luke's feelings! That kiss might only have been a temporary enchantment on his side, born of the moonlight, their happy day, their nearness. If he had declared his feelings, she could have been justified in explaining away a false situation, but what if she explained it and Luke said, 'So what? How can it matter to me?' as, in his present mood, he was capable of doing? He'd thought Ilena had presumed too much. She dared not risk such a rebuff.

She wanted to laugh at Peggy's reaction to Derry. She sat down to lunch with them and wasn't her talkative self at all. Even Josh asked her was she all right. Her eyes went from Derry to Thomasina to Luke as they chatted, as if assessing a relationship she didn't care for. Thomasina insisted on helping with the dishes, visitor or not. She felt the less she had of Derry's company the better.

Peggy said, 'How about you men sitting out on the loggia while we wash up? The Harbour's a dream today, and my brother in Lyttelton said to me on the phone this morning that they're expecting a big new overseas ship in early this afternoon. I want to have a crack with Thomasina about my coming over here an extra day a week. I want to find out which day would suit her writing best.'

Thomasina blinked. After last night's fiasco in the dining-room, she'd thought Luke wouldn't have cared tuppence about that. She looked at him uncertainly. He rose, seized the tray Peggy had just piled up with dishes and bore them out to the kitchen. Thomasina picked up the teapot and milk-jug and followed him. Peggy stayed behind to answer questions about the ship.

Luke put his tray down, said sharply, 'Thanks for the compliment your look of surprise showed. Thought I'd show my displeasure by not conceding you that, didn't you? That would have been rather small-minded, wouldn't it? Or wouldn't *you* think so? Would you think it natural?'

Thomasina felt bewildered. 'You've lost me. I rather think I'm being called small-minded. Why?'

'Why?' his voice sounded weary. 'Because it comes naturally to women, I suppose.'

Thomasina flung her head back. 'I hate either men or women generalizing about the other sex. I've known plenty of men I'd have called small-minded and plenty of women who were big-hearted. And the way you rave on about Anna and Georgiana Swainson, to say nothing of your own mother, whom you appear to adore, it's nothing less than hypocrisy!'

'*Touché*! I shouldn't have generalized. I meant the present generation, as typified by you and Ilena!'

Thomasina said, breathing hard, and trying to keep her voice down, 'I think you'd better get out of my kitchen. Peggy will be here in a moment and if you don't move she'll find us right in the middle of a donnybrook and I don't think I'll be getting the worst of it. I'm fed up to the teeth with your varying moods.'

He turned on his heel at the door and said, '*Your* kitchen?'

Thomasina didn't dare let Peggy see her in so obviously a temper, so she caught up the remains of the salad lettuce and fled with them to the fowl-run. A few moments gathering eggs and she was in control of herself again.

Peggy said, 'My word, your chooks are laying better than ours —look at those, now.'

Thomasina found herself saying, '*My* chooks, Peggy? Better say Luke's chooks, or Ebenezer's!'

Peggy, her arms already wrist-deep in suds, chuckled, 'That's splitting hairs, surely. It's all the same, love. Just a manner of speaking.' Thomasina wished Luke had been there to hear.

Peggy jerked her head. 'How long's that one staying?'

'Oh, just a day or two I hope and pray.'

Peggy looked at her quickly. 'Do you mean that personally, or because you're thinking I don't like visitors because of the extra work!'

'No, you've been so hospitable to everyone who's been here for meals, the Ffoulkes, the Carmichaels, Cousin Ned and his family. No, Peggy. If only I'd been here when he arrived yesterday I wouldn't have allowed him to stay—that is, if I could have prevented Ebenezer asking him.'

'Why?' Peggy was a yes-no person and didn't beat about the bush or excuse herself for curiosity. She took it for granted you knew she loved you and wanted to know for that reason. What a relief not to be painfully anxious to give the right impression!

'Well, he sort of drifted into my life, Peggy, took me out a few times, then made a painless and undramatic exit when Dad and Maddy died and he realized I had responsibilities.'

Peggy looked at her sharply. 'And it didn't hurt?' It was more of a statement than a question, and Thomasina hugged her

152

quickly.

'Oh, bless you, you do understand. No, it was even a bit of a relief. I hate hurting people and knew I'd got to tell him soon that I wasn't serious. He bored me. Anyway, looking at it practically, no one could blame him. He was just starting out in life. Though the kind of man I'd like to marry would be one who'd count the cost and find it worth while. But as far as I'm concerned, Derry is just—' She tried to find the right word.

'Just a blithering nuisance!'

Thomasina giggled and felt better. 'You're dead right, Peggy. Besides which, I think he—' she stopped again.

Peggy had no scruples. 'You think he deems you a better catch now. He surmises you have expectations.'

'Exactly. I don't want to do him an injustice. Anyway, I've told him I'm *not* Ebenezer's heir. He brushed it aside. But he did seem rather too affectionate for someone who disappeared out of my life months ago. But what good would that do *him*, even if I had expectations? He's at the other side of the world, and he seems to have a good job now as assistant to this chap who's one of the heads in a big advisory combine to agriculturists and sheepbreeders.'

'Well, watch him. He's a fly one. Nothing to stop him coming here if he thought there was something in it for you. He's got that look.'

'You've made up your mind about him very quickly, haven't you?'

'Yes, I may have met him only yesterday, but I didn't care for what I found him doing then. The stock firm rang Eb up and he had to go over to the wool shed for some figures or something. He was to ring them back. I'd called out goodbye just before that, walked part of the way to the shed with Eb, then remembering I'd left a basin of stewed rhubarb I was taking over for a pie for ourselves, so I came back. Your rhubarb is much further ahead than ours. That man was in Eb's office, shuffling through the papers and bills on top of the blotter, cool as you please! I stood there till he felt my eyes boring into him. Then I said, icily-like, "Can I help you? Are you looking for something?"

'He said very quickly, "Yes, I wanted some writing-paper and airmail envelopes. Mr. Swainson told me to help myself."

'I looked him straight in the eye in a way that said I didn't believe him and said, "Right in the rack in front of you, Mr.

Ford. See!" He made some laughing remark about how you always miss what's in front of your nose, but he knew fine he'd not pulled the wool over my eyes. I then said firmly, "You'll find it more pleasant writing at the desk in the side window of the dining-room," and I waited till he came out. I marched through, waved at the desk, saw him settled and said, "Just as well I came back, I'd clean forgotten to dust this room." And I made it last till after Eb got back.

'Good for you,' said Thomasina. 'I can't think what he's after, out what a nerve! I mean a conference like that would have access to all sorts of figures. This isn't one of the large sheep-stations—or a stud farm. But I feel better now you've told me this. He was so strange when he arrived. Made it sound sus-picious that I hadn't received two letters from him saying he was making this trip. He made me feel really uneasy, as if I'd been concealing his coming. Why would I? I mean, I can't help it if mail goes missing.'

Peggy considered it, asked just what had been said. Then she said, 'I think he had wind of the fact that you and Luke are falling for each other and he wanted to put a rift in the lute.'

Thomasina blushed delightfully. But, confused, she disclaimed it.

Peggy brushed it aside. 'I won't embarrass you in front of the others, but it's as plain as the nose on your face, and ideal at that. That fellow wants to make it up. Watch him. Trust yon Ilena to dig up something like that when she was away. Have you ever thought she's got the distinct look of a ferret?'

Thomasina burst out laughing. 'Oh, Peggy, don't be absurd. Ilena is beautiful. It's a giddy wonder to me that Derry didn't fall for *her*.'

Peggy said darkly, 'Well, she's got no prospects, and that young man in there has an eye to the main chance. However, neither she nor Derry will be here for ever. Did he say his boss is staying on a little longer in Christchurch because he has rela-tives there? Well, even at the most it can't be more than a few days.'

'No, Ebenezer has asked him to stay tonight and tomorrow night, so I hope that means they fly home next day. Though Derry could join him at his hotel. Peggy, be a sport and ring Elizabeth from your place and ask her to invite me over there tonight to babysit or something. Derry's so apt to engineer situations that I'd rather be out. If they want to talk farming flat out, all night, they can.'

Peggy laughed and promised she would.

Elizabeth rang just after dinner, evidently well primed by Peggy, and in case anyone was near the phone and her voice should carry, said, 'Thomasina, would you be a darling and come over to babysit for the twins? Roddy's out tonight and Jeremy did want me to go over to meet some journalistic bod here from Sydney at the Clarendon. How about it, or can't you leave this friend of yours from England?'

There was an undercurrent of wickedly mischievous laughter in her voice. Thomasina was at the dining-room extension so they were all within earshot. 'Of course, Elizabeth. You and Jeremy mustn't miss that on any account. I'd love to, particularly as I have some typing to get away. May I use your typewriter? Oh, thanks. We've got someone staying here, he's with that U.K. Commission thing, and Luke and Ebenezer and he will be talking farming all night. I'll just wash the dishes and start the children on their homework and be over.'

Thomasina decided she must have a horrible nature because she enjoyed the look of surprise on their faces, especially Luke's. After last night's little episode on which he'd placed completely the wrong interpretation, he was obviously puzzled to think she'd go off, leaving Derry on one of his few nights. That would make him ponder. It might dawn on him that there was nothing in it. Much better than trying to explain.

But she resented it when he actually said, 'Derry had better walk you over.'

'Oh, come, it will only be twilight. And I love rambling round these lanes on my own. I'll go over the stile and through the lane, then through their orchard.' She saw him starting to say something else and added, 'And of course Jeremy will see me home. It will be late. No one's to wait up for me. I'll take a key.'

When she got to Cherrington Lodge, Jeremy was wearing a puzzled look. 'I've just got in,' he complained, 'and Elizabeth tells me you're coming over to babysit, but we're not going out. What on earth are you two up to? She says we're going to enjoy having you all to ourselves, but I'm not to answer the phone if anyone rings, I'm to let you answer it. That much I've got out of her. Would you explain to a poor bewildered editor? I have a feeling my I.Q. isn't what it was!'

Thomasina patted his hand. 'Not to worry, Jeremy, it's just

some crazy feminine ploy. A man I used to know in England arrived here the other day when I was in Akaroa with Luke. Ebenezer, bless him, thinking I'd be pleased to see him, asked him to stay. He's with that U.K. Commission. Very much a junior assistant. He's being a nuisance. I just felt I'd scream if I had to stay over there all night with him. He's only got another night here, I think, so it's not so bad. I thought they might all get the message if I hived off somewhere.'

Jeremy chuckled, then said, '*They* might get it? Don't you mean *he* might?'

Thomasina looked a little confused. 'Well, Luke seems to regard him in the light of a resurrected boy-friend, and I'd rather he didn't.'

Jeremy's warm brown eyes danced. 'Ah . . . complications! Well, if this little deception clears up anything between you and Luke, I'll certainly lend a hand.'

'Oh, it's not like that at all . . . I mean, anything between me and Luke. Oh, no, you mustn't get the idea that—'

He said gravely, 'Then what is the idea, if not that?'

Elizabeth said quickly, 'Jeremy, my love, I think I hear one of the twins. Would you go up and see what's happening now? I've stopped them pillow-fighting, taken each a drink of water, changed Teddybear for Raggedy Anne because it wasn't Teddy's night to be in bed with Rosamond, and parted Tony forcibly from bubble-gum. I will not have them taking gum to bed. They could choke. So have a good look under his pillow, Jeremy, in case he's got some more stashed away.'

Jeremy said suspiciously, 'I didn't hear a thing, and when I looked in on them as I went to wash, they were both flat out to it and looking like angels. I think you just want to get rid of me.'

Elizabeth sighed, 'Well, I didn't succeed, did I? I had an idea Thomasina might want a woman to confide in, not a man.'.

'Well, I'm a lot safer than you. I'm hardly likely to blazon it over the front page of the *Argus*.'

'I can keep secrets every bit as well as you can, Jeremy Ffoulkes, and I—'

'I know you can. You keep them only too well. I didn't mean that. I meant maybe I could help. I know Luke so well. You know, Elizabeth, when it came to our own romance, you bungled that horribly, by being too secretive, bottling things up. One question from you and I could have cleared it up in two minutes and saved us both a lot of real agony of mind. Now hush, will you?'

Elizabeth pulled a face at him, but hushed.

Thomasina said hastily, 'It's not quite the same. Not a romance, just a delicate situation. About money, not love.' She avoided their too-knowing eyes. 'This must be in confidence, because to start with it concerns Ilena, and I wouldn't like anyone to gossip about the way Luke—' she didn't quite know how to put it. Jeremy did.

'The way he choked her off,' he suggested.

'You know?'

'I saw him trying to do it fairly painlessly at one or two local gatherings.'

Thomasina therefore felt heartened to continue. She told them about Ebenezer's missing letter. They had known she'd won the competition, fortunately.

Jeremy said, 'I knew Ebenezer was going to ask you to come and that he'd make it worth your while, because he talked it over with me. It wasn't a sudden whim. You see, it was through the *Argus* that he found you. So he chatted about it a lot.'

By the time she reached the part where she had got into the stables to find herself overhearing the father and mother of a fight, Elizabeth and Jeremy were convulsed. She recounted crouching by the bank, Luke yelled at her and hauling her into the stables, and bawling her out there. In a deeply ashamed voice she said, 'That was when I lost my temper and slapped his face.'

Jeremy guffawed, 'Oh, I'd like to have seen that!'

'But it wasn't funny. It was crude and undignified and humiliating—to me.'

They didn't seem to be shocked. 'I managed to give him a few doubts about my motives in visiting there, and when I hoped aloud that his uncle would know when he'd posted the letter, Ebenezer's head appeared upside down from the loft opening. He'd heard the lot, both rows, but had kept quiet.'

'Well, he'd have enjoyed hearing Ilena get her come-uppance,' said Jeremy, grinning. 'But he'd come to your rescue all right and establish the fact that he'd posted the letter after you left Britain.'

'Unfortunately he did it before, and I could have received it—just. I didn't. But it ought to have been forwarded on, everything else has been. Well, I refused to take anything except wages for the housekeeping and let him keep the children. I'll never touch a penny of Swainson money. When your cousin Louisa returns, Elizabeth, if she can manage with just Peggy, and some help from me with the garden, and let me manage our meals in the little wing, I'll work as a nurse-aide at the hospital. Then we went over to Martensens. Ilena came home that day. She'd met Derry there, teamed up with some of the party, went to Mount Cook with them. She gave me a message from Derry and made my surprise at hearing he was even in New Zealand look phoney. I've the maddest idea it was on purpose. But why?'

Elizabeth said, ' I can tell you—to put a rift in the lute between you and Luke. I've know her for some time. She's a nasty bit of work. *You* can't understand anyone acting like that. *I'd* believe anything of her. And you know, Thomasina, Luke soon stopped feeling sore with you. That morning they fell in the pond he took me aside and said not to publish the follow-up article yet. He had an idea that, given time to think it over, you might just stay on and delight Ebenezer.'

Thomasina looked staggered. ' As soon as that? Well, perhaps, but we quarrelled later on again, but we had a wonderful day at Akaroa.' She coloured, rushed on. ' For the first time I thought we were real friends, and that he now trusted me. Then, to my dismay, we found Derry at home. Oh, it needn't have mattered, but I wish Ebenezer hadn't asked him to stay. You see, his boss is spending a few extra days in Christchurch.'

' I know,' said Jeremy unexpectedly, ' we interviewed him today. We gave him lunch and when we came out Ilena was awaiting him in the lounge. How thankful I was she hadn't turned up earlier. We'd have had to extend her an invitation and quite apart from not being able to stand her, our questions couldn't have been as free in front of her. Not all of them were for publication.'

Thomasina's heart warmed to him. ' I got a great surprise at seeing him at Corrieside, but then Derry made it awkward. He vowed I must know, that he'd written. Oh, it sounds so weak, but I had to say I hadn't got that letter either. It was too much of a coincidence for Derry and Luke to swallow.'

Jeremy's voice was sharp. ' I don't see why. These things happen. Look, as a newspaper man I've reported coincidences all my life—readers love real-life ones. Elizabeth said of one that if she used it in one of her novels, the criticism would be that it was contrived. It was reported all over New Zealand. It was the night the *Royal Family* film was being shown on television. There was a power failure in a small country town, and every viewer was frustrated. They cheered up on hearing it was to be repeated. Accordingly practically the whole community was sitting in front of their sets when the screen went dark again—an accident had brought down a power-pole. Of all the towns in New Zealand it had to be theirs. So why couldn't Luke believe it?'

'Because Derry said he'd written *twice*. That's a bit too thick!'

'Sheer bad luck, I'd say!' Jeremy's voice was savage, 'but why should it matter to Luke?'

She made a helpless gesture. 'It's revived all his suspicions. And Derry has been so strange. He's making up to me again. I think he fancies farming life in New Zealand and if there was a chance I might fall heir, with the children, to half Corrieside, he'd try to make the running. I think Luke now thinks I've just been crafty in refusing it so far and that soon I'll give in to Ebenezer. He thinks I've been in touch with Derry, and that we cooked something up between us. That I was really expecting him, but got muddled about what we'd plotted and fluffed my lines when he turned up. Oh, it's horrible! Derry's so devious. Peggy caught him looking through papers on Ebenezer's desk that very first day. I think Ebenezer talked too openly to him, thinking any friend of mine, knowing our circumstances back home, would rejoice in the fact that now my lines have fallen in pleasant, and promising, places!' Her lip trembled. 'Oh, how I would like to go back home where no one ever doubted my motives! Even if money would be tight, we'd be happier. At least I would. But Edwina and Matthew so love it here. Edwina sits on Luke's knee every night. Matthew listens with glistening eyes to all Ebenezer's stories. How can I deprive them of that? But how can I bear not being trusted?'

Jeremy said decisively, 'You *can't* deprive them of it. I'm a great believer in time taking care of things. I once thought I'd never know happiness again, but now—' his eyes went to Elizabeth, and he had no need to finish that. 'Derry will soon be gone. You've made it plain to him that there's nothing doing. Luke'll soon stop thinking you encouraged him out here. Make sure he realizes you're relieved he's gone. You have only to be adamant in refusing any part of the estate and time will prove you sincere in this.'

'I'm terrified Ebenezer simply sends for his lawyer and does it. I had a feeling last week he might, something I overheard him say to Luke.'

Jeremy grinned. 'Not to worry. Luke's half seas over already. That night at the Sickle he said to me after my second dance with you, "Beetle off, Jeremy. I'd like the monopoly of Thomasina's dances!"'

'But a lot has happened since then.'

'Perhaps so, but many folk suffer at some time or other in their life from false reports being made about them. Yet, left to time, people form their own assessments, trust their own judgements more. Why, even Elizabeth had all sorts of horrible thoughts about me. She believed gossip! But when she realized what a truly bee-yew-ti-ful nature I had, all was well!'

Elizabeth was indignant. 'It wasn't like that at all! I decided I loved him madly, past wickednesses and all, and I'd risk it. It was wonderful to find it was reputation, not character.' She stopped, said, 'Oh, dear, perhaps Jeremy's version was more comforting.'

He said, but affectionately, 'See what I mean? She's a bungler.'

Elizabeth ignored him. 'I'm sure it will come out all right. Derry will soon be gone. Surely he can't do much mischief in a short time? Don't act in a hurry, Thomasina. You could break Ebenezer's heart by leaving. This is a dream-come-true for him, Bessies's great-granddaughter living in Thomas's Corrieside.'

Thomasina agreed. 'I won't, I promise. Unless the situation got really unbearable. And in a way Ebenezer is a double complication.'

'How?'

'He's rushing his fences. He—he wants it too idyllic. He makes it embarrassing. I feel he's pushing me on to Luke.'

Jeremy nodded. 'That must be embarrassing. I'll drop Eb a hint that he ought to let the young 'uns make their own pace. How'd that be? I won't even hint that I've been talking it over wih you.'

Thomasina stood up, dropped a kiss on his cheek, with a saucy look at Elizabeth. 'I'm sure I'm entitled to express my gratitude that way. If it comes seemingly spontaneously from you, Jeremy, I think it could help. I just wish Luke would fall in love with some nice local girl; that would solve everything.'

Elizabeth and Jeremy, as one astounded voice, demanded 'Why?'

Thomasina said flatly but convincingly, 'Because the money involved is too big an obstacle. It cuts both ways. If I appeared to fall for Luke, he might think me devious, pretending I wouldn't take half the estate but setting my sights on the one who'd inherit it.'

Jeremy said, 'Well, you only need to be off-putting with him to disabuse Luke's mind of that idea. It will only make him keener. He isn't the sort to let the girl make the running. He didn't with Ilena, did he?'

Thomasina said, 'It cuts both ways. I'm just holding Ebenezer back from making another will. If he gets the bit between his teeth and does it regardless, Luke would never ask me for fear that in turn, *I'd* think *he* was after the other half of the estate. No, it's a solid barrier.'

There was a silence while they thought it out, then Jeremy said, 'It's a coil, but like I said, let's give it time. And now there's something I'd like to discuss. I want to run instalments of one of your father's books on our Saturday feature pages. *Thunderbolt Pass*. And with your permission, to introduce it serially, I'd like to have another article about you living here, the week before.'

Colour flamed into Thomasina's face. 'Oh, no, Jeremy. It's sweet of you, all cooked up to give me extra money in my pocket, but no, I can't take favours like that.'

Jeremy burst out laughing. 'I'm beginning to have sympathy with Ebenezer over your spirit of independence. You think I'm making the offer on the spur of the moment out of sympathy. You chump! I can prove to you it's nothing of the kind. I've been in touch for quite some weeks with your father's publisher and he's willing to negotiate on your behalf with the *Argus* for second British serial rights. And it's more than likely other New Zealand newspapers will follow suit. I'll show you the letter. I brought it home intending to ring you.'

He came back with it, held it out. The date was nearly a week ago, and in it Graham Whistler said he would be writing 'to Miss Meade at her New Zealand address.'

It lifted Thomasina's spirits as nothing else would have done. It brought her father near. How glad he would have been that those long hours at his desk, often at the last, in pain, still provided for his three children when they most needed it.

CHAPTER X

Ebenezer said to her next morning, ' Well, you look better for your night off.'

She said, rapidly sliding rashers of home-cured bacon, lean and pink, on to the plates beside the eggs, ' Nothing like a spot of solitude for restoring one's soul. Sounds inhospitable, but while I'm gregarious most of the time I have to have some time on my own. I used to roam all round Northumberland by myself, chanting poetry learned by heart, out loud. I can't do that in company. I did it last night, on my way to Cherrington Lodge.'

Ebenezer said, ' I must give you my wife's scrapbook to read. Years ago we had far more New Zealand and Australian magazines entirely contributed to by freelances. Georgiana wrote a bit herself, chatty little pars, some verse, the odd article. She used to cut out all the ones she liked to read over and over. Of course there was only radio, no television, and we did far more reading. Some of those poems will give you a pretty fair idea of what women's life in the backblocks of New Zealand and the outback of Australia was like.

' I often read them over myself. It makes me hear vividly Georgiana's warm Northumberland voice reading them to me. There's one in particular I'd like to hear.' He came back with a fat black book. He leafed through it. ' Here it is. It was a great comfort to me after she died. She wanted to be buried here in St. Stephen's churchyard. It looks down on Corrieside, as you know, and last December when we were cutting our hay I'd look up towards the headstones and I felt she was near and happy. Not that she knew her end was near, but years before, when she first read this poem of Jane East's, she said where she'd like to lie. Here it is. Called *Country Cemetery*.' He read it without undue emotion.

' " O dead, lie happily among the scenes,
    The little sounds, the perfumes you have known !
Honey still clogs the air, and scents of hay
    At evening time are blown. . . .
And not so far away the wheat is tall
    Behind the wires that fence the dusty roads,
And painted waggons from the farms roll past
    With high-piled harvest loads." '

Thomasina looked at him with shining eyes. 'That's perfect, Ebenezer. I think that's why I love Harvest Moon Bay so much. Because the past is never gone and forgotten. It's here, all round us. There's never a day, looking down the harbour, I don't think of those First Four Ships, and their bravery and courage, fighting fears and loneliness and nostalgia and enduring rough conditions. I see the road winding up past the Kiwi and down to the plains and I think of those women and children from here going up through that eerie if beautiful bush, and down to the city to sell their produce. The burdens they carried each way! The times they were lost! Now I'll think of your Georgiana too, think of her sleeping there and waiting while the cycle of the years goes on, the mating, the lambing, the sowing, the reaping, the sunshine and the snow. Everything she loved most.'

For a moment or two she had quite forgotten Derry sitting there, Derry the stranger, the outsider. She added, 'I like to think she knew places I knew too, Hadrian's Wall and the Valley of the Tyne.'

'And St. Peter's in Sunderland,' said Luke. 'Aunt Georgiana was christened in it. Were you ever there?'

'Yes, Dad took us all there, not long before he was taken ill. We reached out and touched a wall that the Venerable Bede might have touched. It seems incredible. And Dad said: "What is time?"'

Into the silence Derry said prosaically, 'I've got tickets for the theatre for us tonight.'

Thomasina said, 'What for, Derry?'

'For *Twelfth Night*, Thomasina. Isn't that good of me? I've never cared for Shakespearian stuff, but I know you do.'

'Thank you, Derry,' she said politely, 'I hope it's what the rest like too. I'll see if I can get a babysitter for the children. I would like to get Peggy; I'll give her—'

Luke said, 'You're taking a lot for granted. It's not a family party, just you and Derry to mark what was to have been his last night in New Zealand. He rang for telephone reserves last night.'

'*Was* to have been? What's happened, Derry? Some hold-up with planes?'

She managed to sound fairly ordinary, but inwardly she was completely dismayed. Derry had done enough damage in the short time he was here. But once he was away it might fade. But in any case, it would probably be just a twenty-four-hour delay.

Derry shook his head. 'No, my chief cancelled it.' He grinned.

'He's fallen for Ilena. He's found he lives quite near her in Surrey. He's just out of Guildford. She'd suit him down to the ground—a very decorative hostess. We were to spend three days in Los Angeles and three in New York. We're cutting out the first. Suits me all right. Gives me three more days here with you.'

Thomasina ignored that. 'You mean that? He's fallen for Ilena? How strange—I mean the way you spoke of him, and seeing he's your chief, I thought he'd be years older than she is.'

'Oh, he is. But very well heeled and fascinating in a way, tough as they come, but irresistible to women, or so I'm told. Anyway, she's certainly not resisting. She'll be off home soon.'

Suddenly Thomasina detested him. He was her friend—or had been, and they might class her with him. In fact Luke already had. Money, money, money!

Thomasina stood up and began to clear the table. Luke and Ebenezer departed. Thomasina could have dispensed with Derry's help with the dishes, but he insisted. She shook so much detergent into the water with the effort she was making to control her feelings that she became foam to the elbows and all the dishes had to be rinsed well. She couldn't trust herself to speak. Three more days of Derry's company! He talked on, praising New Zealand, saying he wouldn't mind a chance here provided it was a good one. She could have screamed.

As she wiped the bench and Derry put the last dish on the table, he suddenly said admiringly, ' I hand it to you, Thomasina, you certainly know how to handle the old chap. All that guff—talking about early history that can't mean a thing to you, laying it on thick about the pioneers and his wife. Sentimental old codger, isn't he, Tamsin?'

She flung down her dishcloth, turned to face him. Her cheeks were flying rags of pure rage. 'Derry Ford! That'll be enough of that! You make me feel insincere, acquisitive! Everything I said was from the heart. *You* ought to know how Father and I revered the past, loved tales of other days . . . they were the things we lived by. I *love* Ebenezer. He's about the only stable thing in an uncertain world for me. I'd love him if he didn't have a sou. And I'll never, never, never touch a penny of his money! Money doesn't come into what I feel for Ebenezer. It's a privilege to live in the same house and that's all I want.

'You're utterly horrible! You smirch and cheapen everything you talk about. Don't get any ideas about trying to push me into taking advantage of my cousin! It wouldn't benefit you at all. I only want you back at the other side of the world. Pity *you* hadn't fallen for Ilena. You've got about the same standards. You had a nerve coming here and taking advantage of Ebenezer's hospitality. The next three days can't go quickly enough for me. I won't do anything to shame you in front of the others, but watch your step! I'll only go out with you tonight because it would cause talk if I refused, and I hate to think of disharmony and embarrassment in this lovely old house that's known over a century of honesty and hard work and good neighbourliness.' By this time she was at the door.

' And Peggy told me she found you going through the papers on my cousin's desk—you stay away from everything private in this house or I'll get them to tell you to go!'

Halfway up the stairs she turned back, leaned over the banister and said intensely, 'And *don't* call me Tamsin! That's a little pet name for the people I love to use. I'd advise you to go outside and help the men. You can't get up to mischief outside!' And she disappeared, fury concentrated in one feminine form.

Oddly enough she felt better for her outburst. She no longer felt weary and disillusioned and without hope. She felt fighting fit. She would not allow Derry to shadow her happiness. Luke was worth fighting for.

Derry, evidently shaken, had gone after the men, on horseback. They were inspecting fences on one of the boundaries. They were late in for lunch. Thomasina was so carefully polite to Derry. He watched his step, made an effort to please, praised her curry, her cheese muffins. Once or twice she fancied Luke was watching her.

After lunch he said, 'I'll run down to see if there's any mail. I saw dust rising as we came in, so I guess it was the van.' He went out, then called out, 'Thomasina, can I see you for a moment?'

She went out. It would be nothing. Some minor request to do with the near-at-hand farm chores, probably. He said, 'I'd sooner you drove to the city tonight. I'm not keen on Derry's driving. I let him drive a bit yesterday. He drives on the brakes. I reckon he'd be a speed merchant.'

'He is,' said Thomasina. 'Dad never liked me out with him. It made him nervous. Suppose I says it as shouldn't, I'll be a lot eaesier on your car than he would be.'

'It wasn't that,' said Luke, brows twitching down. 'I thought he might put you over the bank.' The brows shot up, their eyes

165

met. But it wasn't long enough. Ebenezer appeared. Luke let in the clutch of the utility, went off to the mailbox.

Ebenezer put an arm round her shoulder as they waited. 'You know, sometimes I can't believe it—having you here, and the children. You are like my own granddaughter. The household had got so dull. We were getting set in our ways, Luke and I, rattling round this big house. Even with Louisa there was something lacking. No life about it. I feel ten years younger.'

Thomasina turned and put her young cool hands about his cheeks, reached up and kissed him. 'And I feel so carefree. Even the thought of our cottage getting crushed into the ground doesn't stab so much now.'

Derry strolled out and stood beside them.

Ebenezer said, 'Louisa wants me to take you to see her next week. She's at Elizabeth's sister's. They all love Louisa. And so will you.'

Luke came back, got out. 'Piles of mail, mostly for Thomasina. You're going to be busy answering that lot. I think just about everyone in Greenchester must have written to you, judging by the postmarks. Plus a few business letters by the look of them, and a big one from South Africa.'

'South Africa? I don't know a soul there. Sure it's for me?'

He turned it over, said, 'It's from a Mrs. Golders at Durban, care of a Mrs. Mitcham. Maybe Mrs. Golders is an English friend of yours, having a holiday there. How's that for detection work?'

'Very poor. I don't know a Mrs. Golders.' She was laughing. Suddenly things seemed much better between them. She tore it open and out fell a sealed envelope as well as the pages of a letter. She gazed at the envelope first, somewhat blankly. It was addressed to her, in Ebenezer's writing, had a New Zealand stamp on it and was marked 'Urgent.'

Ebenezer, Luke and Thomasina stared at it. Derry was busy opening a letter from Christchurch Luke had handed him. Thomasina said in a strangled sort of tone, 'It's the letter I didn't get! But—but how in the name of fortune has it reached me from South Africa?'

The two men craned over the letter that was enclosed.

'Dear Miss Meade,

'You'll be amazed to get this from me. I'm a Canadian, visiting my daughter here in Durban. I left instructions with my neighbour before leaving to forward my mail, but said any second-class mail just to send by surface, which isn't really frequent to here.

'I happen to have a friend in New Zealand who sends me pictorial booklets from time to time, and always mails them second-class, not sealed down. When one arrived in Canada, my neighbour sent it as it was, and even when it reached here I didn't get it, because my daughter and her husband had taken me on an extended tour round these glorious game reserves.

'When I shook out the booklet out fell your letter. It must have fallen into it in the post-box—that's all I can think of. When we saw the date on it, and that it was marked urgent, we got really worried. My son-in-law decided to ring Greenchester Post Office and get them to contact you and explain it was on its way and to say we hoped you hadn't been upset about its non-arrival. It seemed to be a small village, they knew all about you, and said you'd gone to live in New Zealand at the address on the back of the letter. They said to send it direct to you there. That all your mail was going there now, as you'd decided to stay.

'I do so trust this didn't cause any serious complications. I imagined all sorts of things, felt it might even have had arrangements inside it for meeting you at some airport in New Zealand. I know it will have sorted itself out by now, but it has worried me. I'd be grateful if you could drop me a line just to reassure me that it's finally reached you. My New Zealand friend lives at Ngahuru-Marama too, which explains the incident, I suppose. You've probably met her by now. She's Mrs. Aaron Copperfield.

'With all good wishes,
'Your sincerely,
'Elsie Golders.'

Luke said, 'It beats all! If you'd posted it in town, Uncle, it'd never have happened, but we haven't got a separate box for airmail here, it's so small a post-office.' His eyes met Thomasina's and he smiled, 'Good job I grovelled that night, isn't it? Or you'd have me on my knees right now.'

Derry said, 'Well, that's one mystery cleared up, but I wonder where my mail to you is. My *two* letters.'

Thomasina knew instinctively that he was enjoying saying that Dog-in-the-manger! He had guessed she and Luke were drawn to each other—or had been—and he was enjoying creating doubts Now he was chagrined because there was nothing in this situation

167

for him, and he probably bitterly regretted having gone away when he did.

She wouldn't let him see it mattered. 'No doubt there'll be an explanation for those two as well. I'll let you know if they arrive. I can believe anything now. This mail looks nice. I'm going right up to my room to enjoy reading it without interruption. You'll be back at three for your afternoon tea, I suppose.'

She put aside the Greenchester ones for leisurely reading when she'd disposed of the business ones. She'd save Mrs. Bruce's to the last, like the icing on the cake. There was one from her father's publisher. That would be about the serial Jeremy was going to run. She slit it open and next moment was gazing at the contents with as much amazement as she'd viewed the South African one. Then she read it again. He was delighted to tell her, he said, that her father's second thriller was to be televised. They had secured excellent terms, an advance would be made almost immediately and filming would not be long commencing. It had been in negotiation for some time, but not till it was completely in the bag would he have raised her hopes. He knew, in view of changed circumstances, that it would mean a lot to her, and he had utmost confidence that her father's other books could merit the same treatment eventually. He had also secured a very good contract for paperback editions to follow the series, and these, of course, would have world-wide sales.

Her very first impulse was to rush downstairs and outside to find Ebenezer and Luke, but she checked it. Not while Derry was here. He would spoil it as he had everything, and it would only serve to make him more determined to cling to her. She wouldn't dare even tell the children, they'd never keep a secret like that. Slowly she became aware that this could make a difference to the situation between her and Luke. Ownership of the farm wouldn't matter. She would have money of her own. The farm could be all his.

She made herself open all the other letters. They were so warm, so friendly, one and all glad she had found a home and relations.

She enjoyed every word of Mrs. Bruce's. Her letters were always full of the little intimate village details that had made up their lives till now. But the most significant piece came at the end, though Mrs. Bruce couldn't possibly have known it mattered so much. It was in a postscript.

'I meant to tell you some time ago that Derry Ford rang for your address. I wasn't in, only my niece was here. She knew vaguely who he meant, and looked up the address book. He was ringing from London, so she didn't want to keep him long. He was going out to New Zealand on a business trip. But the only address in the book was the Christchurch Post Office one, so she gave him that. I had your new address on your letter, which I've been so long in answering, but I hadn't entered it up. She told him she was pretty sure you were going to be visiting some long-lost relation nearby, and that you'd be in Christchurch longer than anywhere. He said he'd just write from where they were having their conference, when he got to New Zealand. I hope he was able to contact you all right. Or do I hope that? I never liked him much, and when he faded out because of your responsibilities, I liked him less. However, you might have enjoyed seeing a face from your old life. But do not trust him, gentle maiden. If ever there's a man with an eye to the main chance, it's Derry Ford.'

Thomasina gazed incredulously at the letter. It seemed quite daft. Why should Derry have made up all that stuff about writing from England to this particular address? And he said he'd called on Mrs. Bruce. And only this morning he'd mentioned that he'd written twice. As if he was disgruntled Ebenezer's had turned up, but he'd wanted to emphasise the strangeness of others going astray. He'd wanted to discredit her in front of Luke. Elizabeth had been right. Ilena must have suggested to Derry when they met in Queenstown that it would be a good idea to put a rift in the lute. She must have been told by someone from Harvest Moon Bay that she and Luke had been seen dancing at the Sickle or something. By now Ilena didn't care about Luke. She had eyes for something bigger. But early in the days of the conference she must have mentioned Harvest Moon Bay and the name had clicked. These things were always happening. So they had plotted.

Thomasina was mad clean through now. But she was glad, glad, glad Mrs. Bruce had written this just when she had. She'd felt at such a disadvantage before. She was going to have a grand showdown with Derry and ask him to leave. And to the devil with harmony. He wasn't going to trade any longer on Ebenezer's hospitality.

All of a sudden she realized something . . . Ebenezer was an old man. He didn't deserve anger and hostility in this lovely old home where, as she had said of Akaroa, the keynote should be peace. You never knew what might happen at his age. He'd come out of the rumpus with Ilena and Luke all right, but then he hadn't been directly involved. He seemed hale and hearty, but how terrible if a confrontation such as she intended to have with Derry gave him a heart attack or a stroke. She made up her mind on a plan of action.

She would go over the hills with him tonight for Christchurch. But once there she would not go to the theatre with him. She'd park the car somewhere and tell him he was not coming back, that she was driving him to his hotel and that she never wanted to see him again. It wouldn't be easy bottling it up till then, but for the sake of this old man who so loved her, it was going to be done.

Then with the irritation of his presence in the house removed, she would return to tell Luke and Ebenezer of the wonderful news of the T.V. series, and of what she'd found out about Derry. How he and Ilena must have plotted to upset things out of sheer envy of the set-up at Corrieside. She wouldn't mention that it was really to put a rift in the lute between a man and a girl. If Ilena was capable of things like this, no wonder Luke had been furious with her, Thomasina, when she had talked of the breach between them being healed. Jeremy had convinced her Luke had never cared for Ilena.

Just then she heard Derry's voice calling her, 'Thomasina, Thomasina . . . are you there?' He came halfway up the stairs and called again. She kept absolutely silent. If she met him now the accusations would positively burst out of her.

He gave a last call, quite near this time, then as only silence resulted she heard him say in a lower tone, 'Ah . . . good!' Now what in the world did that mean? His footsteps faded. She quietly went to her window to see if he went out the front way. He couldn't have gone the back way because it was quite impossible to shut that door quietly. She thought he might have gone outside to look for her. Well, why make a mystery out of it? That was the trouble, once you doubted a person's motives, you were suspicious of everything they did, even the innocent things. She smiled to herself; that had been the trouble with Luke.

But she did wonder if he wanted to ring Ilena when no one was about. But if anyone lifted the downstairs phone, it always made a sound on this upstairs extension, and she heard nothing.

She stole quietly to the landing, leaned on the rail and listened. The faintest of sounds reached her. Was she just imagining those movements were muted, stealthy? Then she heard one she recognized . . . the sound of a drawer being slid open. He was in the farm office!

There must be papers there he was interested in. But why? Yet Peggy had been suspicious and had ordered him out. He hadn't had time to find out what he was after. Thomasina went icily calm. He wasn't going to get away with this!

She slipped off her shoes, and took the side of the stairs against the wall as less likely to squeak. She went very slowly. What she saw from the bottom stair did nothing for her already raised blood-sugar. Derry was scanning a sheet of paper, obviously taken from that drawer, and nodding his head as if something satisfied him. He dropped it down, reached into the drawer again, and, fascinated but unbelieving, Thomasina saw him begin to count a wad of ten-dollar notes. Oh, no, Derry wouldn't! Not that. She blinked and concentrated again.

Ebenezer was very naughty, he kept far too much money in the house, and always in that drawer. Thomasina's mind was working with great clarity. He was counting them to make sure there wasn't an even amount. Derry nodded again, drew out two, put them in his pocket. He put the rest back, slid the drawer closed.

Then with one bound, Thomasina was in the office and confronting him. She said in ringing tones that scared the life out of Derwent Ford, 'Thank you, I'll have those notes back, you rotten miserable paltry thief! I always knew money meant too much to you, but I never dreamed you'd stoop to this, stealing from a man who out of the kindness of his heart offered a stranger hospitality. Give them to me, I say!'

He went deathly white and handed them to her without a word. She said, 'Get out from behind my cousin's desk! *Get out*, I say!'

He moved from behind it. She went round the other side, pulled open the drawer, lifted the little weight that held the notes down, restored the ones he had taken and said, 'Now march upstairs, you, I've something to say to you and I would rather say it in private. My cousin's too old to have encounters and upsets like this.'

He said quickly, 'That paper was out of there too. On top of the money. Look, Thomasina, don't be too hasty. It was a sudden temptation, that's all. I was really watching your interests—you look at that paper. It's to do with a new division of the estate and very much in your favour—look!'

She gave it one horrified glance and stuffed it on top of the
171

notes. 'I don't want to know anything about it. I said : March!'

She rushed up the stairs after him, motioned him in to his own room. 'Now . . . Peggy told me you were going through papers on your very first day. I expect you saw money there then—probably took some. No, don't bother to deny it. I wouldn't believe you. I've no way of proving it, but one thing I can do and that is prevent anything else going, by getting you out of my cousin's house. I'll deal with you myself. Certainly Luke could, but then Ebenezer would have to be involved and Luke is a man of action. He'd throw you over the cattle-grids.'

Derry said imploringly, 'Oh, please, Thomasina. Do try to be understanding. Money just melts. I've never had half I wanted. I feel the old boy has so much he'd never miss a note or two.'

'He earned every penny of it. Time was, during the Depression, when he never saw the colour of money. They just lived off the land and kept out of debt. Oh, don't bother to excuse yourself. Most men would think themselves pretty lucky to get a trip like this, all expenses met and a continuing salary. And you pilfer a miserable twenty dollars! I just hope, Derry, it's a lesson to you. If you go on like this you're bound to be caught, and your life will be ruined. It will follow you always. It looks to me as if you have a promising career ahead of you. *If you stay honest!*'

A gleam of hope lit his eyes. 'You mean you aren't going to give me away? I promise if—'

'I don't want your promises. What you do with the rest of your life is nothing to me, except that I wish you well. And that means being honest. I am, however, going to tell Ebenezer and Luke, but not till you're safely out of the house. It's nearly tea-time. I'm coming in to watch you pack your things in case you take a fancy to any of the rather choice things in that room. Thank heaven you haven't got much. You can go down and put them in Luke's Holden, then when he and my cousin come in, you're to tell them your chief rang and wants you back as there's some urgent business to attend to tomorrow morning early, and that I'll be dropping you at your hotel after we've seen the play.'

'You're still coming with me?'

'Not likely. That's just what I'm telling them. After I deliver you to the hotel I'm coming back here to tell them what I've done and why. The children will be in bed by then. I want them to know nothing of this. I've something else to tell them too, nice, exciting news, to take the nasty taste out of their mouths. But I'm warning you, one more attempt from you to queer the situation

172

between myself and Luke, with your lies, and I'll blow the whole thing in front of everybody! Now I must get the dinner on as soon as you've thrown your things in your case. Don't waste time or they'll wonder why I'm here, and I won't look compromised *this* time. I'll tell them exactly why if they arrive.'

He wasted no time. Thomasina was hoping she'd stay mad clean through because she was terrified she'd start feeling sorry for him, and you could be too kind to people, so that they carried on with their underhand dealings.

Mercifully time flew. What a blessing there was cold mutton, a salad, just potatoes to peel, and she had made a cold pudding this morning. She wasn't capable of concocting a super meal tonight.

The children came in, had a cookie, departed to do their chores. She heard the men coming. Luke said, ' I didn't think we ought to be late when you're going out. Derry didn't come back. Is he here?'

'Yes, he's showering. He didn't go back to you because just after he came in for whatever he wanted, his chief rang. Some business has cropped up and he needs him early tomorrow morning, so he's all packed up and I'll drop him at his hotel after the play.'

Luke's voice was carefully regretful, though she was sure an inhospitable gleam of pleasure shot into his eyes. ' Oh, pity he's had to cut his break short. But he'd better take a taxi from the theatre. That hotel is right out by the airport, and it's late enough for you to be driving back over these hills. Leave a bit early and take his things to the hotel then. I'll tell you the way. Then he could probably pick up a taxi from the theatre. You may be parked some distance away.'

Well, she wouldn't be at the theatre, but she agreed. The children's chatter helped and the thought that Derry would be gone for ever from Corrieside in a matter of an hour or so helped Thomasina's spirits rise.

When she came down, Edwina, now more clothes-conscious than Thomasina, said, ' Oh, I thought you'd have been wearing a long dress. Why don't you put on that turquoise cotton with the purple flowers? I love you in that.'

Thomasina said, ' Oh, no need to dress up. Only a few people will be in long dresses and they're horrid for driving in.'

It was Luke who complimented her on her appearance. ' Surely the turquoise can't be more striking than that, Edwina?'

173

Thomasina laughed. 'It was one of the dresses that came with the competition. I'm fond of it myself. It's the nearest to orange I can wear. My hair is just reddish enough to put some shades out of court.'

It was filmy and soft in creams and browns in a big splashy pattern with a low waist girdled with a poppy-gold swathed sash. Big covered buttons of the gold went right down the left side and tiny ones of the same buttoned the long tight cuffs to the elbow, where the sleeves suddenly fulled into leg-o'-mutton ones. She had scooped up her hair at the back of her head and fastened it with one of Edwina's clasps, gold daisies, with brown centres. She saw a reluctant, perhaps rueful, admiration in Derry's eyes.

They all trooped out to the courtyard to see them off. Sunset was painting the sky above the Seven Sisters with trailers of colour as bright as her dress, and Mount Herbert across the harbour was purple with shadow. The sea below was pewter-grey, as if night had reached there, but not here yet. The sky away out to the open sea was celadon green and every little cloud there had caught the reflection from the west and was as pink as candy-floss rimmed with silver light. Thomasina looked about her with beauty-loving eyes. 'I'm sure the weather-man's wrong. It looks like anything but rain. I daresay it will be another nor-wester tomorrow and as hot as today.'

'I doubt it,' said Luke, 'when you get over the other side you'll not see a nor'-west arch over the Alps tonight. Look south . . . see those clouds breaking up from a solid mass into shoals and fanning out? That means a wind change. It'll swing round to the sou'-west during the night. Now mind, Thomasina, straight home after the play. You've got that short white coat, haven't you? It may be cold coming home.' She felt happed about with their concern for her. Things were coming right, fast. She mustn't dread this trip too much. It would be over soon.

She slipped behind the wheel, wound down the window, leaned out to say to Edwina, 'You can watch T.V. till nine *if* you get your homework done first, and, Matthew, no skimping your teeth.'

Luke said, laughing, 'Oh, get away with you, girl. We'll see to all that. You sound like the old woman who lived in a shoe.'

Suddenly, as if overcome by a sudden impulse, he leaned in, said, in the lowest tones, meant only for her and Derry, 'By the way, I owe you an apology, Tamsin.' The brown eyes looked deeply into hers. 'For getting all upstage with you the other night

174

when I found you and Derry in the dining-room. I realized yesterday that you really had come down for that book. Because you must have been hunting for it before Derry went in, because you knew exactly where it was, mad and all as you were with me. So it wasn't an assignation.'

Derry said nothing, naturally. Thomasina said softly, her mouth curving into a smile, 'I'm so glad you worked it out for yourself. Though I was going to tell you exactly how it had occurred, later tonight.'

Then to Thomasina's great astonishment, he leaned down and kissed her full on the lips. 'Have a pleasant evening,' he said.

Thomasina felt dazed—happily dazed. Out of the back window, through the mirror, she saw Edwina standing on her head, a sure sign of excitement. Edwina had liked Luke kissing Thomasina. 'That's one in the eye for that Derry,' she said to her brother in an undertone, but Luke caught it, and they all burst out laughing. 'Poor Derry,' said Matthew, 'Edwina loves him not. He once called her an in—um—incorrigible brat.'

'And she is too,' said Luke, swinging Edwina up, 'but we love her, mischief and all.'

Derry began to talk immediately. It was natural. He didn't want her to say anything to Ilena about taking the money. 'She's right in with my chief and he—'

'As far as the money's concerned that's a closed book. I wouldn't dream of blackening your character. I don't want to be too scathing, Derry, because though I've had precious little of it till now, money's never been a real temptation to me. But I'm prepared to admit it might be to some people. I don't know if you've ever done it before or not, but I've been thinking of something. When your mother came to see me that time—after you'd gone away—she begged me to take that money for a fund for the children from the Greenchester people. She said she would feel so safe if you married me. That I was a strong character. I felt embarrassed. I'd not thought of myself in that light. Then she said something I thought was queer. She added : "And you're as straight as a die, so honest." It makes me wonder. Your parents are perfect darlings, Derry. If they have any suspicion at all about this weakness of yours, they must often know hours of fear for you. It's possible to cut it right out. Otherwise you'll walk in fear all your life long. That I do know.

'The great thing for you is that in a few days you'll be away from all this. Now, I'd rather not talk about any more controversial things while driving, but I have something to say to you about another subject, when we get to the parking area of the hotel. But I don't like to get all het up driving. It's not fair to other people on the road.'

It was still twilight when they drew up at the hotel. The light lasted longer on the plains. Thomasina drew out Mrs. Bruce's letter and read it to him. 'I've a fair idea why you did it, but I'd like to hear your version. It's only right. Why did you try to get Luke to think we'd been in touch and that I knew you'd be seeing me?'

He looked sullen, then said reluctantly, 'Ilena thought of it. I found out she lived at Harvest Moon. That niece of Mrs. Bruce's said it had a romantic name, and came out with it, but had no idea where it was. I had intended writing to Christchurch Post Office. That was true enough. But then she confided in me a bit, said she was in love with Luke, and would like to drive a wedge between you. Not ethical, according to your standards, I know, but then we aren't all made of your fine clay!'

Thomasina ignored that. She felt bewildered. 'But I never met her in my life till she came *back* from Queenstown. I wonder had someone hinted that Luke and I might be falling for each other. Though it was anything but apparent at first.'

'Luke wrote. She was livid. He praised you up to the skies. That nothing was further from your mind than trying for a share in the estate, that you were a brick, and only wanted a home for the children. And he said she was to cause you no unpleasantness when she came back to the Bay—she was to stay clean away from Corrieside.'

Happiness flooded over Thomasina. Luke had done that, for her! Then he had soon lost his distrust of her. That day at Akaroa had, indeed, been the beginning of a romance.

Derry added, 'She thought what would appear to be an old boy-friend turning up might make a rift in the lute, especially if I could make it appear you *were* on the make and had kept me a secret.'

Thomasina added for him, 'And you began to get ideas of your own. You thought I might play up to Ebenezer, consent to him leaving me half of Corrieside, and that you might be able to persuade me to marry you, after all. But you struck a snag. I wouldn't take any of it. Luke has shouldered three-quarters of the work for years, so it all belongs to him.'

How was it she had never noticed what a mean mouth Derwent Ford had? He said, 'Very laughable. Except, of course, that you hope to marry him. That way you get the lot. But do you think you'll ever really be sure of him?'

'What on earth can you mean?'

'Sure of *his* motives. Isn't he just thinking it's expedient to marry you? Because some day you might just give in to Ebenezer. It would please the old man. Luke could quite easily *imagine* he was in love with you.'

Thomasina hadn't been going to allow herself the satisfaction of telling him of her father's posthumous success, but it was too much for her. 'If Luke asks me to marry him, and I'm pretty sure after tonight he will, I'll accept. I always believed in my father as a writer, and now it's been entirely justified. Luke and Ebenezer don't know yet. It's been quite a day. The books are to be televised. I'll never take a share of the farm. We meet on equal terms. Now get out, you despicable hound! You've done all you could to spoil my happiness. I want to get back to tell them the sort of guest they've been entertaining unawares.'

She got out of the car, opened the back, thrust his case at him. 'And just in case Ilena tries to do Luke or myself any more harm I'm going straight to that telephone box over there, to ring Harbourage and tell her I found you out, and her. Oh, not about the theft of the money. It's nothing to do with her and she seems so friendly with your chief, it wouldn't be fair. It looks as if she's found bigger fish to fry now. Pity she hadn't met her tycoon a bit sooner, then she mightn't have tried this on. But I daresay it was sheer spite. Even when she transferred her interests, she carried on. She fooled you too. You played her game, and if she had succeeded in discrediting me, with Luke, there'd have been nothing in it, for you. Anyway, I'm going to spike her guns just in case she tries to do the Corrieside folk any more harm.'

She walked away from him.

She hoped desperately that Ilena wasn't out with Derry's chief tonight. But she thought not. He would hardly have taken her to visit his relations here.

Ilena answered the phone and sounded surprised when she knew who it was. She said hastily, 'I can't chat. I'm expecting an important call any moment.'

'What I have to say won't take long, Ilena. But I've no intention of cutting it short, believe me. If you hang up, I'll call Conrad and tell him to tell you. You might like to know I've just

177

deposited your fellow-conspirator back at his hotel. I don't want him at Corrieside again. I've found out about this business of pretending I'd known he was coming to New Zealand. You thought it would make Luke suspicious. Luke's pretty astute, and he and I understand each other pretty well. It gave Derry a shock to know I really meant it when I said I would accept no share of Corrieside. Besides, I don't need to. My father's books are being televised. I'm quite independent now. But I just wanted you to know I found out what you'd been up to, and if I were you I'd stay away from Corrieside. If you try to do the people there any more harm, I shall make public what you and Derry tried to do.'

Ilena's voice said quickly as if someone had come into the room, 'Oh, I ought to tell you I'm leaving. Yes, I'd like to be back in the hub of the universe again. Wilfred—Derry's chief—wants me to travel back with them. He's pulling strings to get me on the same plane. He's promised me three wonderful days in New York. It's the chance of a lifetime. He lives just a matter of a few miles from us in Surrey. So I won't have time to make a round of goodbye visits. Say goodbye to the Corrieside people for me, will you?'

Thomasina could have danced for joy. Before she could reply Ilena added : 'Conrad came in. He's gone now. Thomasina, I don't want Wilfred to know anything about this. I—'

Thomasina's tones were contemptuous. 'He won't hear of it from me and Derry would hardly be likely to say anything. If it's any comfort to you, none of us will mention it to the Martensens. Ruth and your mother have had a lifelong friendship. It would be a pity to spoil it, but watch what you do in the meantime. Don't try me too far. Goodbye, Ilena.'

As she crossed to her car, something from her subconscious rose up and hit her. It had all the glory of a sudden rainbow. That paper Derry had thrust at her . . . she'd stuffed it back too hastily to register it at the time. It *was* to do with the division of the estate, deeding the Meades a share. But it wasn't in Ebenezer's precise hand, it was in Luke's scrawl. *He had been planning it in conjunction with his uncle!* She felt dazzled with joy.

Soon, soon, she would be home. Yes, it would be home, for always. She looked down at the spare coins still in her hand and, on impulse, rushed back to the phone-box. She would ring Elizabeth and Jeremy. They would be thrilled. She wouldn't mention the theft. Just that she had found out the deception about the letters and Ilena's part in it and her nearing departure.

And she was dying to tell someone about her father's posthumous success. Elizabeth, as a writer, would be thrilled.

She was. Thomasina told her that last. Elizabeth said, ' Could you bear to postpone your journey home for a few moments? It so happens Jeremy is working back. He mentioned, among other things, that he's going to make a preliminary notice about the forthcoming serial, and if he could mention at the same time that another book by the same author is to be seen on the screen in time to come, it would boost it. If I do it by phone he'll be cagey, think I haven't got it straight, but from you, it will be authentic.'

' It will. I signed the contract right away and I'm going to drop it into the Chief Post Office in the Square, so I'll go across the office right after. I thought after that horrible business of Ebenezer's letter going into an open envelope I'd like this to go in an airmail slot! I'll come over tomorrow to tell you how Luke and Ebenezer took the news.'

Jeremy was delighted. She showed him the publisher's letter. He sent for some coffee for her. How different she looked already from the other night when she had had great shadows under her eyes. 'You'll feel so close to your father as you see episode after episode. I'm so sorry your father and stepmother didn't live to enjoy his success, but you'll feel them very near to you in it.'

He walked downstairs with her, looked up at the sky above the slender spire of the Cathedral in the centre and said, ' That's a stormy sky. But I shouldn't think it would break before we're home. I'll only be another hour or so after you. But anyway, be careful, though Luke tells me you're a wonderful driver.'

The shops were all lit, the windows full of delightful wares. Some Christmas stuff was already in. Thomasina knew she'd be able to spread herself this year on presents for the children. She went happily from window to window. She didn't want to get home till the children were in bed and asleep. Nothing must spoil her big moment. From there they would pick up the threads again.

By the time she started the climb up Dyer's Pass, the windscreen was so streaming with rain that the wipers could hardly cope. Soon the houses were left behind, and the force of the wind buffeting the car as she emerged from plantations of pines, or turned a bend, was almost frightening. In the glare of the headlights, the tussocks were bent over with the force of the wind. As she went through the Kiwi cutting she felt the car sway and rock. Then she gained the shelter of the hills to the sou'west.

She was glad when she was past Governor's Bay. She knew this part of the road so much better. Not long now. This was almost like a cloudburst. She sat bolt upright and peered through the streaming water. The windscreen wipers were squeaking horribly. Then suddenly the sqeaking stopped. The wipers weren't functioning any more. She knew what had happened; the cable had gone.

She had no vision at all. She dared not go on. She dropped to a crawl, because she couldn't stop here, too near a bend, and wound her window down and stuck her head out into the drenching rain. She saw about twenty yards on was a widened-out piece of road, where it would be safer to stop, and carefully edged out on to it. With a flash of relief she realized that, with the time she'd spent in town, Jeremy would be along any moment. There was always a torch in the car, she could wave him down with that. Of course with a downpour like this, there was the chance it would stop just as suddenly, then she'd be able to go on.

She wound up the window, snapped on the inside light, found the torch. Now all she had to do was wait till she saw Jeremy's lights come round the big bend that would be visible from here, and she'd have plenty of time to leap out. They'd have to leave this car on the road till morning.

It was eerie; she seemed in a small enclosed world, surrounded by miniature waterfalls. She hoped the first car would be Jeremy's. She hadn't passed a single one on the way over.

Then she saw lights coming. As soon as they disappeared round the next bend she got out. Better to get a drenching than miss him. If she did she'd have to walk, and two miles in this would be horrible. She must be careful to wave it across the road, not into the car itself, or she'd dazzle him. She walked about two paces back from the car. Further than that she couldn't go as it would mean getting on to the macadam and it wouldn't be safe. One thing, whoever the driver was, he'd be proceeding slowly. The wind tore at her, swayed her back, screamed down the gully above her again. Really, she'd never heard a wind roar like that! It sounded as if the whole hillside was moving down. Her scalp pricked. *But it was!*

The awareness of danger came just too late. She tried to pierce the darkness, to gauge the direction of the landslip, this dark terrifying mass that was bearing down on her. There was no time to avoid it, nowhere to run. Thomasina knew a moment of extreme terror, made a swift turn, then it was on her, a mass of boulders from the stream-bed, mud, scrub, bushes, and she was borne over the edge, screaming as she went, heard a chilling sound of protesting metal and knew the car was going over too, and threw herself aside. Her last conscious thought was, oh, if only that relentless tide sweeping her down had been water, she'd have had a chance. Then she knew nothing more.

Jeremy Ffoulkes came round that bend, sitting upright and straining for visibility. His powerful headlamps picked up something on the road that oughtn't to have been there. Not at that height . . . tree branches, and a tangled mass of debris. He braked cautiously, aware of the film of water on the road, came to a stop about three feet from the thinned-out edge of an indescribably menacing river of mud and uprooted trees and shingle, and saw with horror that it was still moving.

The water was already banking up against it. He reversed with extreme care, took several attempts to get round and knew a great release from fear when he was headed once more in the direction whence he'd come. Another five minutes and he'd have copped that lot. He must go like hell for the nearest phone, ring Governor's Bay, get them out on the road to stop traffic coming that way, and ring Harvest Moon to do the same. What a blessing Thomasina had left when she did. She'd be safe home ages ago.

He knew every house on the road . . . Akens would be nearest. They were off the hill to the right, a fairly long drive, but he'd sound his horn halfway down and that would bring them out at the double. No time must be lost. Minutes could mean a life gone. He turned in, put his hand on the horn. As he drew up at the door the outside light came on and out rushed most of the family.

They went into action immediately. Once Governor's Bay and Harvest Moon were alerted, they rang the Kiwi to stop anyone coming over the Pass, and Lyttelton and the Bays between, and Christchurch. The whole network of emergency road services would swing into efficient movement. Then Jeremy rang his wife. Elizabeth was shaken at his narrow escape, but thankful it had happened at the time it had. Jeremy said, 'I saw Thomasina, of course, but she'd be nearly an hour ahead of me. It must have just happened, because it was still moving fast. But get hold of Corrieside and just check, will you, darling? I don't want to keep

181

this phone out of action.'

Luke answered the phone. He was amazed when Elizabeth without preamble, asked, ' Is Thomasina home yet?'

' No. We don't expect her for ages. The play won't be out til nearly eleven. I've decided to take Uncle's car over and wait outside the theatre. I don't like her driving home in this. We can leave the other car at a garage. I—'

' Luke, be quiet! She didn't go to the play. I can't go into it now, but she dumped Derry at his hotel and that was it. She found out something about him, rang me, and as she had a bit of news besides that that I thought would interest Jeremy, I asked her to call in. He was working late. She left before he did—about an hour, so she ought to be home. He's just rung from Akens'. There's a slip across the road at Blowhole Gully. Oh, Luke, what are we to do? He's rung the village. They'll be out on the main junction now stopping traffic, but—oh, Luke, you do think she'll be between here and the slip, don't you?'

Luke said, ' I'll get the Land Rover out now. Elizabeth, get hold of Aaron if he's still home. Or anyone you can. Alert Andrew. Get him to the slip just in case. I'm on my way.'

He told his uncle in a few terse words. ' Get hold of Josh, tell him to follow me. Oh, she must have got past it if she left an hour before. But there may be smaller slips between Blowhole and here and she may be stranded between and terrified. You'll have to stay with the children. I'm off.'

He yanked a sou'wester off a hook, oilskins. Ebenezer thrust a rug at him, imploring him to take care. There could be other slips. ' You'll serve her best if you stay in one piece yourself.' Then he was gone.

He paused at the road-block to tell the men Thomasina was on the road, somewhere, and Aaron Copperfield, a giant of a man, leapt into the Rover with him. Others would follow.

Luke's voice in its savage horror was almost unrecognizable. It was only a croak. ' If it caught her she'd never get out of the car. I wonder how far it would go. It might get caught by trees. But she would be injured. She'd have her safety-belt fastened, of course. That might save her a bit. But if it went over Aken's Bluff the car would be—' He didn't finish that. He said, ' Oh, damn this rain, damn it! I can't see a thing!'

Aaron said, 'Steady, man. Steady. Easy does it. She'll have need of all our resources, don't let's expend them yet. We don't know that she *was* caught in it. Not yet. She may just be caught between two slips, a minor one this side.'

But they took the three bends between them and Blowhole Gully and the road was clear all the way. And they both knew as they turned the corner, and saw it ahead of them, that she *must* be over the edge.

There was little movement in the slip now, which meant it had piled up against the trees further down the gully below the road. Pray God it had, before reaching the Bluff. That all of it had. But it was deep, horribly, sickeningly, slimily deep.

They brought the Rover as close as was consistent with safety, beaming its lights over the edge. Luke hadn't forgotten to snatch up a couple of powerful electric farm lanterns. They both began scrambling down the side of the slip, slanting the beams this way and that, appalled at every glimpse of the mass of debris they could see in the beating, pitiless rain.

There was nothing to be seen save rubble and bushes and great boulders, any of which, crashing on a car hood with a girl inside, could have crushed her to death. Suddenly, as if someone had turned a tap off, the rain ceased. They worked their way diagonally across the slip, swinging the beams from side to side. Suddenly Aaron made a sound, brought his lantern back from a wide arc, steadied it, focused on something. There was the car against a tree, slewed sideways, so that though the roof was stove in and the windows shattered, it wasn't crushed to a pulp.

They slid and slithered their way down to it, fighting beastly conditions every inch of the way, hideously obstructed by trees that sought to entangle them, and patches of deep slime they couldn't negotiate. They swore and cursed as branches slapped their faces, lawyer vines clung and scratched. But none of it mattered save for the time it was taking.

They reached it together, braced themselves for what they might find; shone a torch through the shattered window, peered inside, then made incredulous sounds. Aaron brought the other torch into play. No battered and broken body. No one. Nothing except her bag lying tumbled on the floor.

Luke said hoarsely, unbelieving, 'She's *gone*!' He swung the torch madly from side to side, not heeding the jagged remnants. Aaron said, 'She'd been able to undo the safety belt, so she wasn't too badly damaged, and—look—there's no blood.'

Luke said, 'But she'd never have got the door open—look, I can't even do it from here. It's twisted and jammed.' He went on wrenching at it. 'I mean, imagine trying to push it open from the position she'd be in, flung to the side of the car that's resting against the tree. Aaron, she must have seen the landslide coming, got out and tried to run for it. Then—Oh, God—she got caught!'

They both lifted up their voices and shouted: 'Thomasina, Thomasina, are you there?' Then because it was so long a name to shout, Luke began again, 'Tamsin, Tamsin, Tam . . . where are you? We're here, Luke's here!'

But there was no sound except for the wind, battering at them, the lashing of the standing trees, the agonized creaking of the branches of the uprooted ones. They stopped yelling and looked down at the river of debris and neither of them could speak.

Then Aaron said, 'I'll do this side, you do that. Keep calling.'

Luke searched desperately, but he had no hope in his heart, only a determination to rescue her broken body from this sickening slime and tangled debris. As he crawled up over a huge mound that barred his way he saw car lights coming from the Governor's Bay side. More to search. And the more there were, the sooner it would be over. He checked a sob that tore at him. He must save his breath to keep shouting her name, though he knew she'd be past hearing.

The next instant his urgent torch-beam lit up something. He pounced on it, tugged. It was a golden sash, mud-stained, saturated, but still gleaming a little. He bent down and scrabbled badly at the slush. It came away in his hands, intact. But it hadn't been attached to anything!

He raised his voice, 'Aaron . . . Aaron . . . quick, she must be somewhere near. I've found something!'

He could hear the rush of Aaron's scrambling while he went on digging frantically with his hands, saying her name over and over. Aaron bent over, directing his light, said, 'It's not deep here—you're right down to solid earth—I think she lost the sash and tumbled further down, but there's hope, man, it's thinner here and there are trees further down, standing—'

Luke had the more powerful lantern, so he snatched it and swept the light out in a huge semi-circle, downhill, and suddenly, against a huge rock, they could see something that lay like a rag doll flung limply down on the playroom floor.

The next moment they were across to it. Aaron, a great fear and pity in his heart, directed the beam full on her. She was an indescribable sight, but she was on *top* of the debris. She wasn't even partly submerged because the rock she'd been borne against was so firmly embedded in Mother Earth that it had deflected

184

ost of the evil-flowing tide away from her. Some of the stains
her face were blood, they thought, but most of it was mud.

Luke had put a hand each side of her face. Aaron would never
rget the emotion in his voice as he cried, ' She's *warm*! She's
ive !'

They could hear voices coming towards them from the Harvest
[oon side. Luke said, ' We dare not move her yet. It must be a
retcher. There may be broken bones.' He was struggling out of
s oilskins, peeling off his jacket, his jersey, his shirt. He
ratched the ooze out from under Thomasina's head, holding it
mly against movement, pushed the jersey under it. He covered
r drenched body with the other things, took more from Aaron.

He looked up and there was Andrew, stolid, comfortingly
nowledgeable, with expert hands that felt slowly, surely, as
.ey held the lights. He was extremely thorough.

He said, ' Impossible to tell what damage may have been done,
ut at least no major bones have been broken. And there's no
gn of head damage, so it's probably concussion. I hope she
ays out to it till we get her up. The stretcher is following. I said
get one down, in case you found her. I want her moved very
owly and carefully. We've a station wagon here. We'll have her
ack to Cherrington Hospital in no time.' He put a hand on
uke's shoulder. ' It's all right lad. She's got every chance. It
ould have been a lot worse.'

Luke was seized with a fit of violent shivering reaction.

Suddenly Jeremy was there, with the others from that side.
here were plenty of helpers now. Luke asked one to go back to
kers and ring Corrieside to tell an old man his darling was
und and she was alive.

Although the distance wasn't far in actual length, the going
as hideous, bearing a stretcher. Then they gained the edge of
ie road, others lifted it over, the doctor ordered them to put
neir burden down while he made another examination by the
ght of headlamps.

He grunted in a sort of satisfied way, said, ' I think she'll do.
he'll be horribly bruised and sore, and we'll take X-rays, but it's
iore than a miracle she came out of it alive. I'd think this was
oncussion. She could come out of it any moment.'

' Like now, for instance,' said a weak voice from the stretcher.
I heard all that.'

Luke was still on his knees, so was the doctor. They peered at
er. Thomasina's lips twisted in a travesty of a smile. ' My face

185

won't be scarred, will it?' she asked anxiously.

The doctor gave a snort of mirthful relief. 'Women! Vain even at moments like this. No.'

The next moment Thomasina said, 'Oh, it's still raining.'

Luke's voice answered her. 'It isn't, Tamsin. That's me crying.' He didn't mind admitting it in front of all those men. He didn't mind anything. She was alive, she was alive!

She put up a hand, clasped his, said, 'Don't. I'll be all right. Oh, is that Jeremy? Then you're safe. I got out of the car—my wipers had failed. I was trying to stop you with a torch. Then it happened.'

Jeremy said grimly, 'I'm safe, yes, but if you hadn't come to give me that news. you'd have been on your way and safe home long ago.'

She tried to shake her head and winced. 'You're not to think that. It was my fault. Like the doctor said, vanity. You told me to come straight home. I window-shopped up and down Colombo Street first—lovely clothes, and things for Christmas for the kids. But wasn't I lucky to be out of the car? And not in the middle of the slip! I sort of rode it down, but caught my head a crack.'

The doctor put an end to the talking, except that as he and Luke rode beside her on the floor of the station wagon, he asked a few questions, mainly about her sore places.

The efficiency and cleanliness of the hospital seemed heaven after the conditions out there.

Elizabeth and Ebenezer were there; because Peggy was with the children. Ebenezer put his arms about her, mud and all. 'My girl, my girl.'

The nurses bathed Thomasina, washed the mud out of her hair, dried it softly. She was quite obviously only bruised. She was lying back in a small room, white, but happy. Elizabeth and Ebenezer talked to her for a short while—Andrew said it might get it out of her system—then, by mutual consent, they left her alone with Luke, except for Andrew, who was busying himself at a table, writing up her report, presumably.

Suddenly Thomasina felt terribly shy. It had been so pointed, as if they all anticipated an engagement now. Ever since she had found out that Derry and Ilena had definitely planned to discredit her, she had been filled with happiness. Now doubt struck at her. Had she read too much into the situation? Mightn't it have been just a case of friendship between herself and Luke?

186

e had been almost manoeuvred into an engagement once before,
e might resent things being taken too much for granted.

She said, awkwardly, 'What a terrible thing I did to your
.r. It might have been a lot safer with Derry, after all.'

Luke said blankly, 'Oh, the car.' He waved a dismissing hand.
That's what insurance is for.'

He turned and grinned at Andrew. 'Andy, you're decidedly
e *trop*. I want to propose to your patient. It's long overdue. We
t our lines crossed. So would you mind?'

Andrew grinned. 'No, I don't mind, Luke. But you're going to
nd the going hard, man.'

Luke said, 'What do you mean? Oh, I know we've been at
ts, but not any longer.'

'I don't mean anything of the kind. I mean I've given her a
ery strong sedative and I don't reckon she'll be able to hold out
gainst it long enough to say yes.' He chuckled. 'Thomasina,
ut him out of his misery and say yes before he asks you and
efore that takes effect. You might as well. Innes and Elizabeth..
ink you were made for each other, and that's a pretty powerful
ombine.'

Her voice was already blurred and her eyes hazy, but she tried
resist it. 'I will *not*! I mean—I won't say yes. At least I won't
ay it *now*. I want a . . . I want a . . . proper proposal. At
—Corrieside. Place I love best . . . in world.' All of a sudden
er voice got a bit clearer and she giggled. 'Luke, you said once
hat a girl would certainly know it when you proposed . . . Oh
ear, I'm all woozy . . . I don't think I'll even remember it.'

She was dimly conscious of lips touching hers, but she couldn't
ee. Her lids were too heavy. to lift—they must be Luke's.
Couldn't be the doctor's, oh, no, doctors don't kiss patients. She
made a tremendous effort. 'Goo'-night, Beetle-brows,' she said,
nd knew no more.

CHAPTER XI

When Thomasina woke next morning, save for stiffness an
bruises and a few scratches, it was hard to believe it ha
happened. Andrew Carmichael was in audacious spirits. 'You'
to be allowed home this afternoon. I've been in touch wit
Elizabeth and told her it's the most important afternoon of you
life—so far—and she's to go up to the homestead and pick ou
your very prettiest dress. And Ebenezer is going to see that n
one else is around, not even him, though he'll be in his offic
to keep callers and telephone at bay. There'll be just Luke. An
Elizabeth will bring your things up here and drive you home.'

Thomasina went rosy. 'Couldn't I just walk?'

'Let my patient walk after what she went through last night
Not much. But why?'

'Oh, I suppose it doesn't matter really. I just had a yen t
walk up the lane instead of going in by the main gate, and t
go through the spinney and the stable-yard, just as I did when
first arrived.'

'Then Elizabeth can drop you up the lane. I'll fix it.'

She clutched him. 'Doctor, don't!. It sounds too arranged.'

He burst out laughing. 'Perhaps you hardly knew what wa
going on last night. But why not too arranged? After all, I goose
that poor bloke's proposal for him last night by administering
sedative at the wrong moment. I like things done in true romanti
fashion.'

She gave him a saucy, reassured look. 'You must tell m
exactly how you proposed to Innis!'

He groaned. But a reminiscent smile touched his lips. 'It's
sore point. A doctor works against great odds. I planned t
propose to her on Four Winds Headland. I got called out at thre
that morning and didn't have a moment to spare from dir
calamity, births, minor injuries, surgery hours and what-have-yo
till nearly three the next morning. I was dog-tired and jus
going to bed when the phone rang. Another confinement an
one that wasn't to be delayed, they said.

'It would have been all right if Innis hadn't been on call tha
night. I got overcome. I blurted it out in the middle of pro
ceedings—well, not exactly the middle. The baby was born an
attended to, but the patient was still out to it. Or so I thought

ter that wretched woman told the whole ward exactly what
said. We tried to pretend it was hallucinatory, due to the
aesthetic, but it was no go. We just had to announce it there
i then before we'd even chosen the ring. I've never heard the
of it.'

was a glorious November day. The first of the roses were out
nting the air, as Elizabeth dropped Thomasina. 'You're to go
ough the old drawing-room to the loggia. Ebenezer is in his
dy keeping everyone away. Make the most of it. We give you
t an hour.'

Elizabeth had brought her turquoise dress. It had soft, full
hop sleeves that concealed the plaster on her arms and the
p white pointed collar set off the ruddy tints of her hair to
fection. She had set her hair this morning dressing it high,
l tying it with a turquoise ribbon, and letting the back strands,
led at the ends, fall to her shoulders. The turquoise brought
the vivid blue-green of her eyes. The scratch on one temple
s barely noticeable. How wonderful it was just to be alive!
Bellbirds and tuis were singing from the kowhai trees in the
nney, and thrushes with creamy speckled breasts whistled as
passed. The whole day seemed vibrant with life and beauty
d joy. There had been a horrifying moment last night when
had thought she was going to be engulfed, when she had
ught that for her there would be no more tomorrows and the
ldren were going to be left quite alone . . .
She crossed the stable-yard, glanced at its doorway remi-
cently, began to mount the steps. The lavender was fully out
w. She stopped to pick a few stalks, pinched the flowers to
ng out the fragrance. All her life the perfume of lavender
uld evoke for her the memory of Luke's first kiss.
The garden was a mass of colour, blues and purples, pinks and
ds . . . Thomasina went along the passages, into the drawing-
om where the pictures of Thomas and Anna, Edwin and Bessie
l their children adorned the walls. The French windows were
n. Luke was standing on the loggia, one hand on the post, his
k to the scene below, waiting and watching for her.
She stopped in the doorway. He seemed rooted to the spot.
looked his fill. She waited, smiling.
He said, 'I can't believe it—that you're here, like this. I—
't deserve it, the doubts I entertained of you, the way I treated
. Last night I thought you'd never know how much I love

189

you. I could only hope that you'd read into my parting words la
night all I was going to say to you on your return. Late
searching frantically, I kept thinking if only I'd refused to l
you go with Derry. If only I'd—'

She held up a hand, still smiling. 'You were meant to ha
those doubts. It was a conspiracy entered into by Ilena ar
Derry. I'd like you to let me explain about it before—' sl
sketched a little gesture with her hands to indicate happiness
come.

He shook his head. 'Not before anything. It can wait.
doesn't matter—I can guess. Listen, my love, this thing starte
when you overheard that slanging match between Ilena ar
myself. It finished completely when *I* overheard *you* telling Der
what you thought of him the other morning when he calle
Ebenezer a sentimental old codger. I heard the lot. If only I
whisked you away then, taken you into the office or somethir
and locked the door. Only—well, I'm a sentimentalist too.
wanted him out of it and Corrieside returned to normal befo
I asked you to be my wife. And it nearly brought you to yo
death, that delay!' He passed a hand over his face as if to shu
out something.

His look made one thing crystal-clear. Thomasina knew the
not only that he loved her but *how* he loved her.

He said, almost inconsequentially, 'You wouldn't let him ca
you Tamsin. I knew then that you'd never loved him, hadn
wanted him in New Zealand, didn't know he was coming.'

He smiled and held out his hands to her. 'I said everythir
else could wait. Well, are you coming to me, Tamsin?'

He was silhouetted against the beauty of the harbour wher
just over a hundred and twenty years ago, four little sailing shi
had come to safe anchorage. A harbour where, to forget h
brother's wife, Thomas Swainson had come, penniless, to me
his true love and to found a family. In so doing he had, all ur
knowing, created for Edwin and Bessie's great-granddaughte
safe harbouring after storm.

Luke's arms closed about her . . .

It was more than three-quarters of an hour before they came bac
to earth, and then only because they could hear voices nearir
the house. They went to the end of the long loggia and looke
out towards the village across the croquet lawn of long ag
Here they came. Ebenezer must have gone to meet them. Ha

ere ever been a more handsome old man, erect, tall, his silver
ir shining in the sun, smiling, radiating happiness? Elizabeth
s holding his hand. Andrew had Innis with him; Drusilla had
heepish Jake in tow, there was Aaron and his wife, Peggy and
sh, and Edwina and Matthew, schoolbags swinging.
'How's that for an instant engagement party?' said Luke.

Each month from Harlequin

8 NEW FULL LENGTH ROMANCE NOVELS

Listed below are the latest three months' releases:

ALL BOOKS 60c

These titles are available at your local bookseller, or through the Harlequin Reader Service, M.P.O. Box 707, Niagara Falls, N.Y. 14302; Canadian address 649 Ontario St., Stratford, Ont.

A